W9-ACU-590

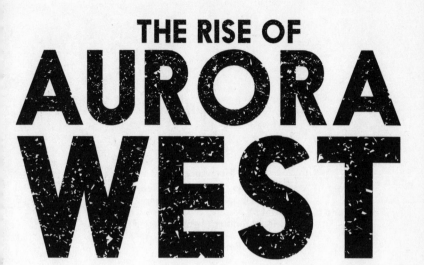

THE RISE OF
AURORA WEST

First Second

Copyright © 2014 by Paul Pope
Published by First Second
First Second is an imprint of Roaring Brook Press, a division of Holtzbrinck
Publishing Holdings Limited Partnership
175 Fifth Avenue, New York, New York 10010
All rights reserved

Cataloging-in-Publication Data is on file at the Library of Congress

Paperback ISBN: 978-1-62672-009-1
Hardcover ISBN: 978-1-62672-268-2

First Second books may be purchased for business or promotional use. For
information on bulk purchases please contact Macmillan Corporate and
Premium Sales Department at (800) 221-7945 x5442 or by email at
specialmarkets@macmillan.com.

FIRST
EDITION

First edition 2014

Art by David Rubin
Story by JT Petty and Paul Pope

Type set in "PPope," designed by John Martz
Book design by Colleen AF Venable and John Green
Printed in the United States of America

Paperback: 10 9 8 7 6 5 4 3 2 1
Hardcover: 10 9 8 7 6 5 4 3 2 1

THE RISE OF AURORA WEST

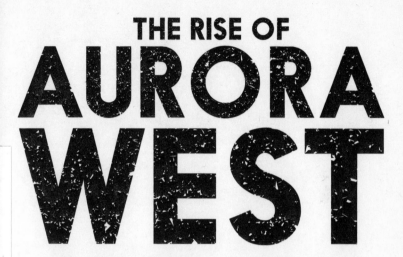

Written by JT Petty and Paul Pope

Art by David Rubín

First Second
New York

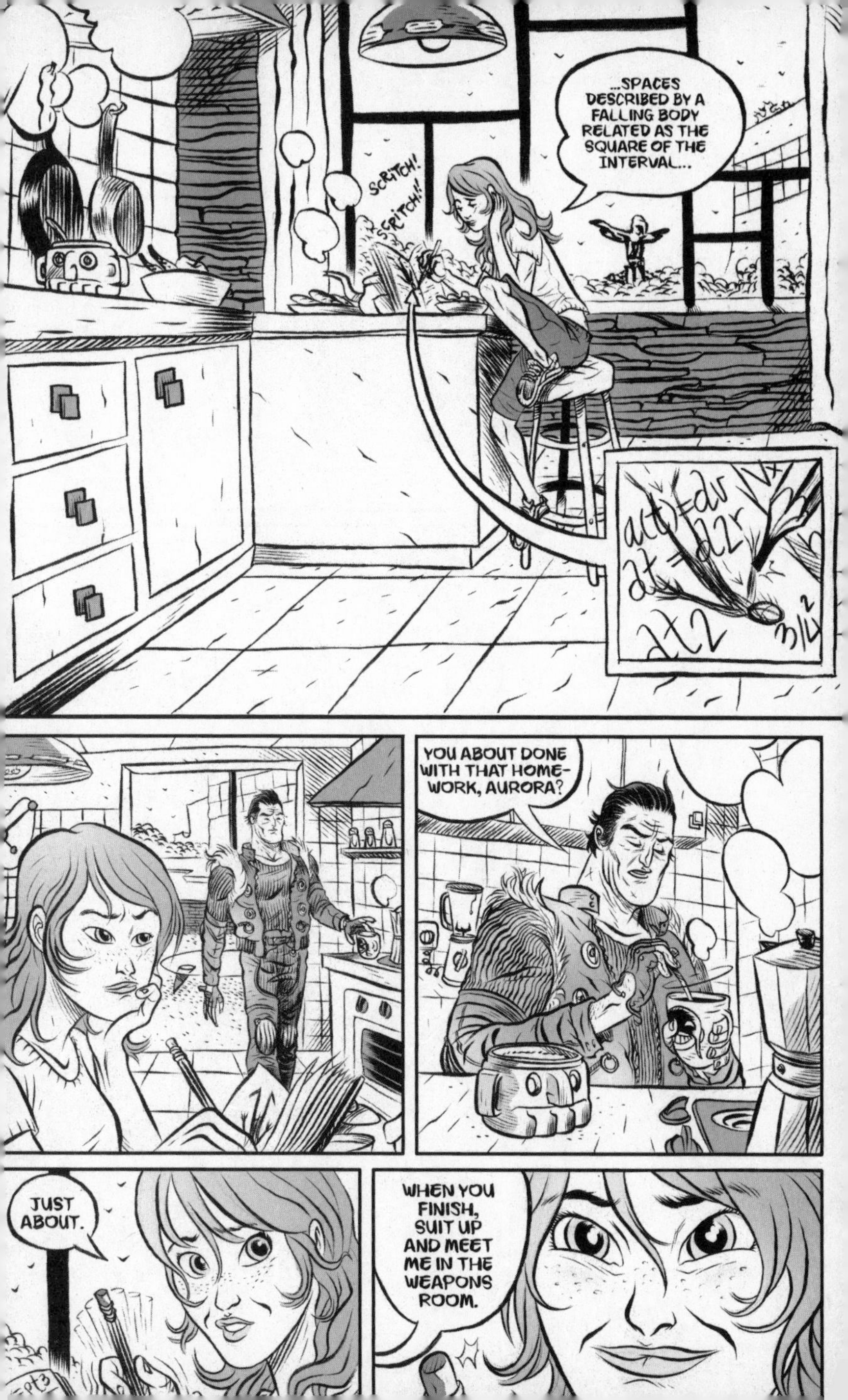

SCRITCH!
SCRITCH!!
...SPACES DESCRIBED BY A FALLING BODY RELATED AS THE SQUARE OF THE INTERVAL...
YOU ABOUT DONE WITH THAT HOME-WORK, AURORA?
JUST ABOUT.
WHEN YOU FINISH, SUIT UP AND MEET ME IN THE WEAPONS ROOM.

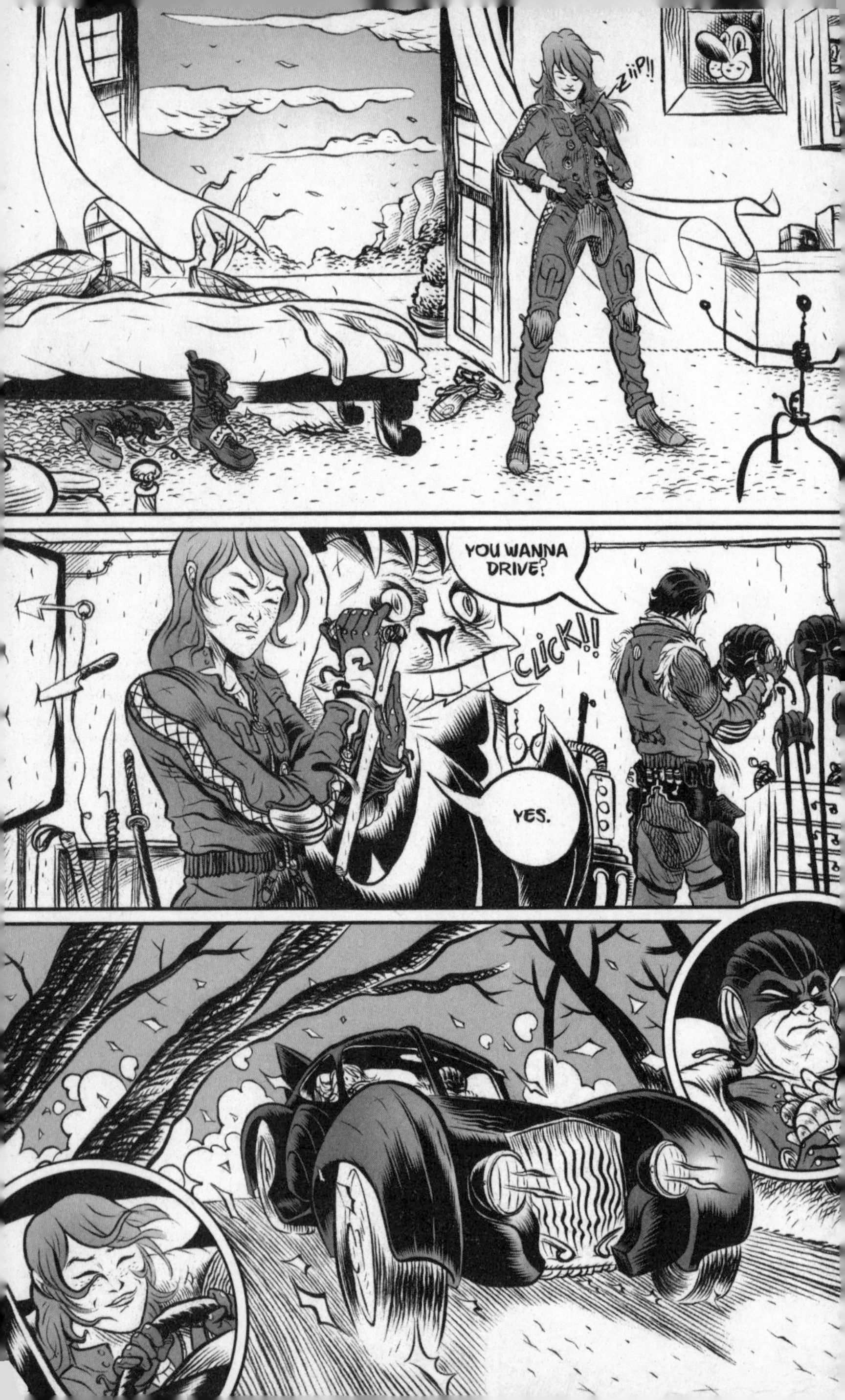
ZIIP!!
YOU WANNA DRIVE?
CLICK!!
YES.

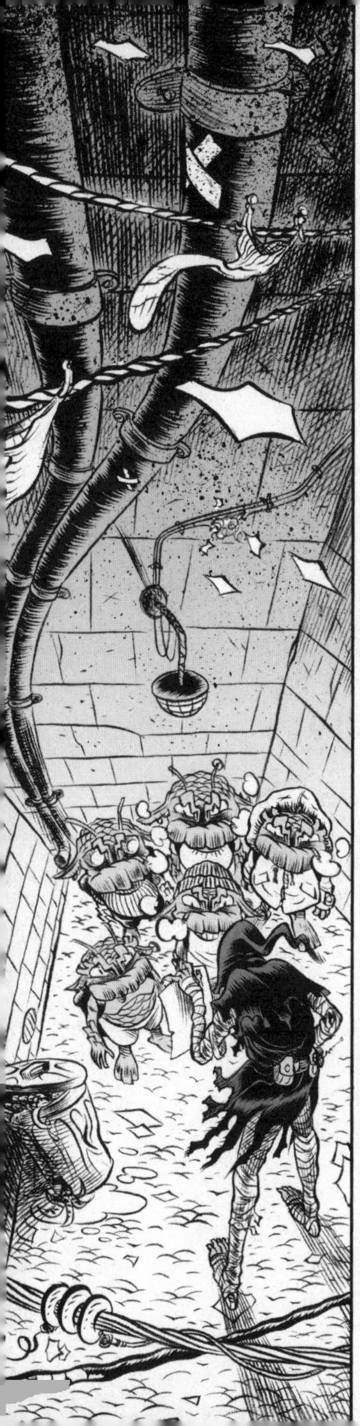

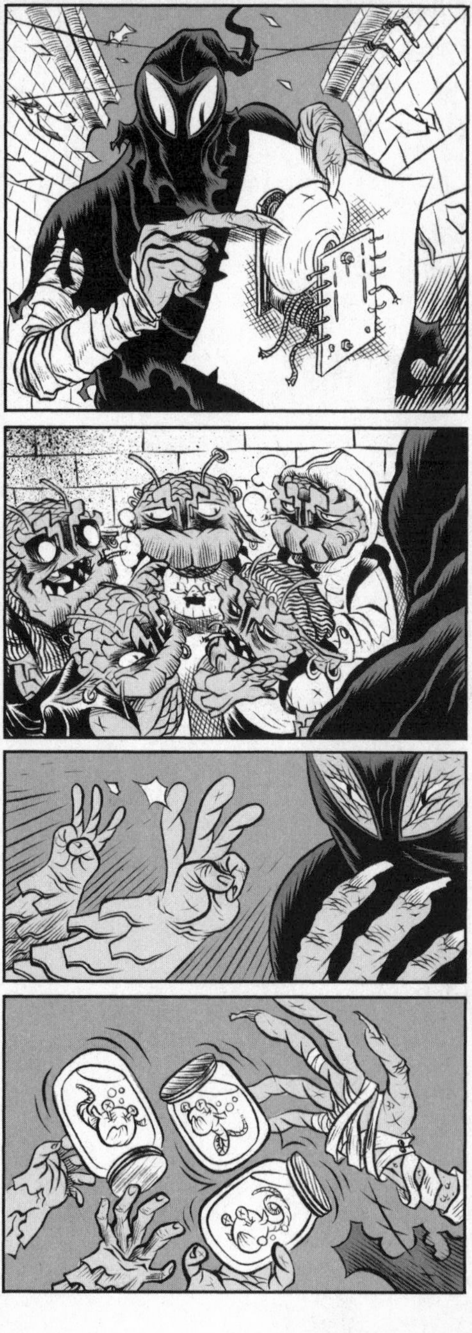

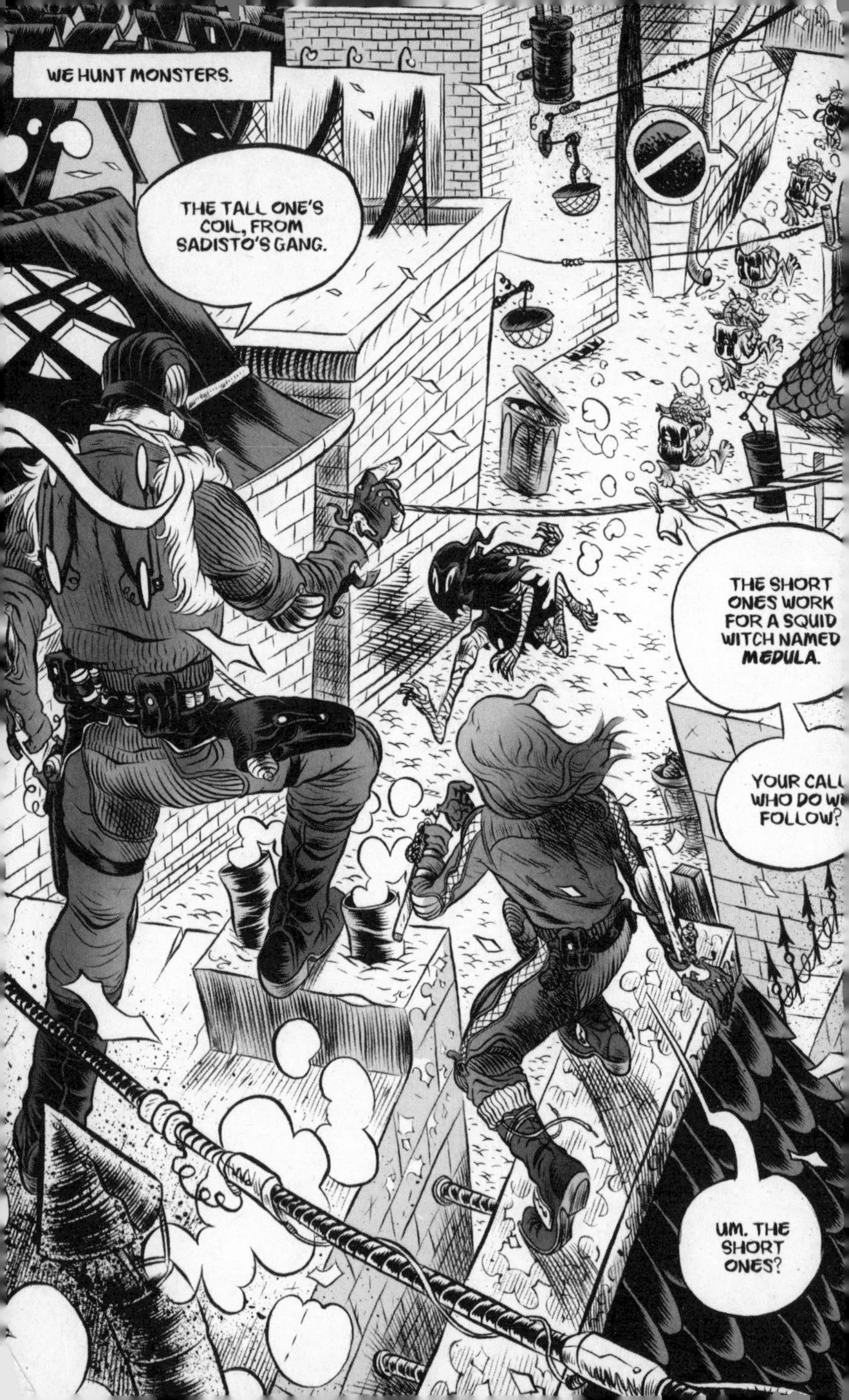
WE HUNT MONSTERS.
THE TALL ONE'S COIL, FROM SADISTO'S GANG.
THE SHORT ONES WORK FOR A SQUID WITCH NAMED **MEDULA.**
YOUR CALL WHO DO W FOLLOW?
UM. THE SHORT ONES?

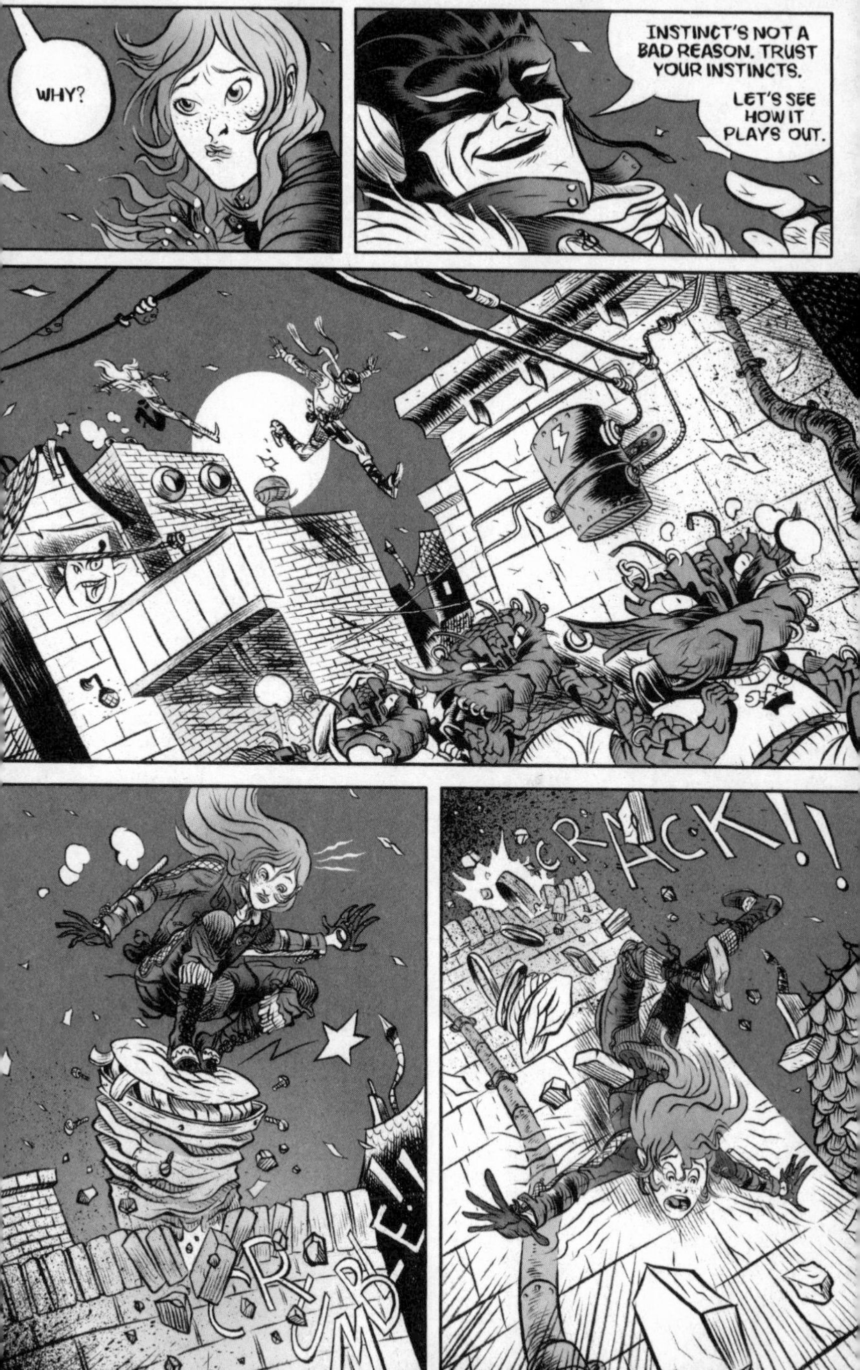
WHY?
INSTINCT'S NOT A BAD REASON. TRUST YOUR INSTINCTS.
LET'S SEE HOW IT PLAYS OUT.
CRUMBLE!!
CRACK!!

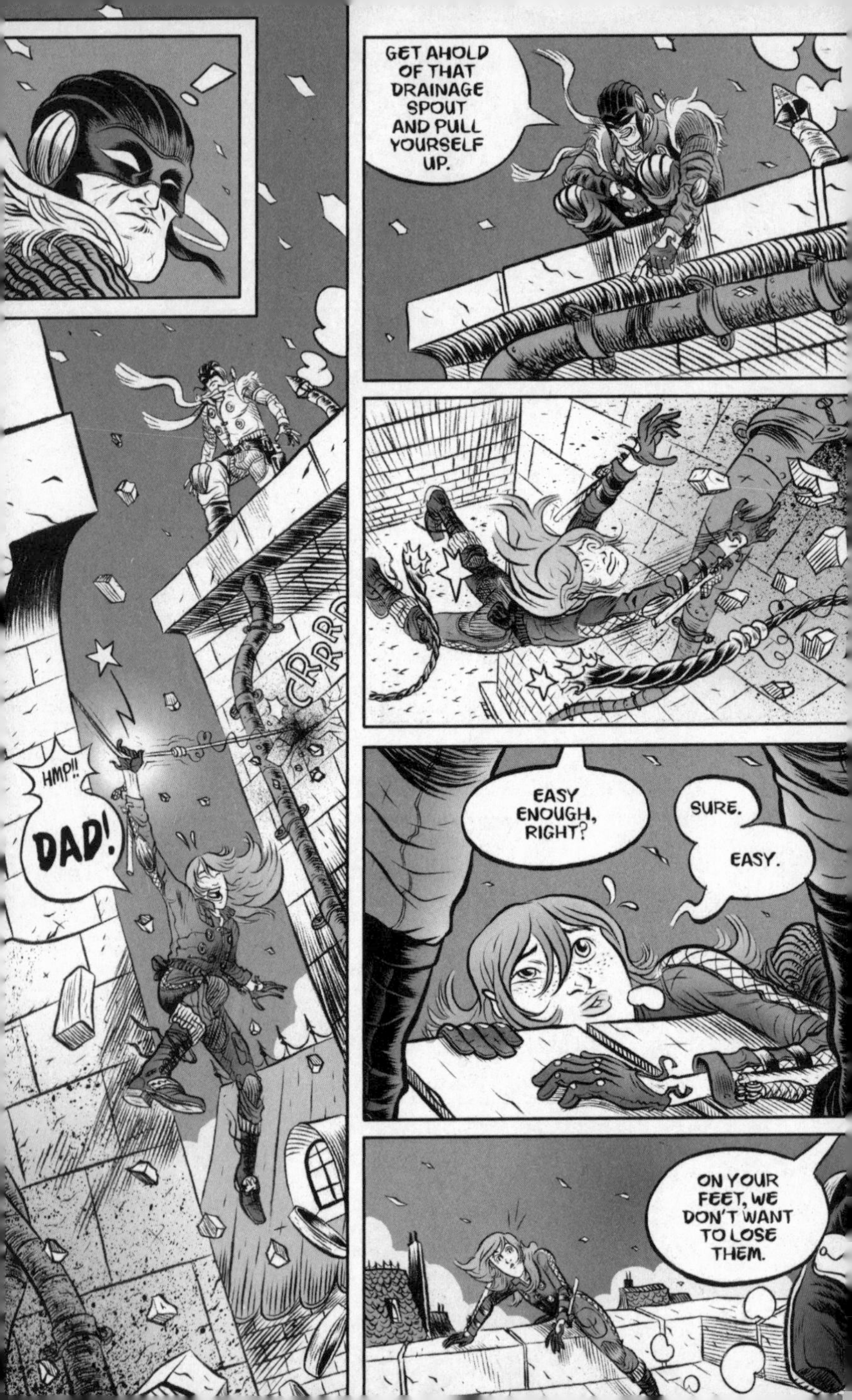
CRRRR
HMP!!
DAD!
GET AHOLD OF THAT DRAINAGE SPOUT AND PULL YOURSELF UP.
EASY ENOUGH, RIGHT?
SURE.
EASY.
ON YOUR FEET, WE DON'T WANT TO LOSE THEM.

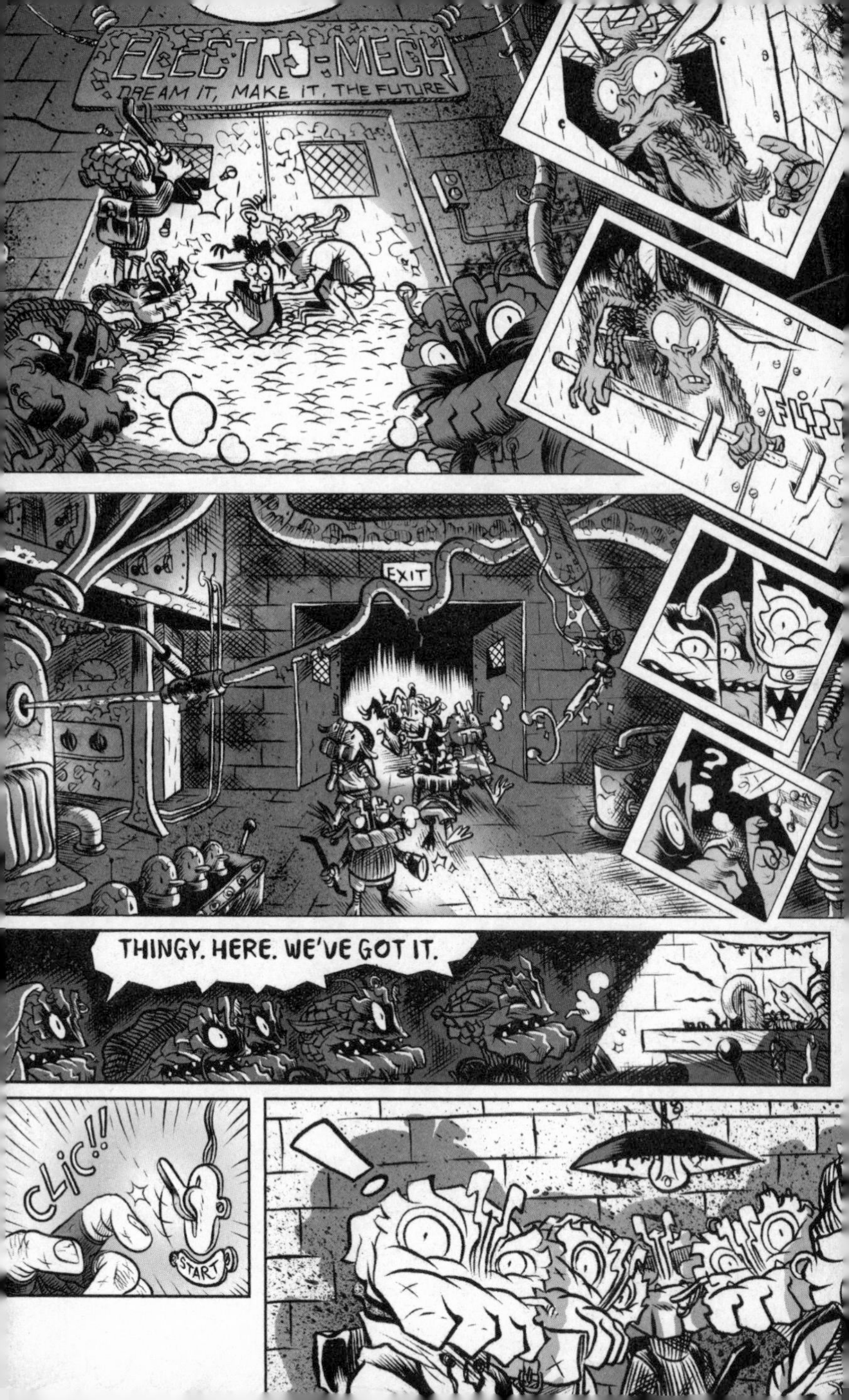
ELECTRO-MECH
DREAM IT, MAKE IT, THE FUTURE
FLIP
EXIT
THINGY. HERE. WE'VE GOT IT.
CLIC!!
START

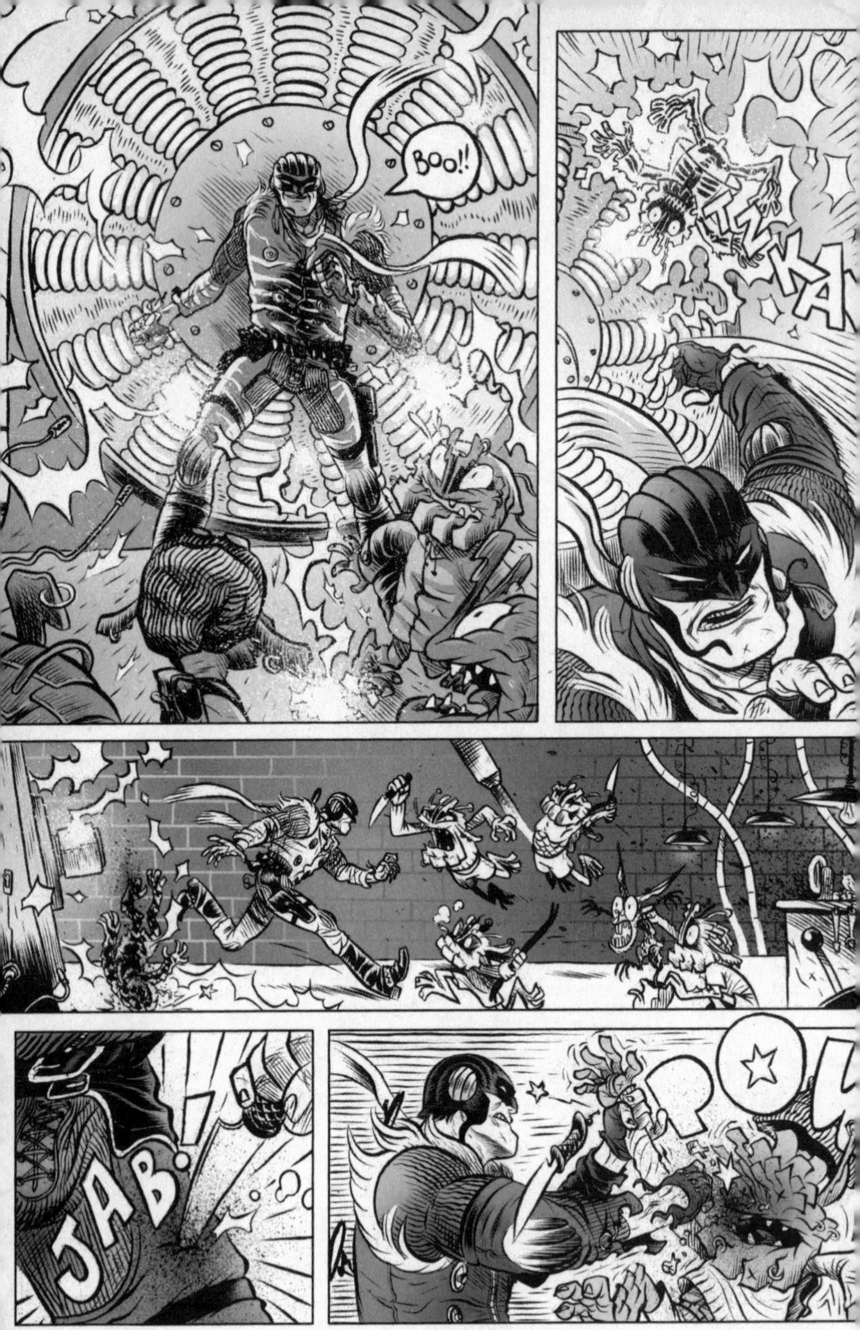
BOO!!
TZKA
JAB!
PO

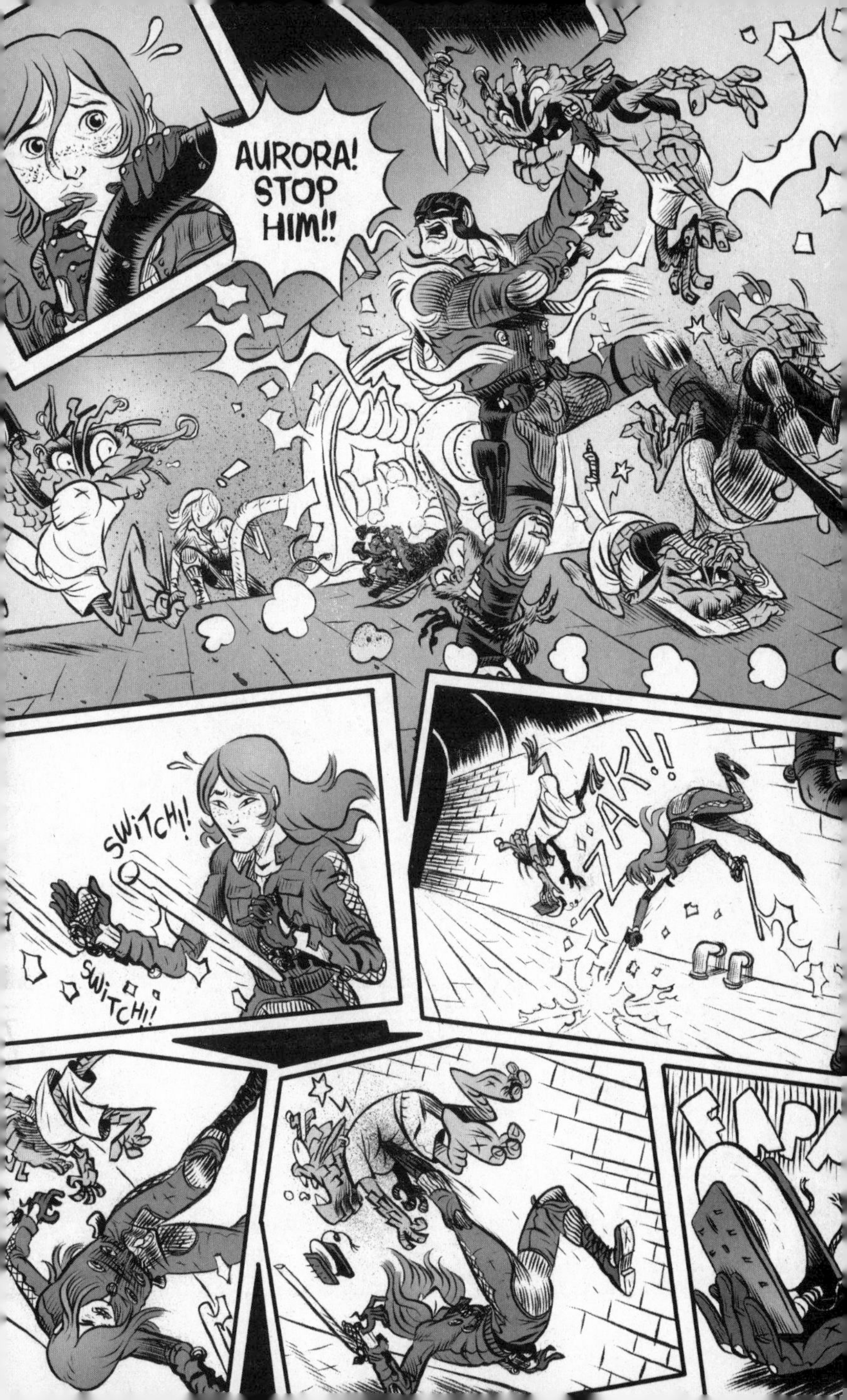
AURORA! STOP HIM!!
SWITCH!
SWITCH!
TZAK!!

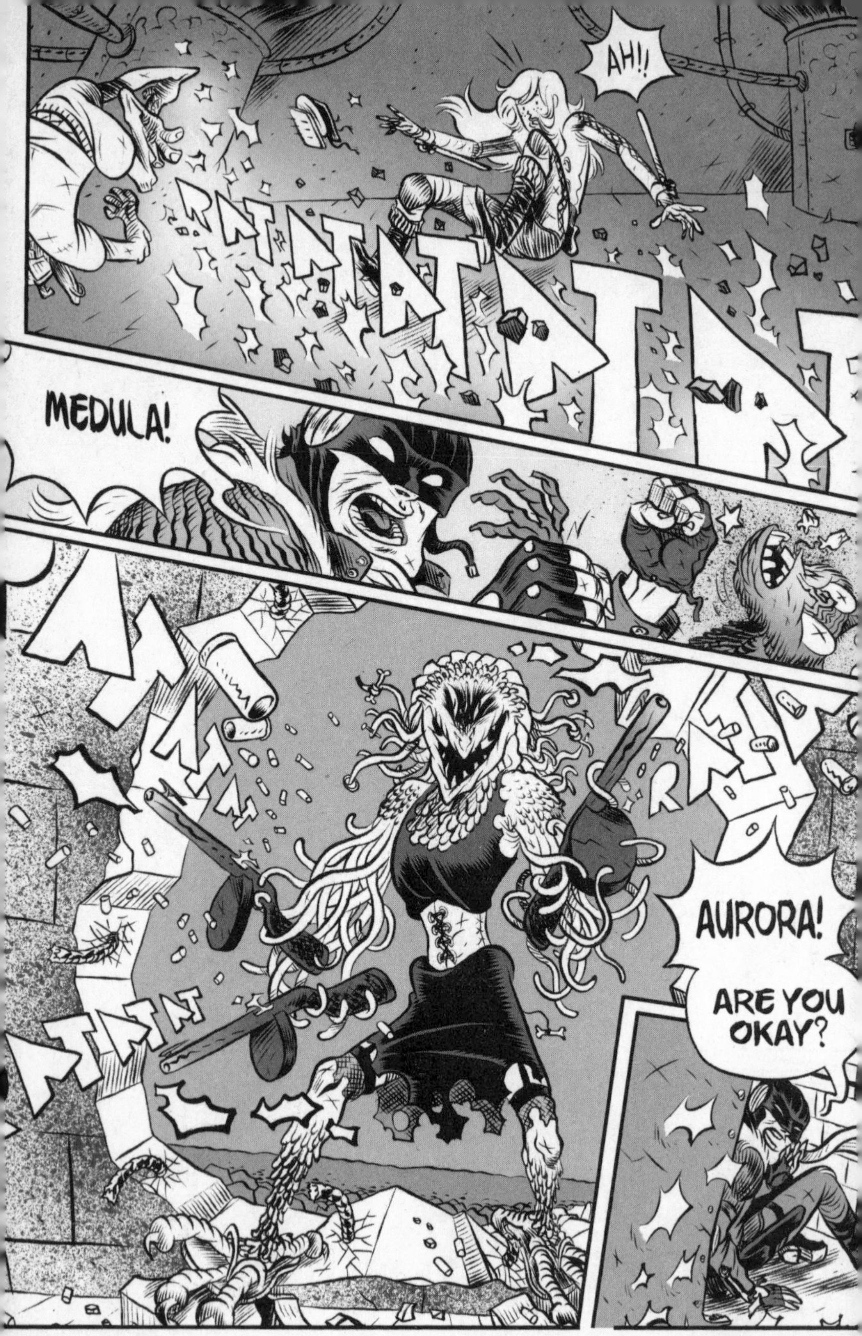
AH!!
RATATATATAT
MEDULA!
AURORA!
ARE YOU OKAY?

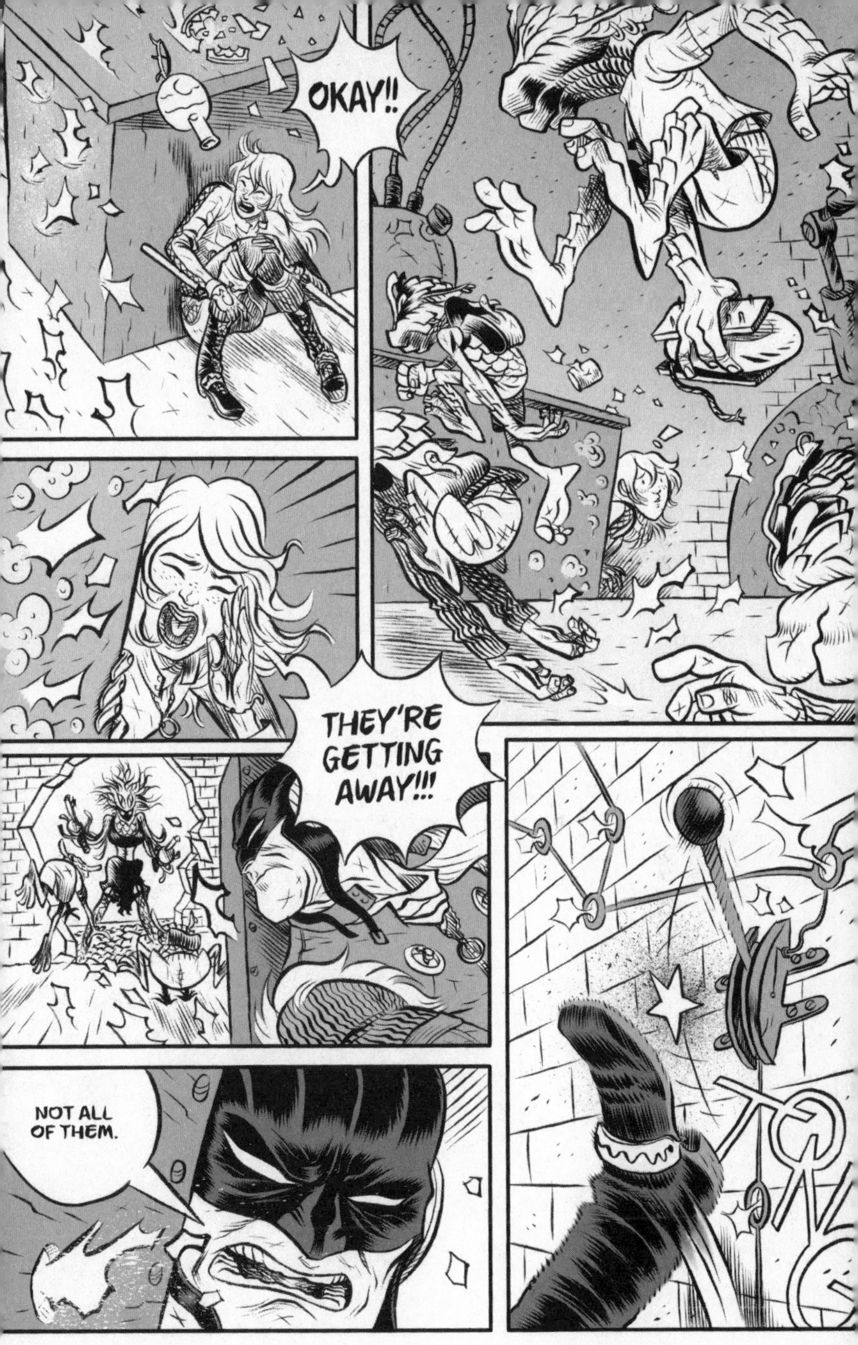
OKAY!!
THEY'RE GETTING AWAY!!!
NOT ALL OF THEM.

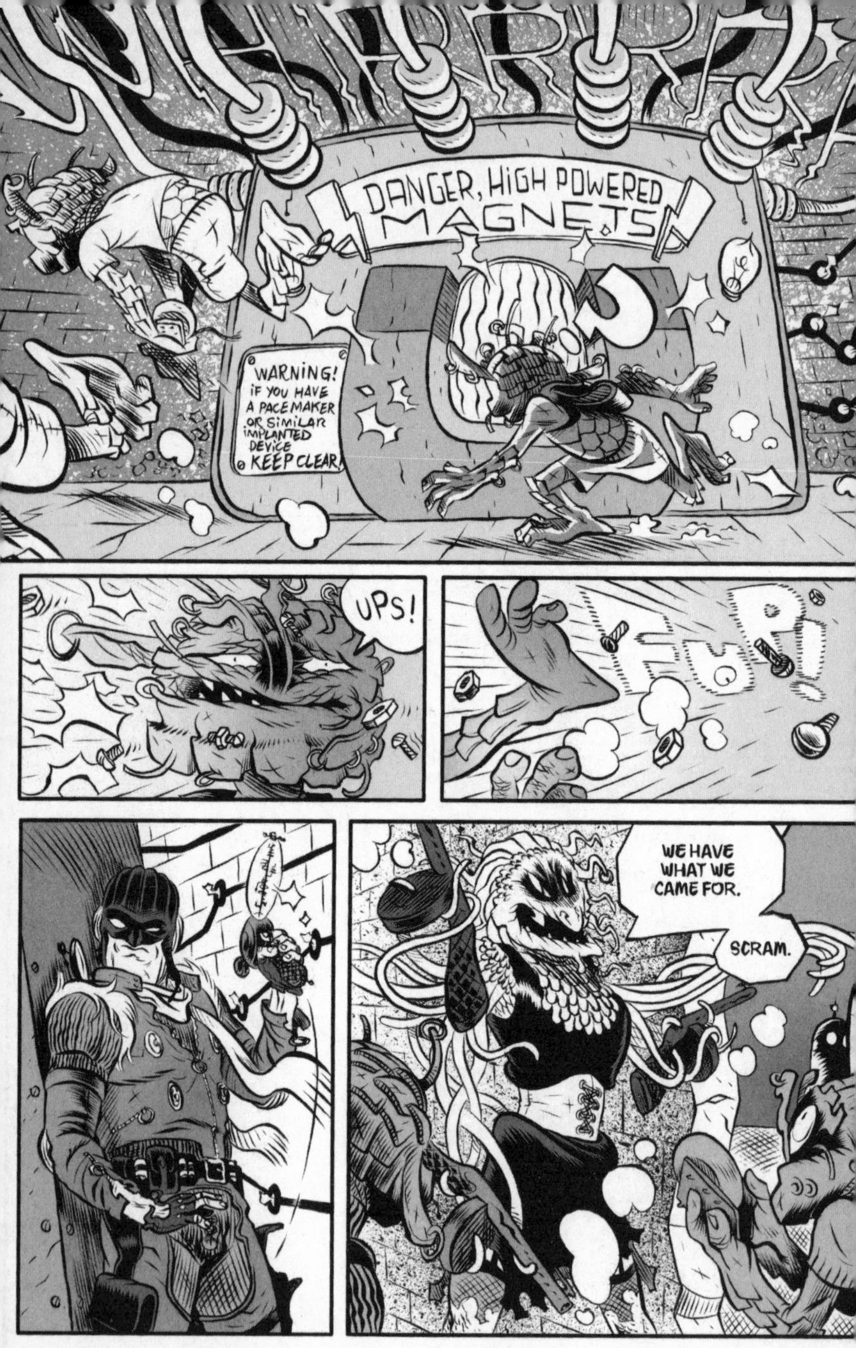
DANGER, HIGH POWERED MAGNETS
WARNING! IF YOU HAVE A PACEMAKER OR SIMILAR IMPLANTED DEVICE KEEP CLEAR!
UPS!
WE HAVE WHAT WE CAME FOR.
SCRAM.

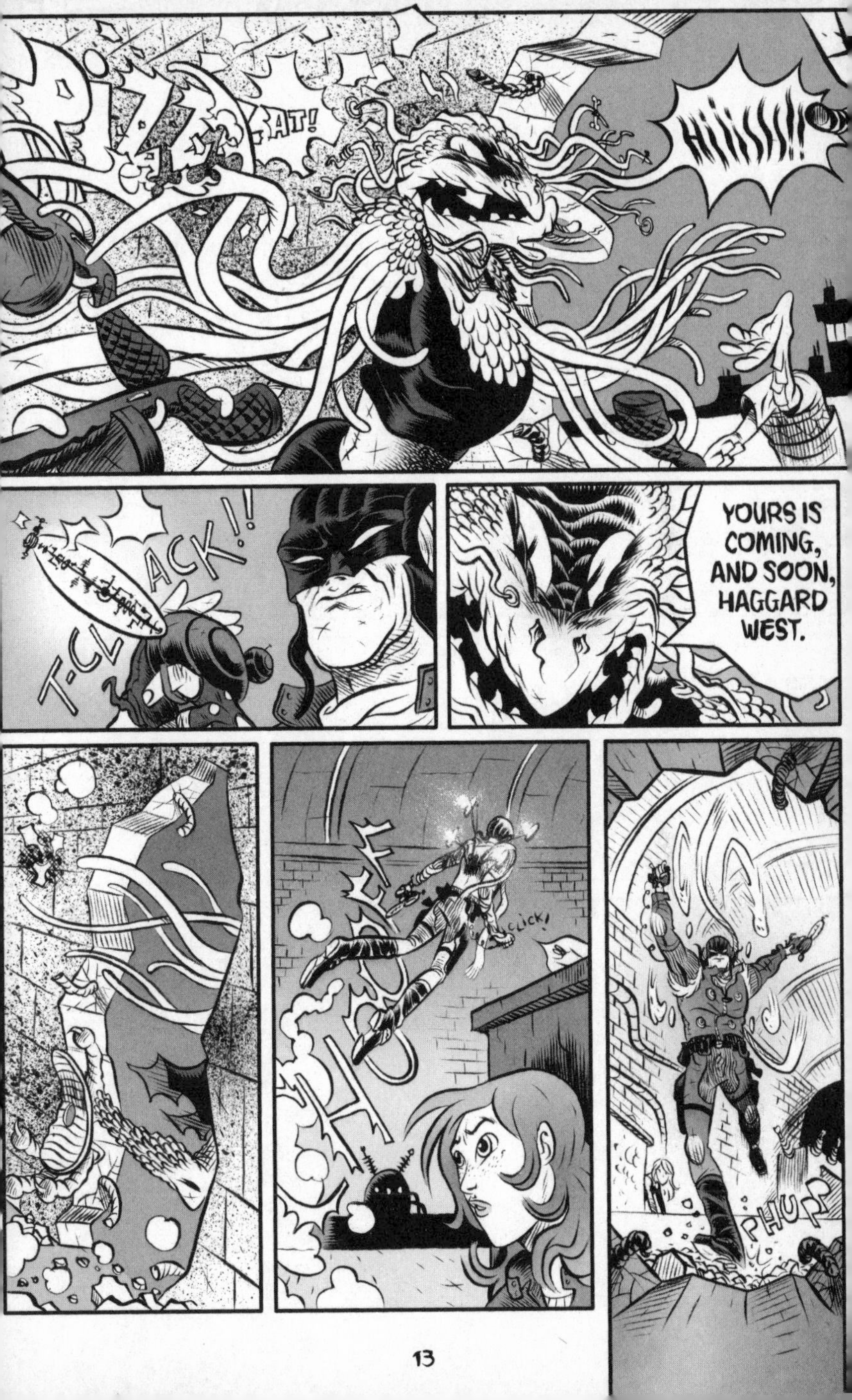

AT!
HIIIIIII!!
T-CLACK!!
YOURS IS COMING, AND SOON, HAGGARD WEST.
CLICK!
PHUP

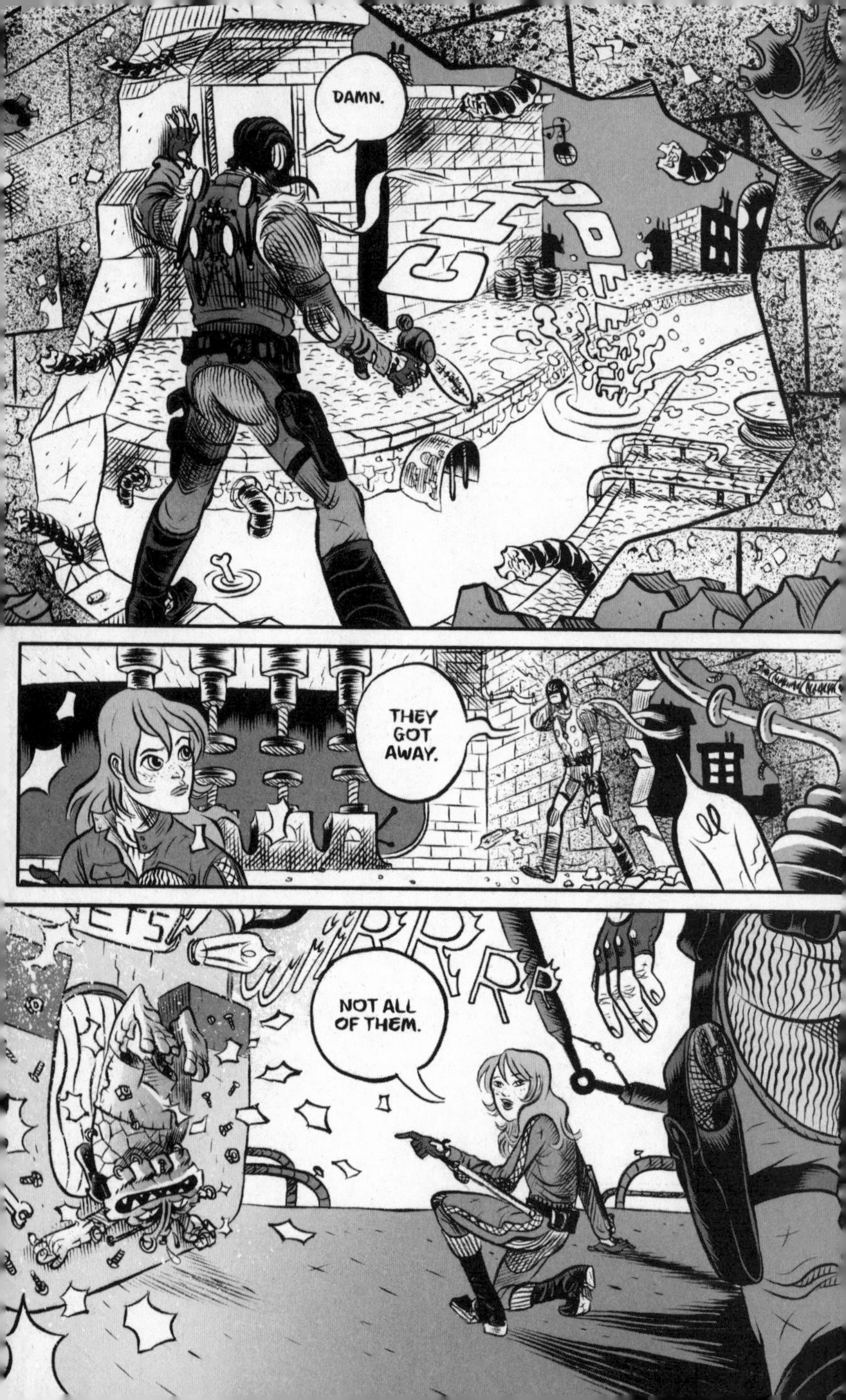
DAMN.
THEY GOT AWAY.
NOT ALL OF THEM.

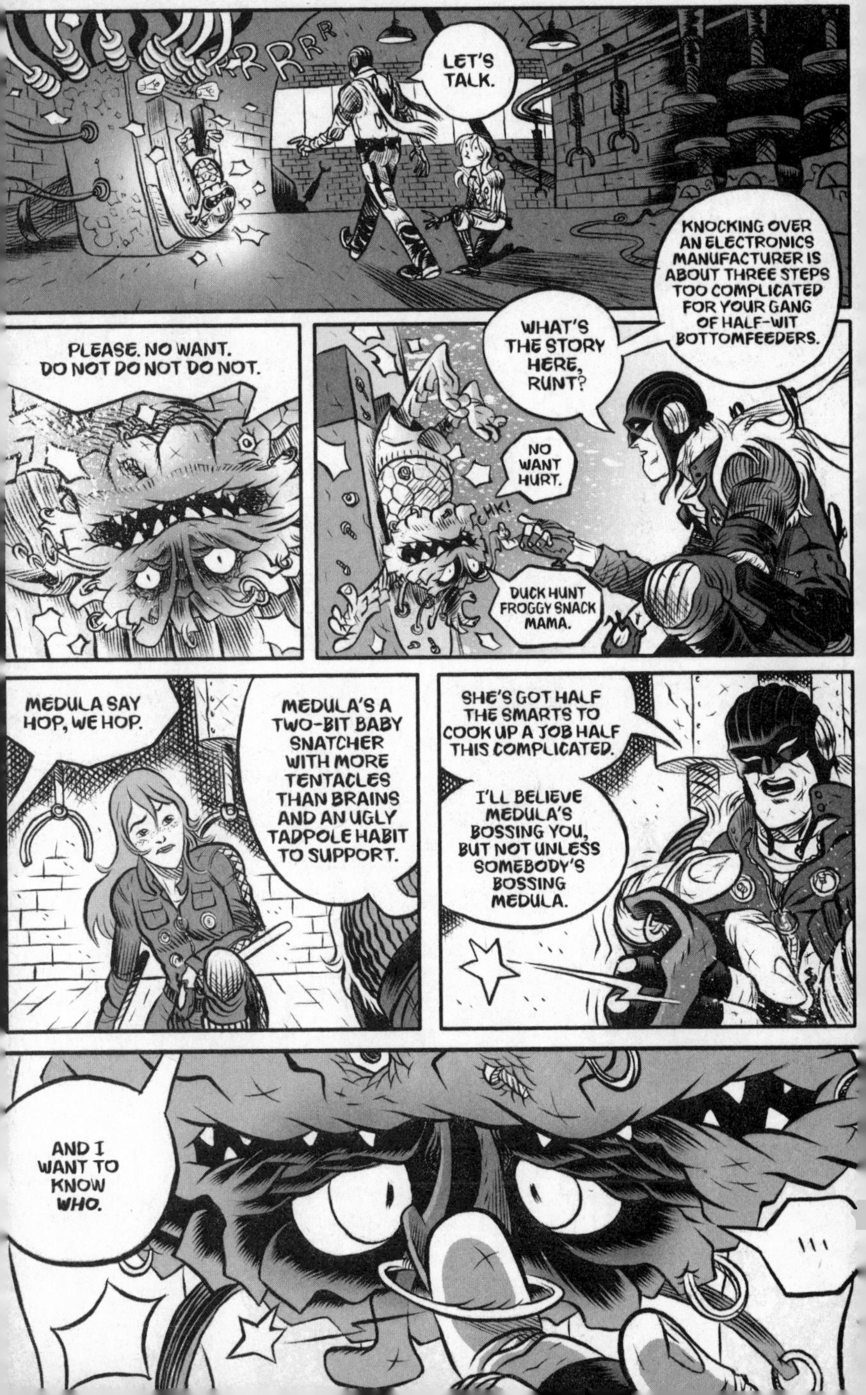
RRRRRR
LET'S TALK.
KNOCKING OVER AN ELECTRONICS MANUFACTURER IS ABOUT THREE STEPS TOO COMPLICATED FOR YOUR GANG OF HALF-WIT BOTTOMFEEDERS.
WHAT'S THE STORY HERE, RUNT?
PLEASE. NO WANT. DO NOT DO NOT DO NOT.
NO WANT HURT.
CHK!
DUCK HUNT FROGGY SNACK MAMA.
MEDULA SAY HOP, WE HOP.
MEDULA'S A TWO-BIT BABY SNATCHER WITH MORE TENTACLES THAN BRAINS AND AN UGLY TADPOLE HABIT TO SUPPORT.
SHE'S GOT HALF THE SMARTS TO COOK UP A JOB HALF THIS COMPLICATED.
I'LL BELIEVE MEDULA'S BOSSING YOU, BUT NOT UNLESS SOMEBODY'S BOSSING MEDULA.
AND I WANT TO KNOW WHO.

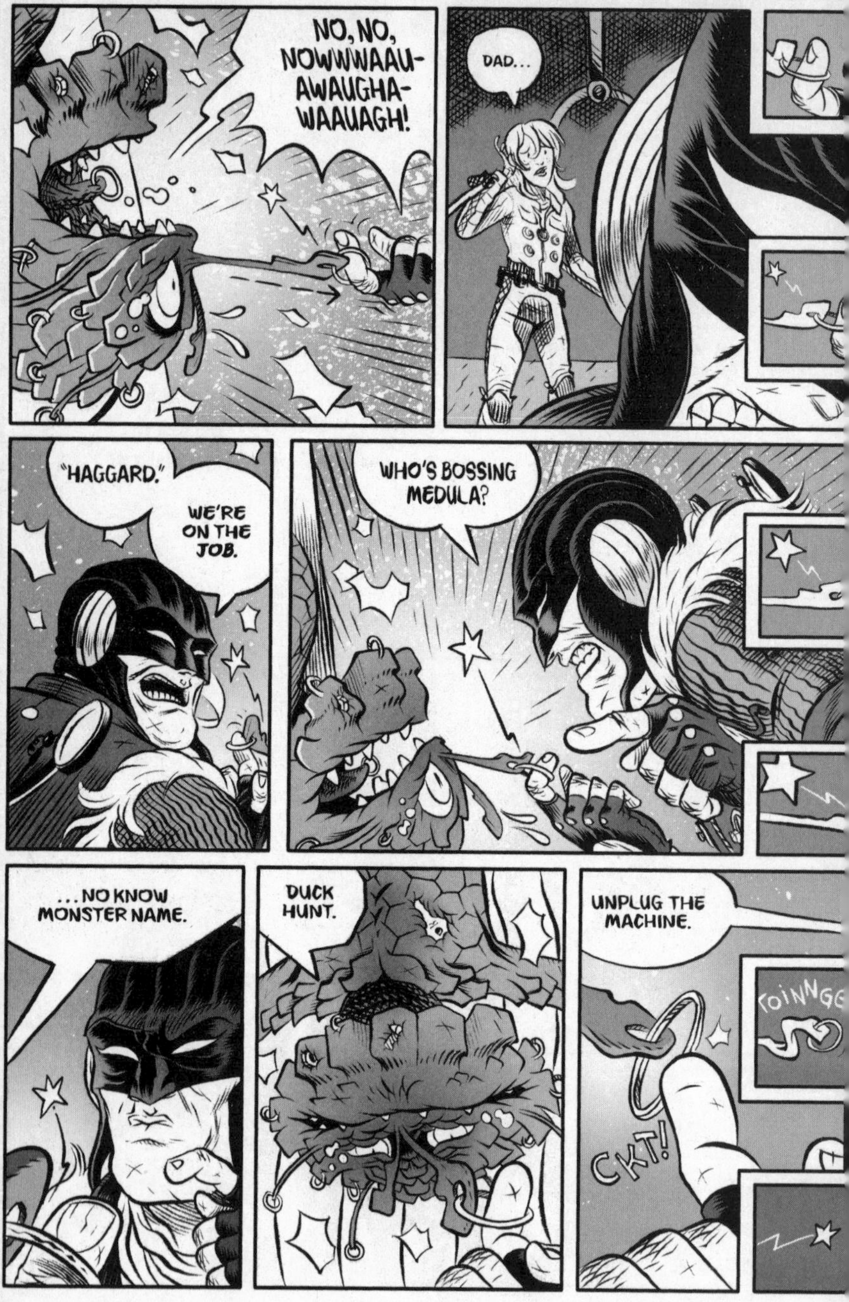
NO, NO, NOWWWAAU-AWAUGHA-WAAUAGH!
DAD...
"HAGGARD."
WE'RE ON THE JOB.
WHO'S BOSSING MEDULA?
...NO KNOW MONSTER NAME.
DUCK HUNT.
UNPLUG THE MACHINE.
CKT!

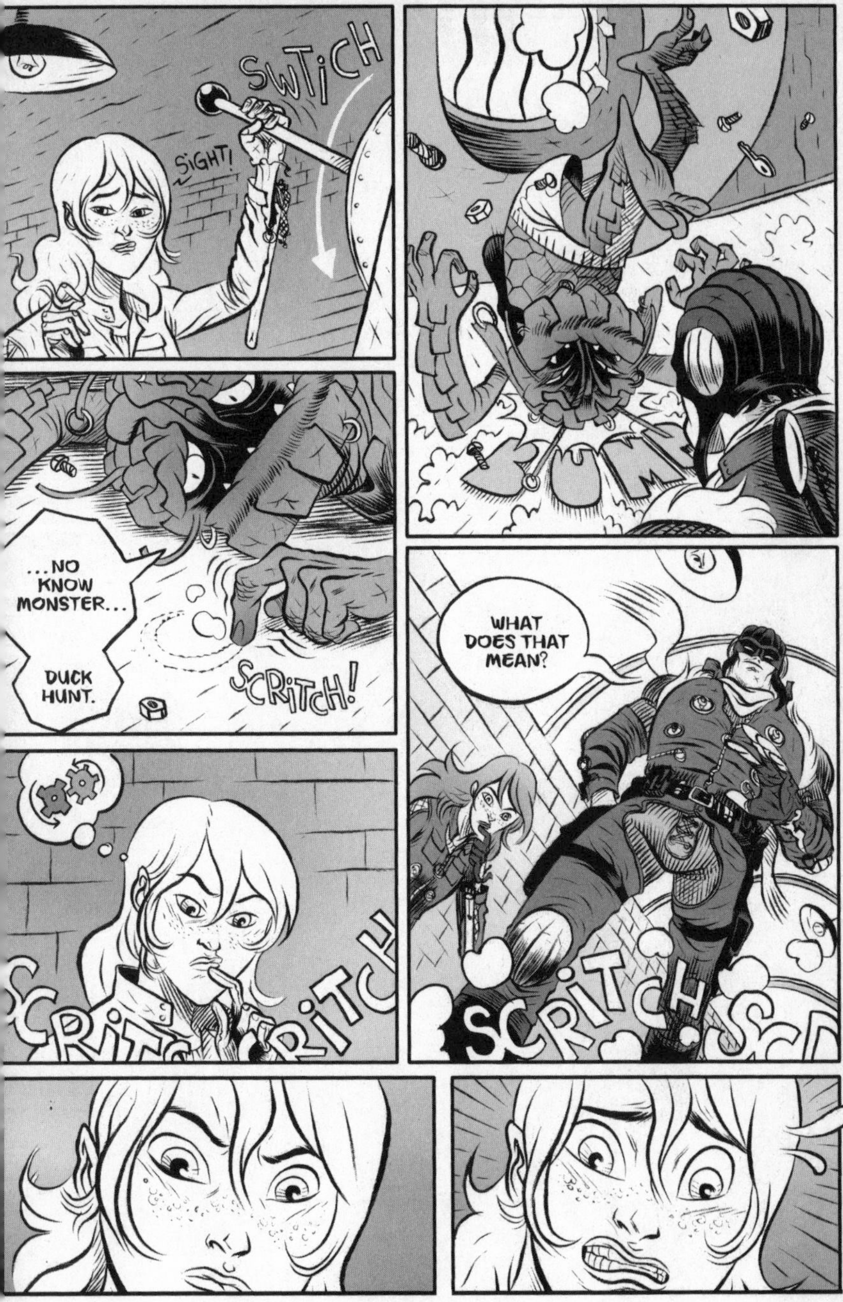
SWTICH
SIGHT!
...NO KNOW MONSTER...
DUCK HUNT.
SCRITCH!
WHAT DOES THAT MEAN?
SCRITCH SCRITCH
SCRITCH

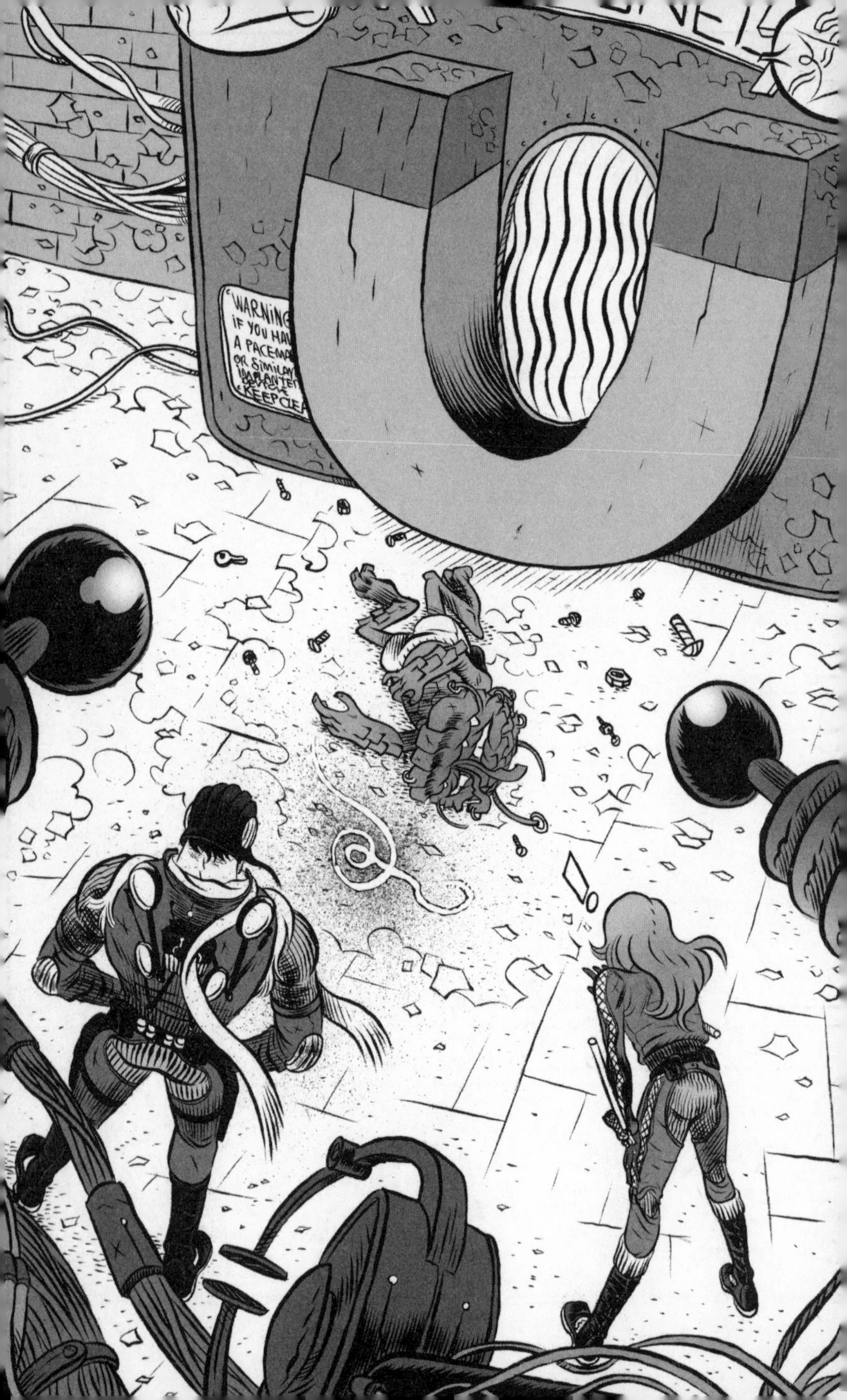
WARNING
IF YOU HAV
A PACEMA
OR SIMILAR
IMPLANTED
DEVICE
KEEP CLEA

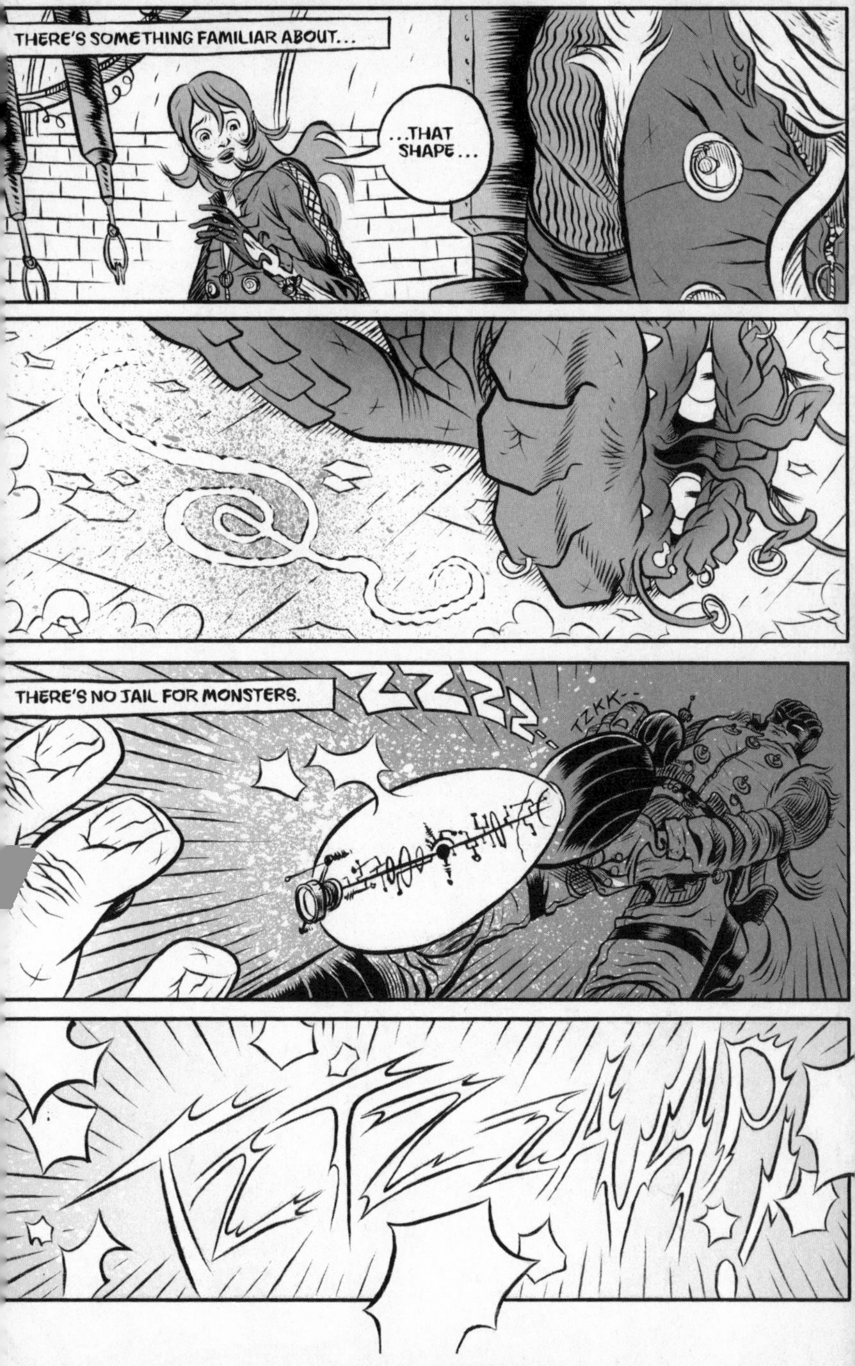
THERE'S SOMETHING FAMILIAR ABOUT...
...THAT SHAPE...
THERE'S NO JAIL FOR MONSTERS.
ZZZZ...
TZKK--
TZZZAAP

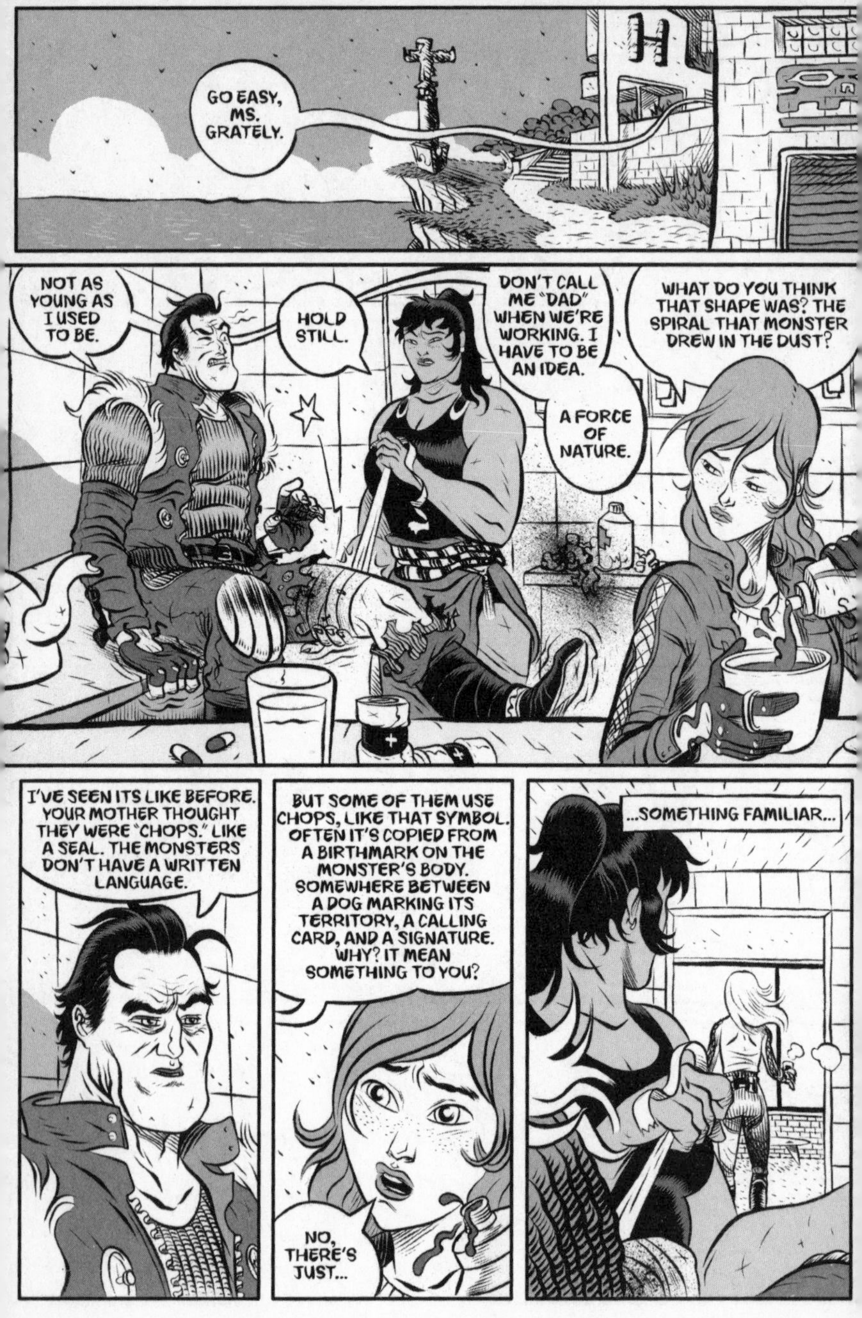
GO EASY, MS. GRATELY.
NOT AS YOUNG AS I USED TO BE.
HOLD STILL.
DON'T CALL ME "DAD" WHEN WE'RE WORKING. I HAVE TO BE AN IDEA.
A FORCE OF NATURE.
WHAT DO YOU THINK THAT SHAPE WAS? THE SPIRAL THAT MONSTER DREW IN THE DUST?
I'VE SEEN ITS LIKE BEFORE. YOUR MOTHER THOUGHT THEY WERE "CHOPS." LIKE A SEAL. THE MONSTERS DON'T HAVE A WRITTEN LANGUAGE.
BUT SOME OF THEM USE CHOPS, LIKE THAT SYMBOL. OFTEN IT'S COPIED FROM A BIRTHMARK ON THE MONSTER'S BODY. SOMEWHERE BETWEEN A DOG MARKING ITS TERRITORY, A CALLING CARD, AND A SIGNATURE. WHY? IT MEAN SOMETHING TO YOU?
NO, THERE'S JUST...
...SOMETHING FAMILIAR...

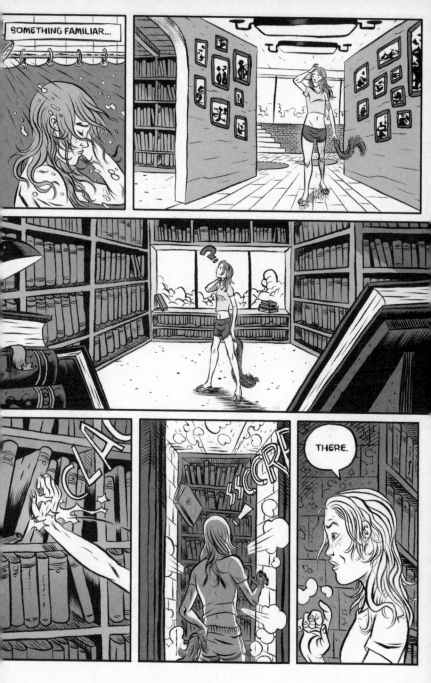

SOMETHING FAMILIAR...

THERE.

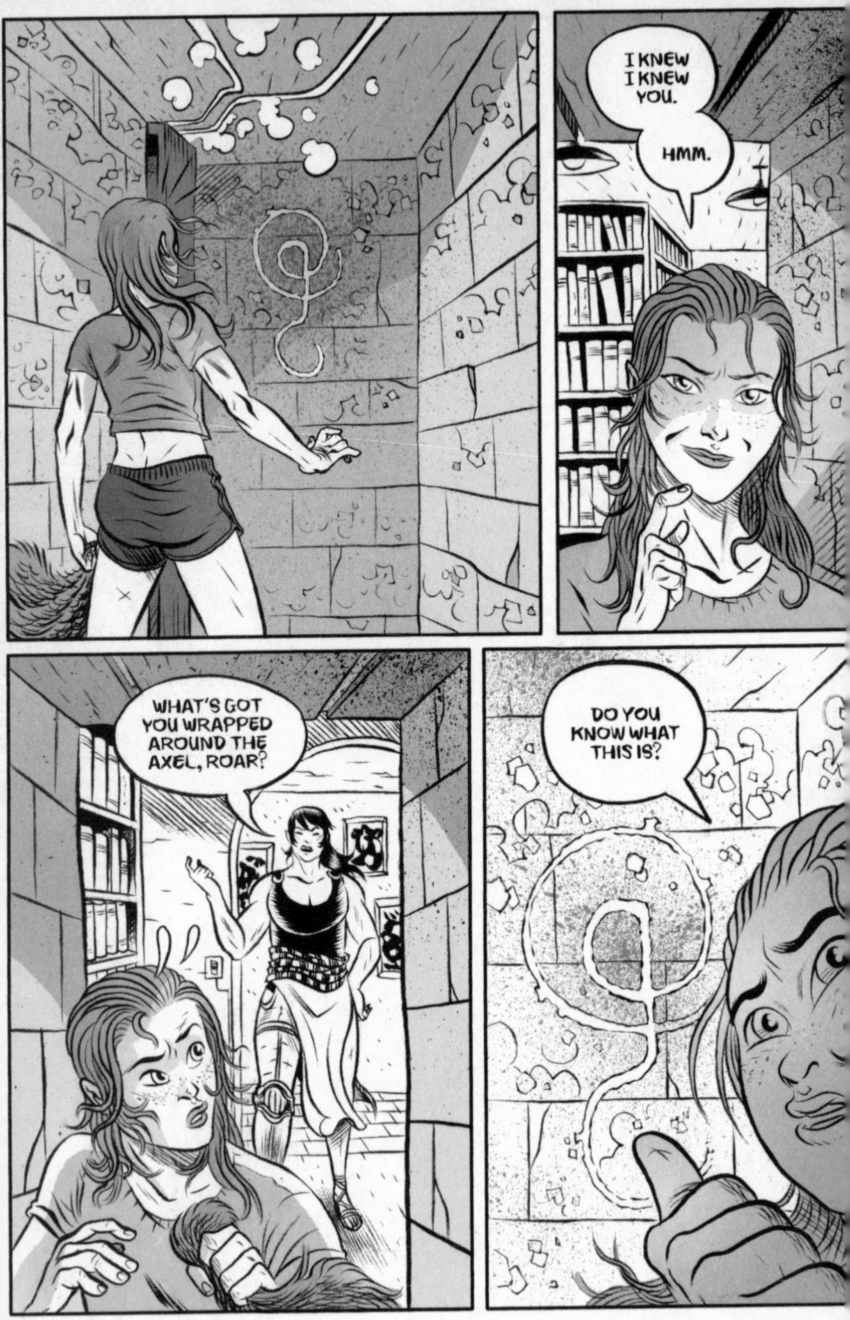
I KNEW I KNEW YOU.
HMM.
WHAT'S GOT YOU WRAPPED AROUND THE AXEL, ROAR?
DO YOU KNOW WHAT THIS IS?

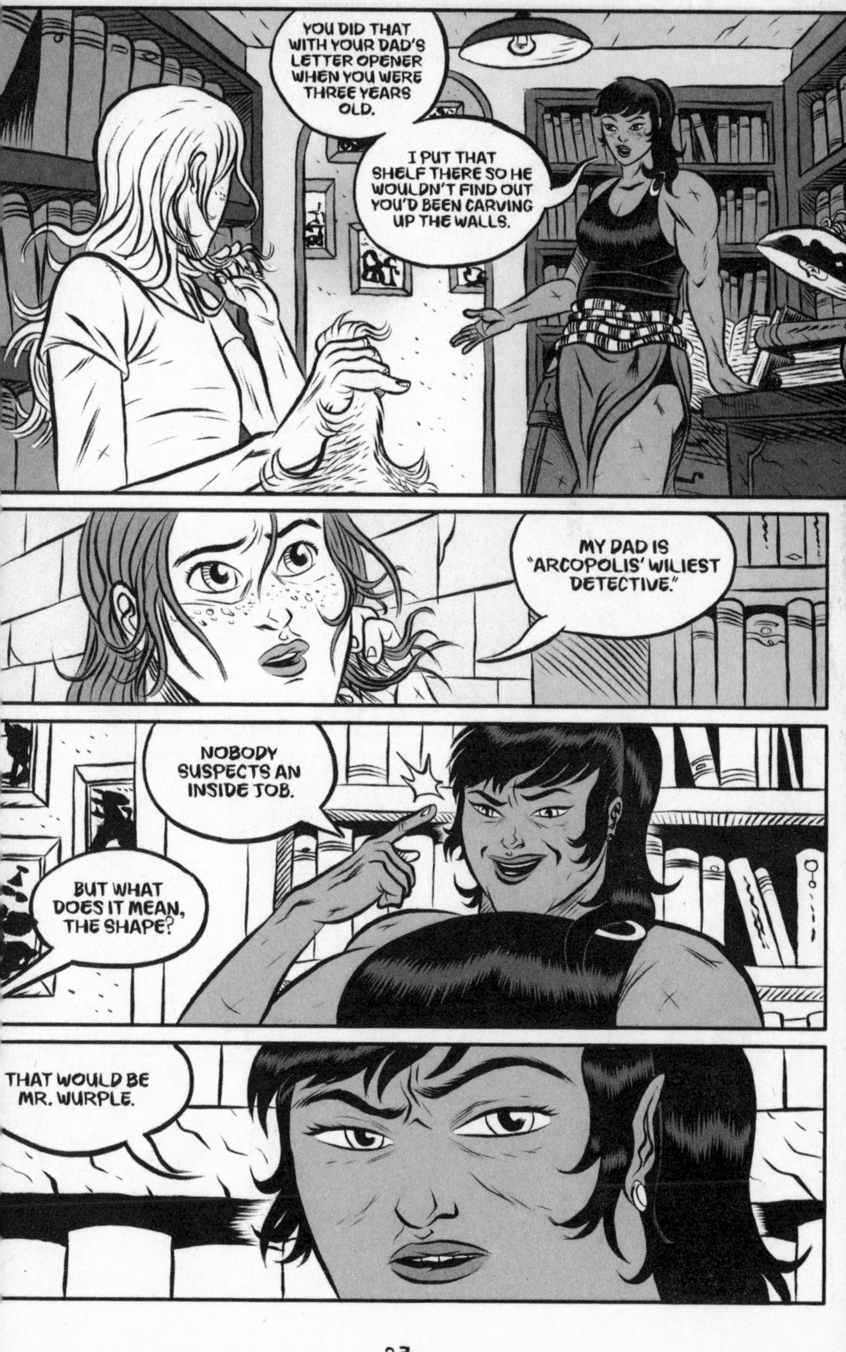

YOU DID THAT WITH YOUR DAD'S LETTER OPENER WHEN YOU WERE THREE YEARS OLD.
I PUT THAT SHELF THERE SO HE WOULDN'T FIND OUT YOU'D BEEN CARVING UP THE WALLS.
MY DAD IS "ARCOPOLIS' WILIEST DETECTIVE."
NOBODY SUSPECTS AN INSIDE JOB.
BUT WHAT DOES IT MEAN, THE SHAPE?
THAT WOULD BE MR. WURPLE.

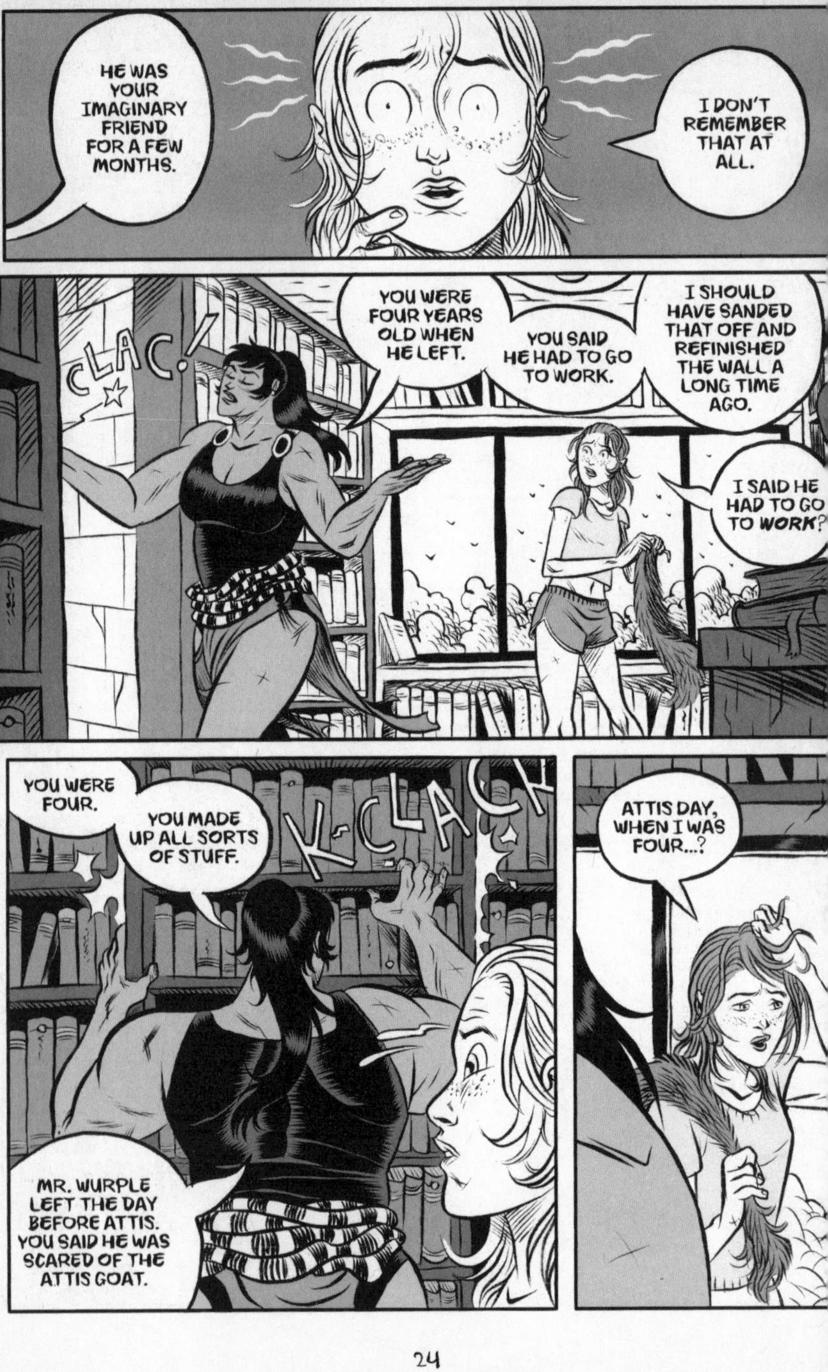
HE WAS YOUR IMAGINARY FRIEND FOR A FEW MONTHS.
I DON'T REMEMBER THAT AT ALL.
CLAC!
YOU WERE FOUR YEARS OLD WHEN HE LEFT.
YOU SAID HE HAD TO GO TO WORK.
I SHOULD HAVE SANDED THAT OFF AND REFINISHED THE WALL A LONG TIME AGO.
I SAID HE HAD TO GO TO WORK?
YOU WERE FOUR.
YOU MADE UP ALL SORTS OF STUFF.
K-CLACK
MR. WURPLE LEFT THE DAY BEFORE ATTIS. YOU SAID HE WAS SCARED OF THE ATTIS GOAT.
ATTIS DAY, WHEN I WAS FOUR...?

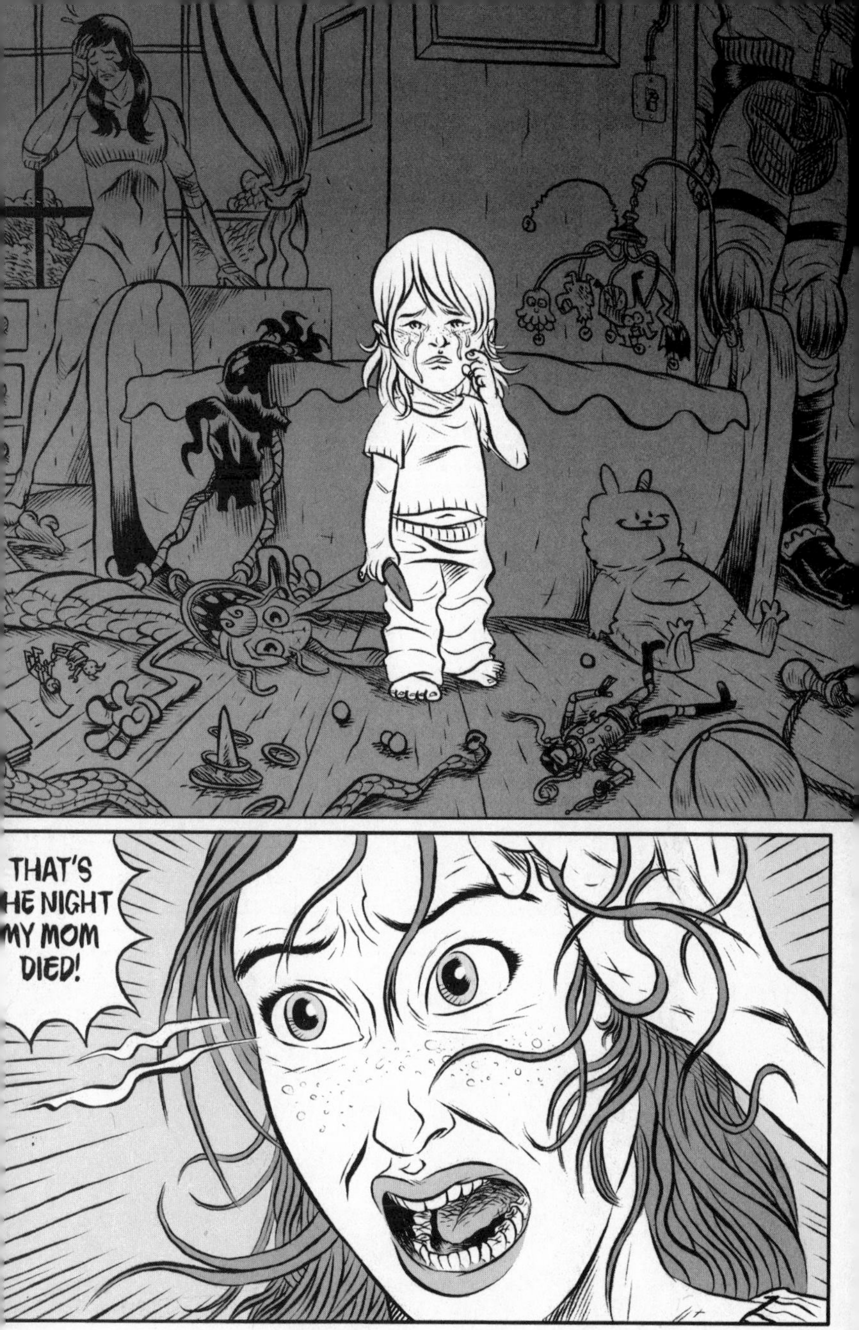
THAT'S
HE NIGHT
MY MOM
DIED!

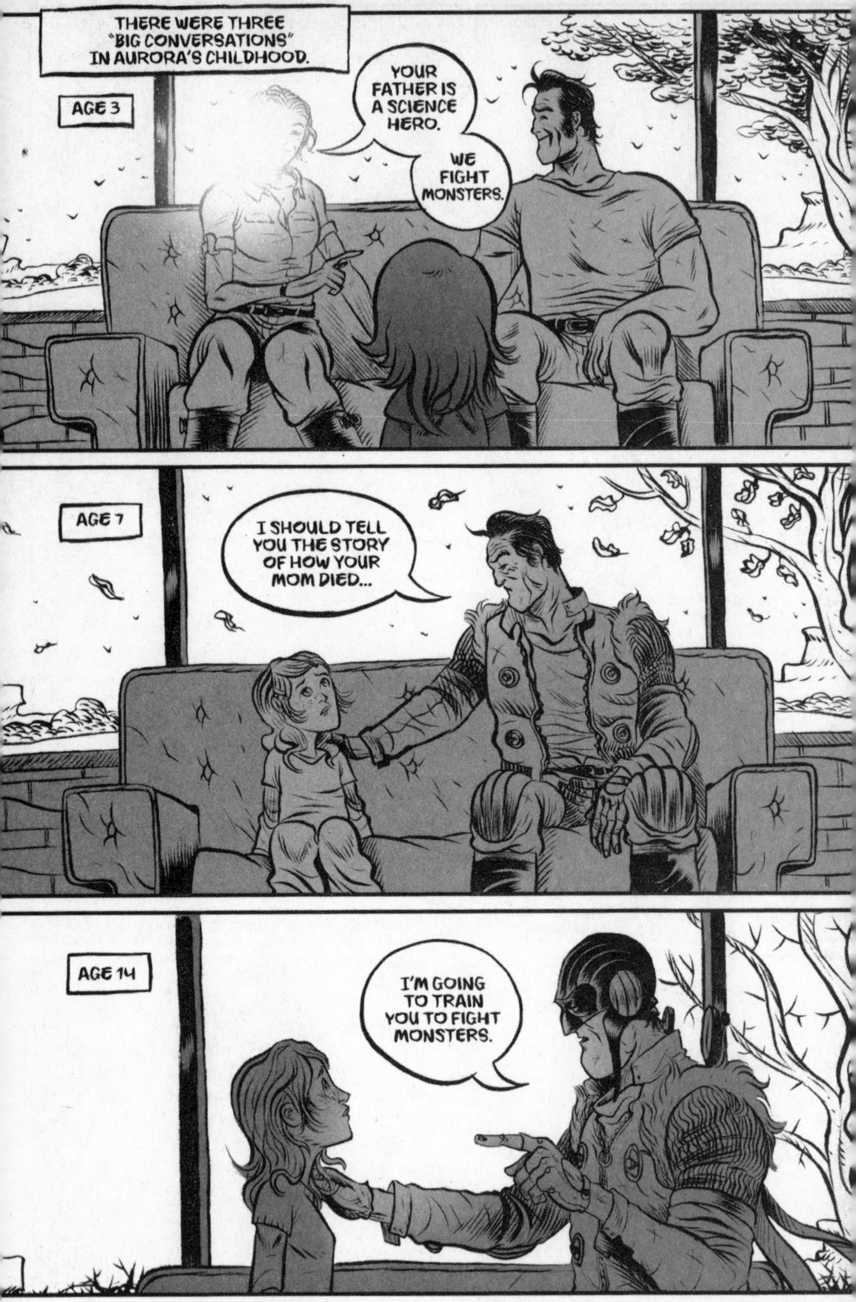
THERE WERE THREE "BIG CONVERSATIONS" IN AURORA'S CHILDHOOD.
AGE 3
YOUR FATHER IS A SCIENCE HERO.
WE FIGHT MONSTERS.
AGE 7
I SHOULD TELL YOU THE STORY OF HOW YOUR MOM DIED...
AGE 14
I'M GOING TO TRAIN YOU TO FIGHT MONSTERS.

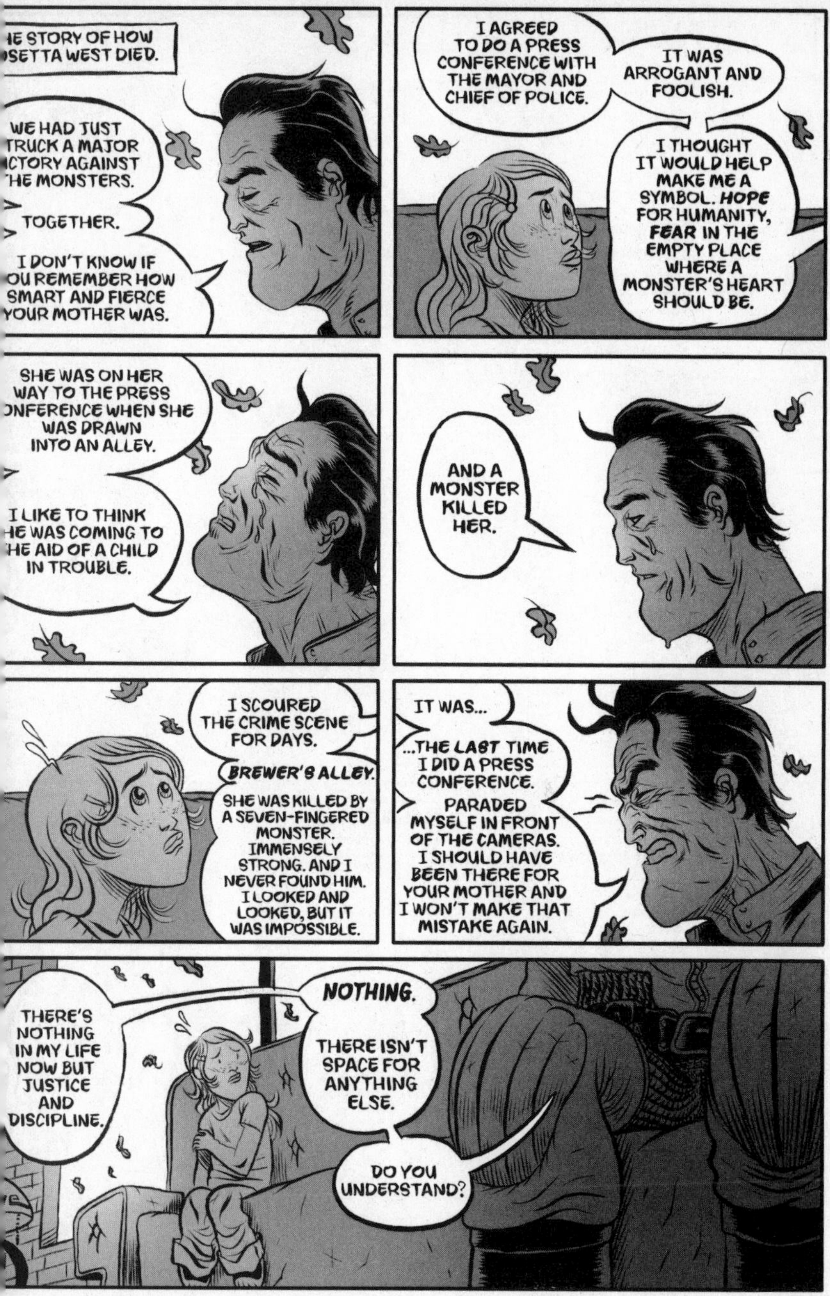

IE STORY OF HOW
)SETTA WEST DIED.
WE HAD JUST
TRUCK A MAJOR
ICTORY AGAINST
HE MONSTERS.
TOGETHER.
I DON'T KNOW IF
OU REMEMBER HOW
SMART AND FIERCE
YOUR MOTHER WAS.
I AGREED TO DO A PRESS CONFERENCE WITH THE MAYOR AND CHIEF OF POLICE.
IT WAS ARROGANT AND FOOLISH.
I THOUGHT IT WOULD HELP MAKE ME A SYMBOL. HOPE FOR HUMANITY, FEAR IN THE EMPTY PLACE WHERE A MONSTER'S HEART SHOULD BE.
SHE WAS ON HER
WAY TO THE PRESS
ONFERENCE WHEN SHE
WAS DRAWN
INTO AN ALLEY.
I LIKE TO THINK
HE WAS COMING TO
HE AID OF A CHILD
IN TROUBLE.
AND A MONSTER KILLED HER.
I SCOURED THE CRIME SCENE FOR DAYS.
BREWER'S ALLEY.
SHE WAS KILLED BY A SEVEN-FINGERED MONSTER. IMMENSELY STRONG. AND I NEVER FOUND HIM. I LOOKED AND LOOKED, BUT IT WAS IMPOSSIBLE.
IT WAS...
...THE LAST TIME I DID A PRESS CONFERENCE.
PARADED MYSELF IN FRONT OF THE CAMERAS. I SHOULD HAVE BEEN THERE FOR YOUR MOTHER AND I WON'T MAKE THAT MISTAKE AGAIN.
THERE'S NOTHING IN MY LIFE NOW BUT JUSTICE AND DISCIPLINE.
NOTHING.
THERE ISN'T SPACE FOR ANYTHING ELSE.
DO YOU UNDERSTAND?

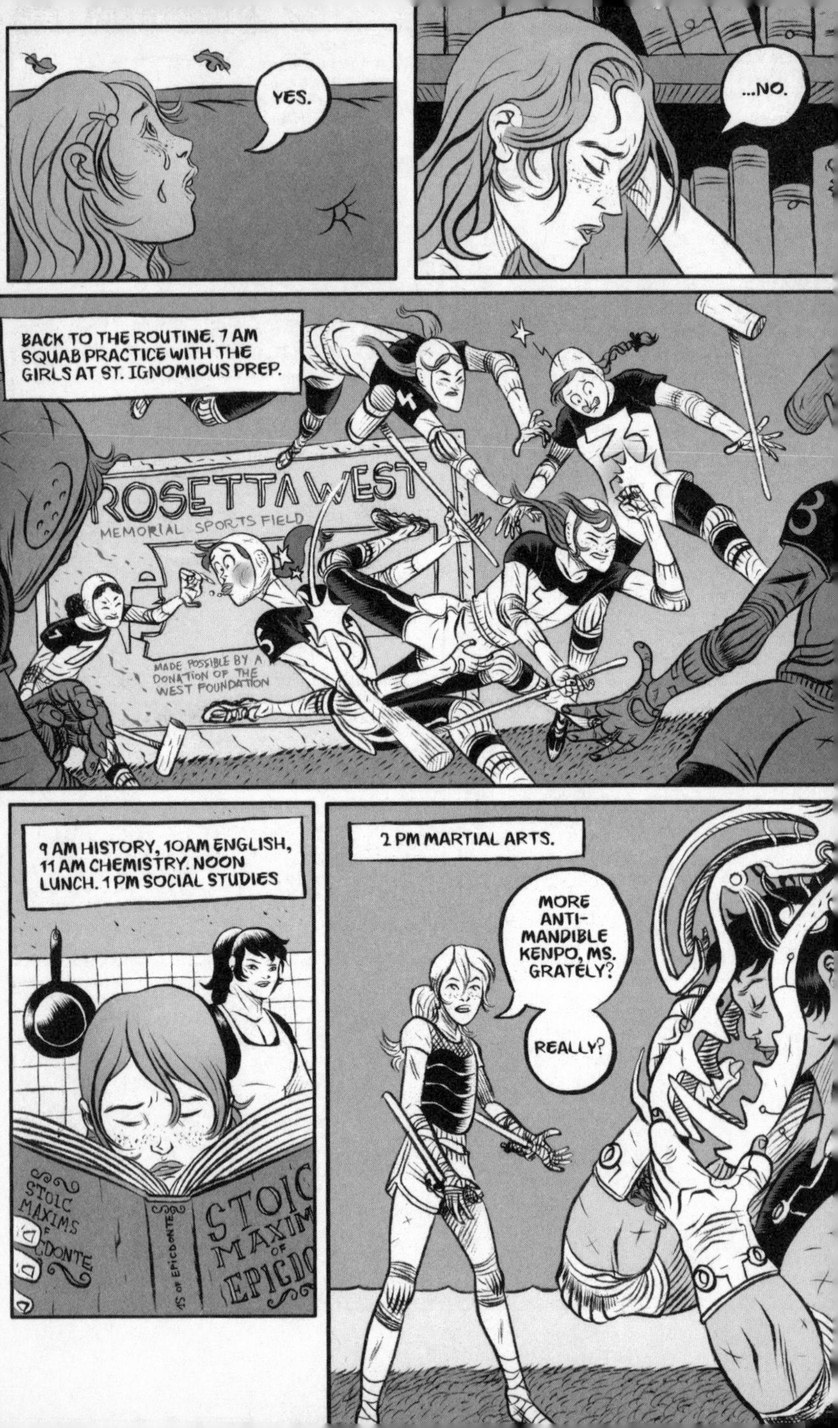
YES.
...NO.
BACK TO THE ROUTINE. 7 AM SQUAB PRACTICE WITH THE GIRLS AT ST. IGNOMIOUS PREP.
ROSETTA WEST
MEMORIAL SPORTS FIELD
MADE POSSIBLE BY A DONATION OF THE WEST FOUNDATION
9 AM HISTORY, 10AM ENGLISH, 11 AM CHEMISTRY. NOON LUNCH. 1 PM SOCIAL STUDIES
STOIC MAXIMS OF EPICDONTE
2 PM MARTIAL ARTS.
MORE ANTI-MANDIBLE KENPO, MS. GRATELY?
REALLY?

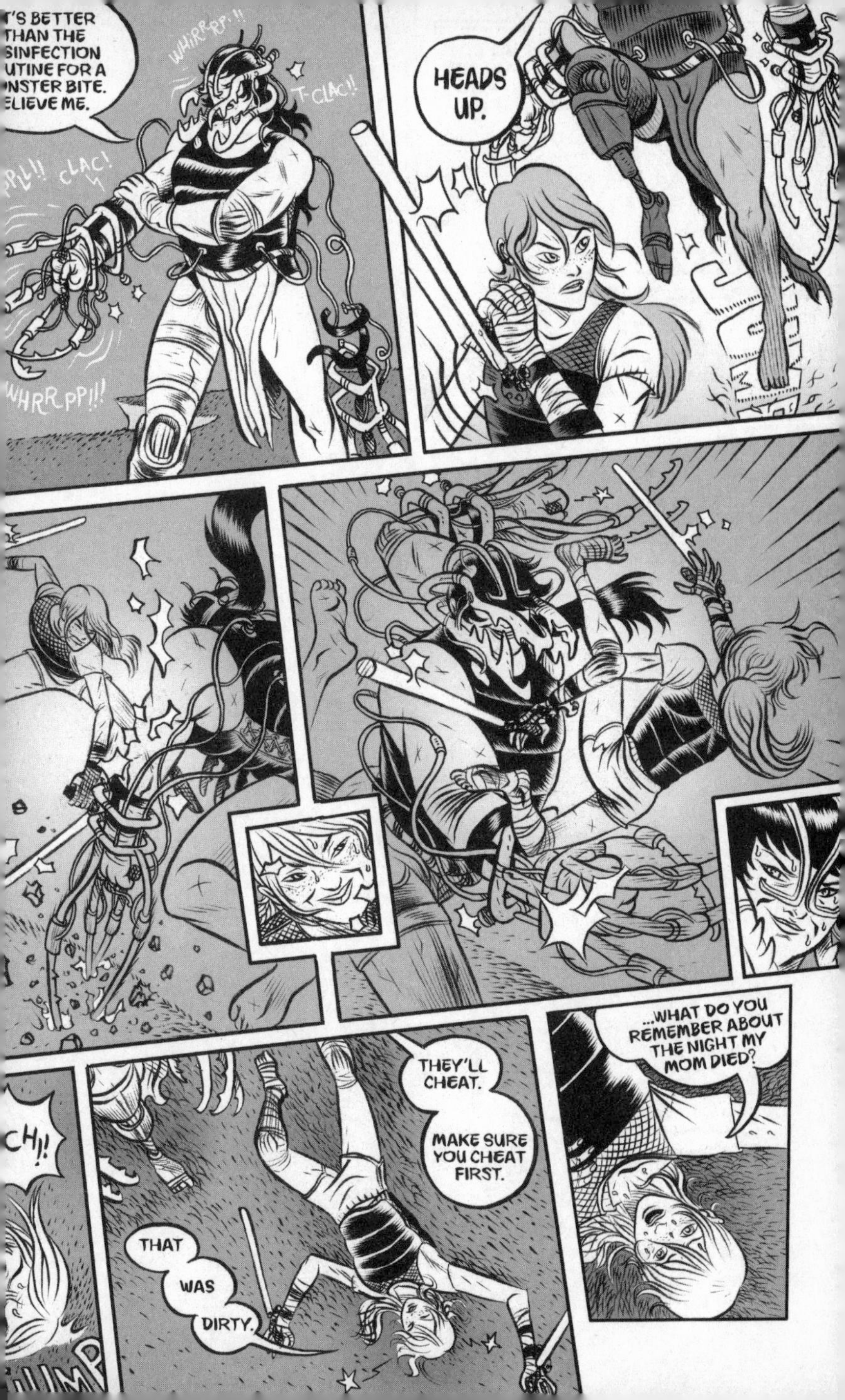

'S BETTER
THAN THE
SINFECTION
UTINE FOR A
NSTER BITE.
ELIEVE ME.
WHIRRRPP!!
T-CLAC!!
PPLL!! CLAC!
WHRRPP!!!
HEADS UP.
THEY'LL CHEAT.
MAKE SURE YOU CHEAT FIRST.
THAT
WAS
DIRTY.
...WHAT DO YOU REMEMBER ABOUT THE NIGHT MY MOM DIED?

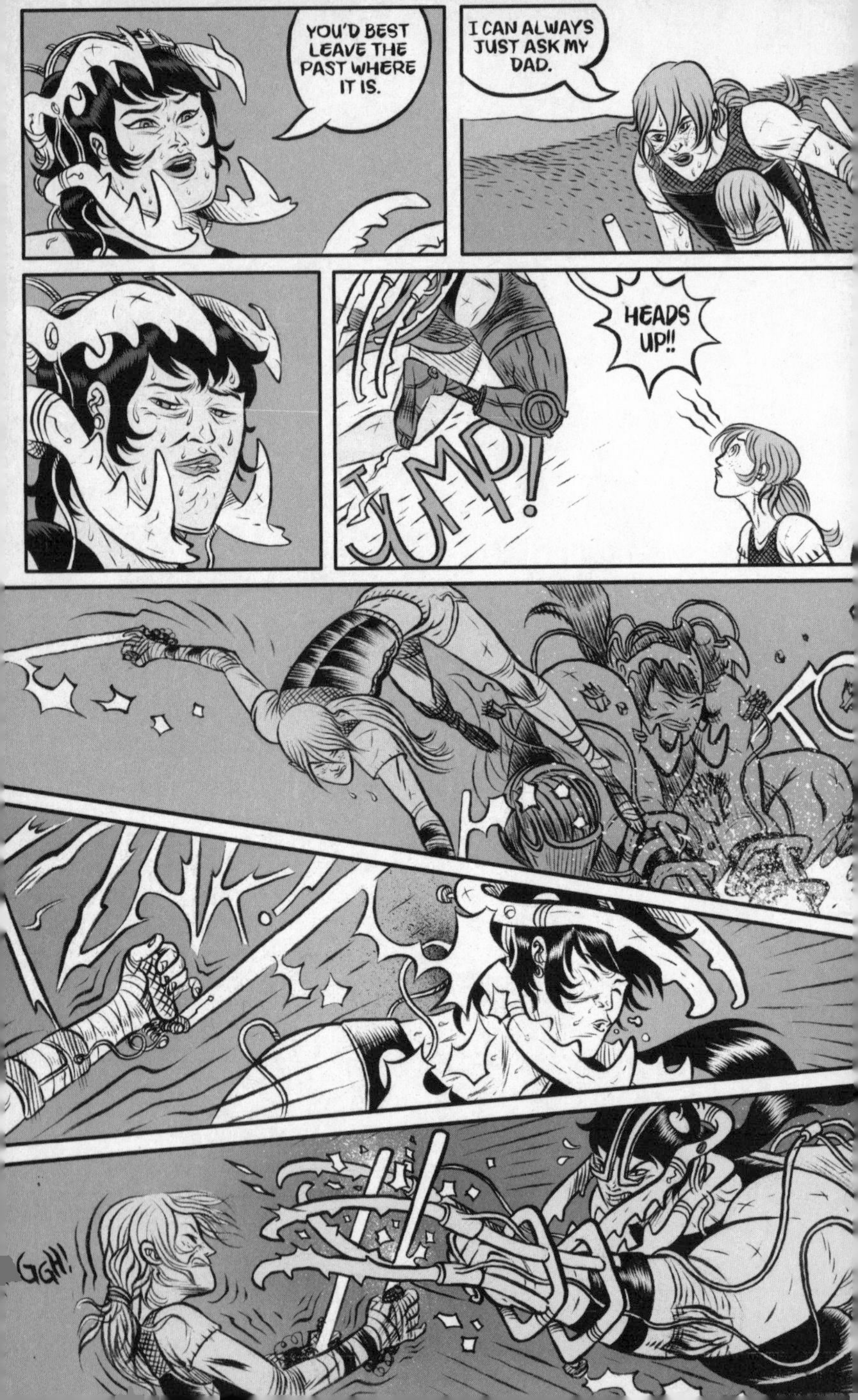
YOU'D BEST LEAVE THE PAST WHERE IT IS.
I CAN ALWAYS JUST ASK MY DAD.
HEADS UP!!
JUMP!
GGH!

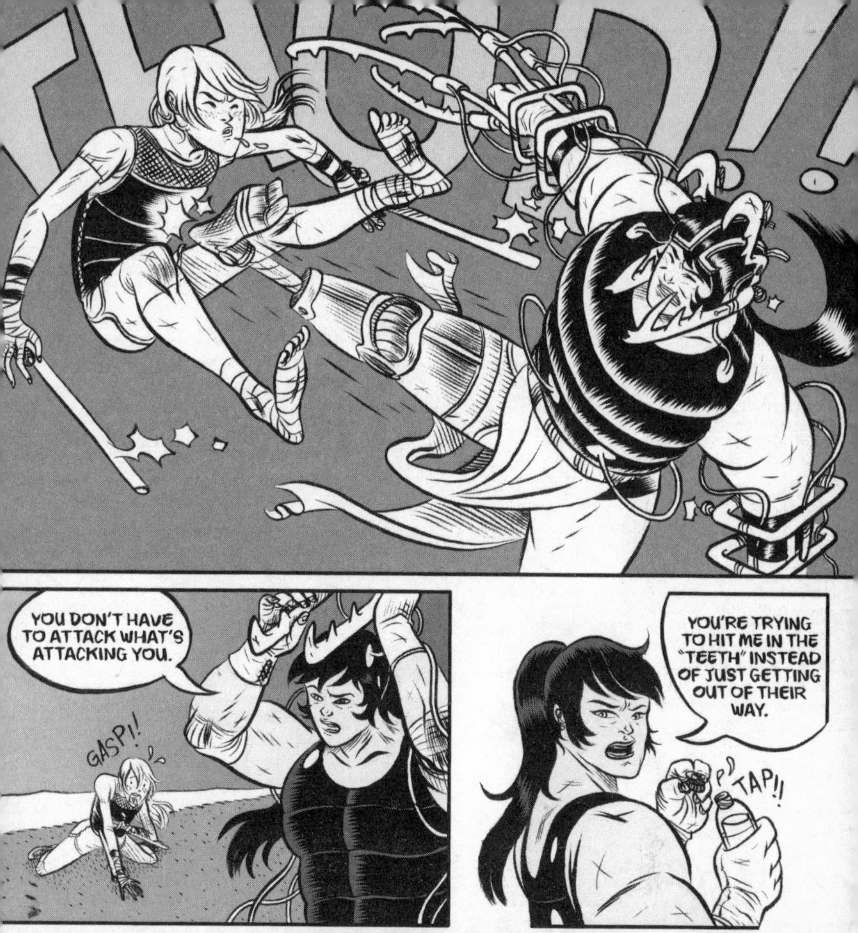
YOU DON'T HAVE TO ATTACK WHAT'S ATTACKING YOU.
GASP!!
YOU'RE TRYING TO HIT ME IN THE "TEETH" INSTEAD OF JUST GETTING OUT OF THEIR WAY.
TAP!!
DODGE THE TEETH AND IT THE BELLY. OR THE LEGS. OR THE GROIN. YOU'RE A SMALL TARGET, TAKE ADVANTAGE OF THAT.
AND ABOUT YOUR MOM...

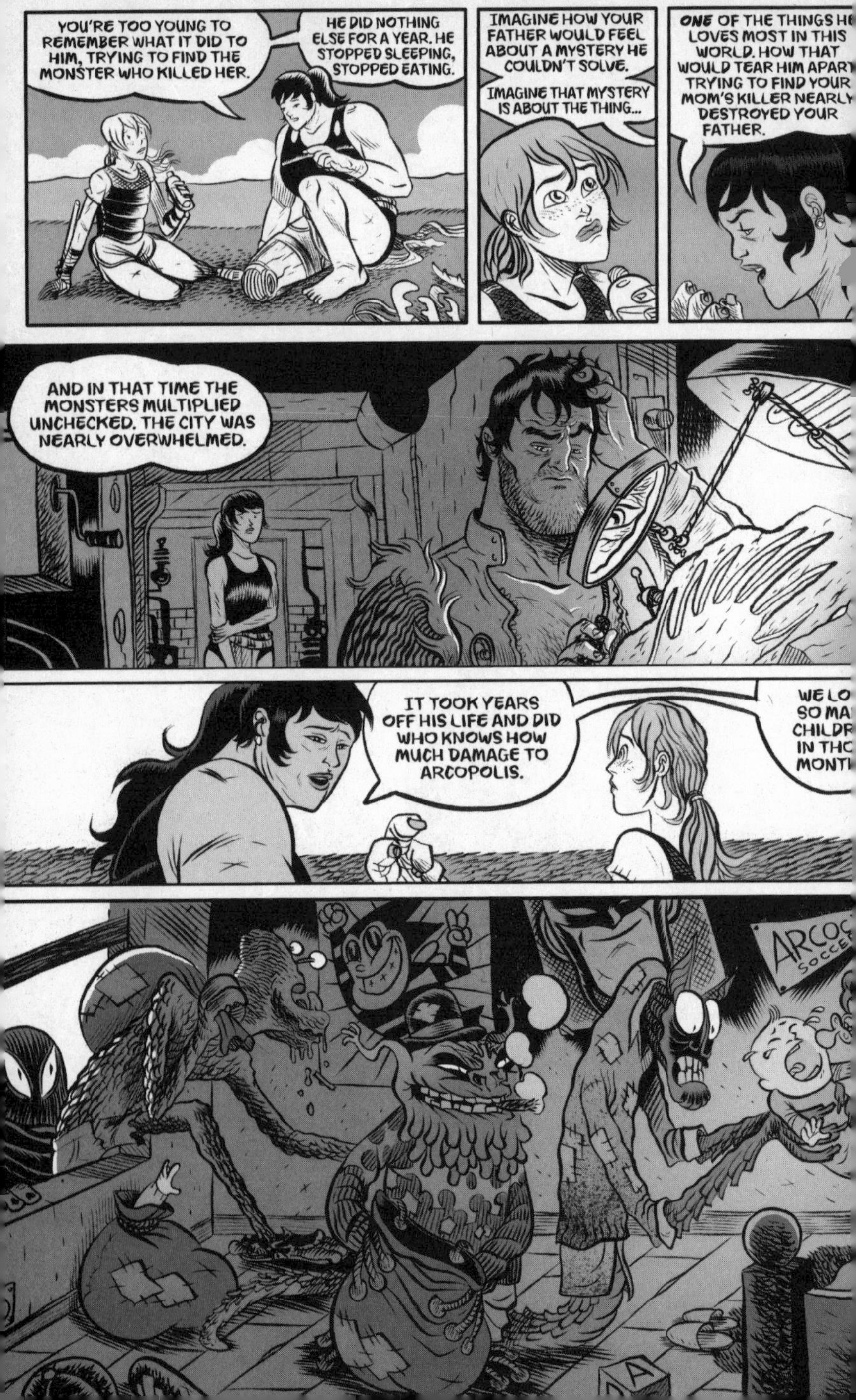

YOU'RE TOO YOUNG TO REMEMBER WHAT IT DID TO HIM, TRYING TO FIND THE MONSTER WHO KILLED HER.
HE DID NOTHING ELSE FOR A YEAR. HE STOPPED SLEEPING, STOPPED EATING.
IMAGINE HOW YOUR FATHER WOULD FEEL ABOUT A MYSTERY HE COULDN'T SOLVE.
IMAGINE THAT MYSTERY IS ABOUT THE THING...
ONE OF THE THINGS H LOVES MOST IN THIS WORLD. HOW THAT WOULD TEAR HIM APART TRYING TO FIND YOUR MOM'S KILLER NEARLY DESTROYED YOUR FATHER.
AND IN THAT TIME THE MONSTERS MULTIPLIED UNCHECKED. THE CITY WAS NEARLY OVERWHELMED.
IT TOOK YEARS OFF HIS LIFE AND DID WHO KNOWS HOW MUCH DAMAGE TO ARCOPOLIS.
WE LO SO MA CHILDR IN THO MONT

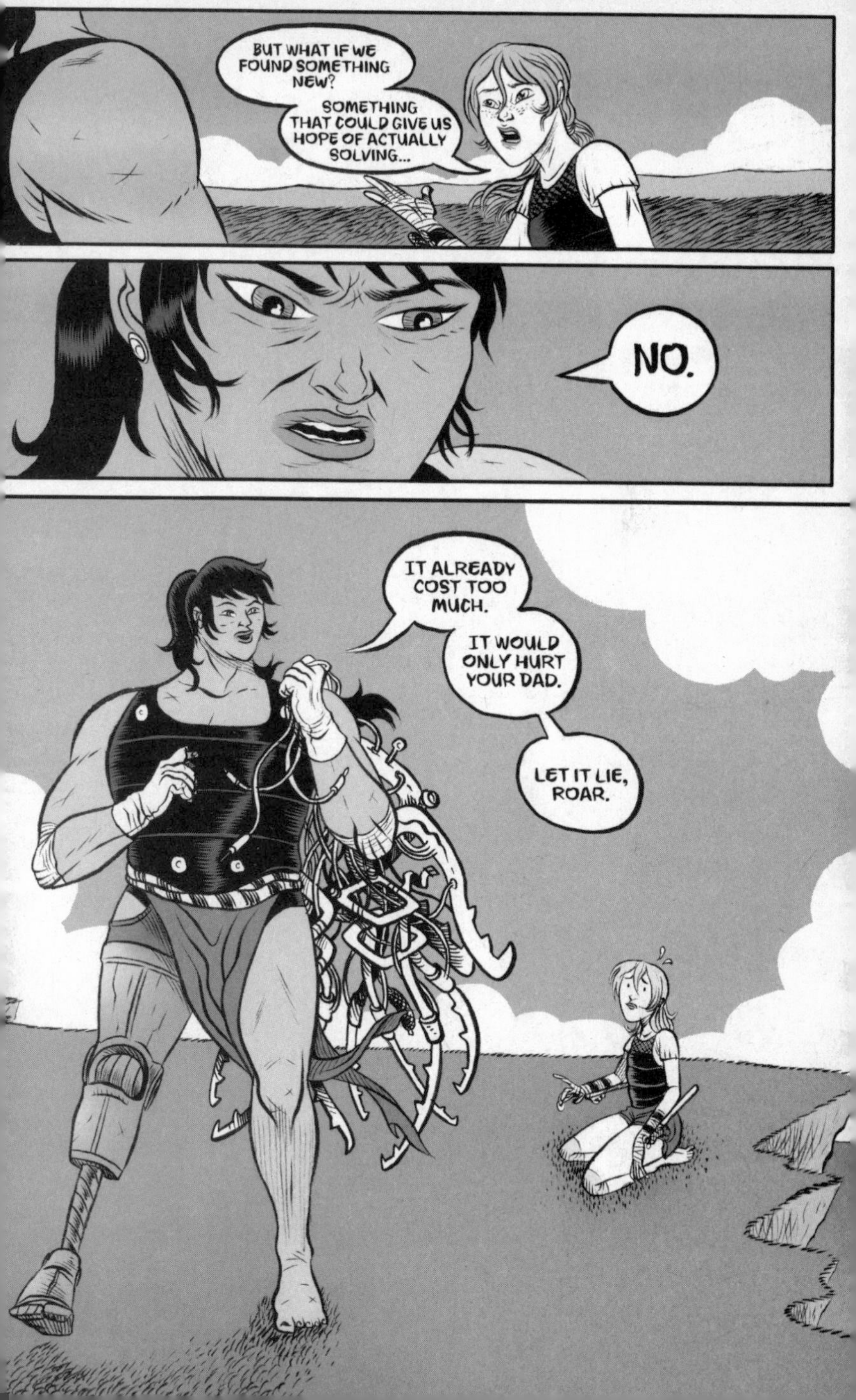
BUT WHAT IF WE FOUND SOMETHING NEW?
SOMETHING THAT COULD GIVE US HOPE OF ACTUALLY SOLVING...
NO.
IT ALREADY COST TOO MUCH.
IT WOULD ONLY HURT YOUR DAD.
LET IT LIE, ROAR.

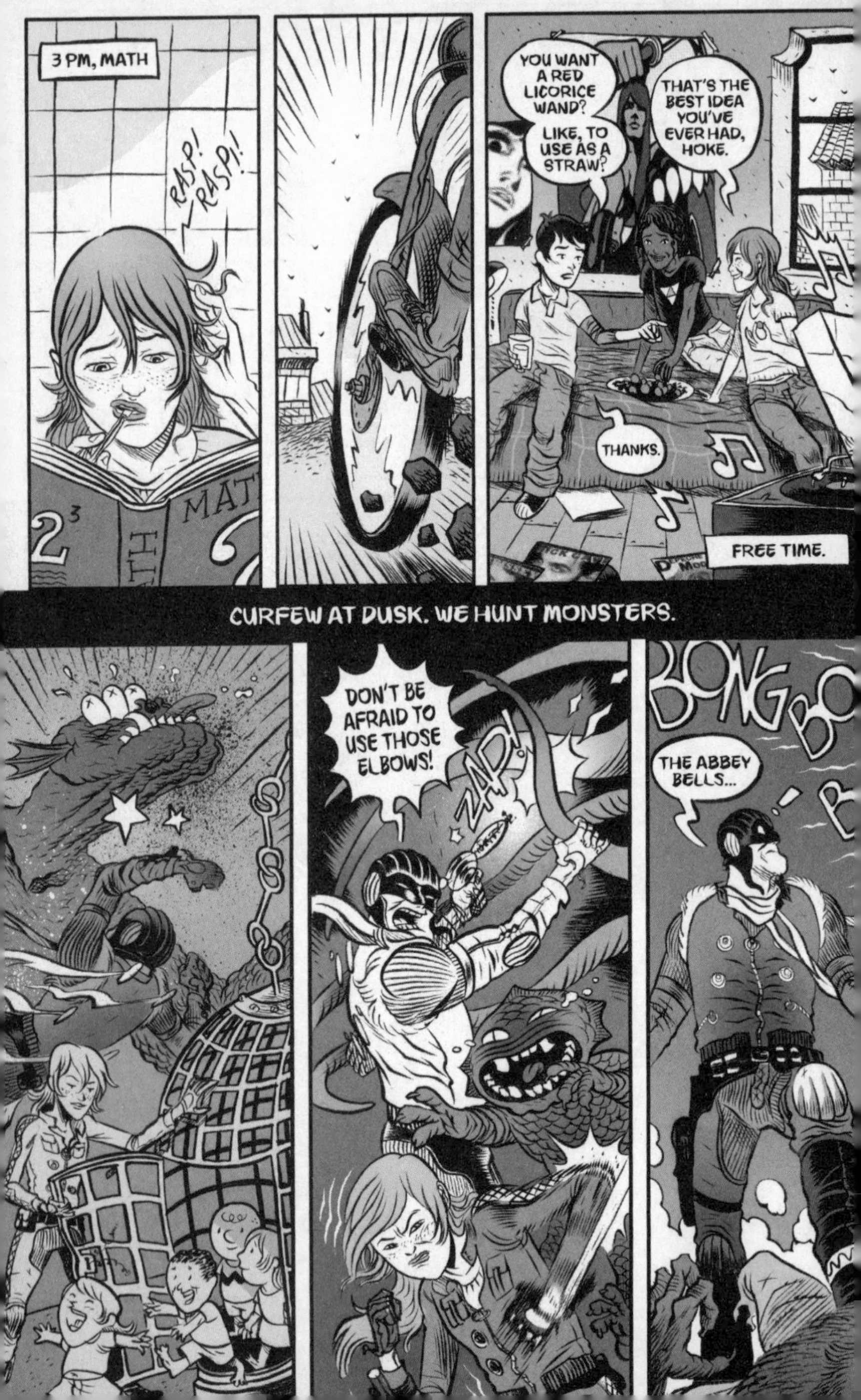
3 PM, MATH
RASP! RASP!
YOU WANT A RED LICORICE WAND?
LIKE, TO USE AS A STRAW?
THAT'S THE BEST IDEA YOU'VE EVER HAD, HOKE.
THANKS.
FREE TIME.
CURFEW AT DUSK. WE HUNT MONSTERS.
DON'T BE AFRAID TO USE THOSE ELBOWS!
ZAP!
BONG
THE ABBEY BELLS...

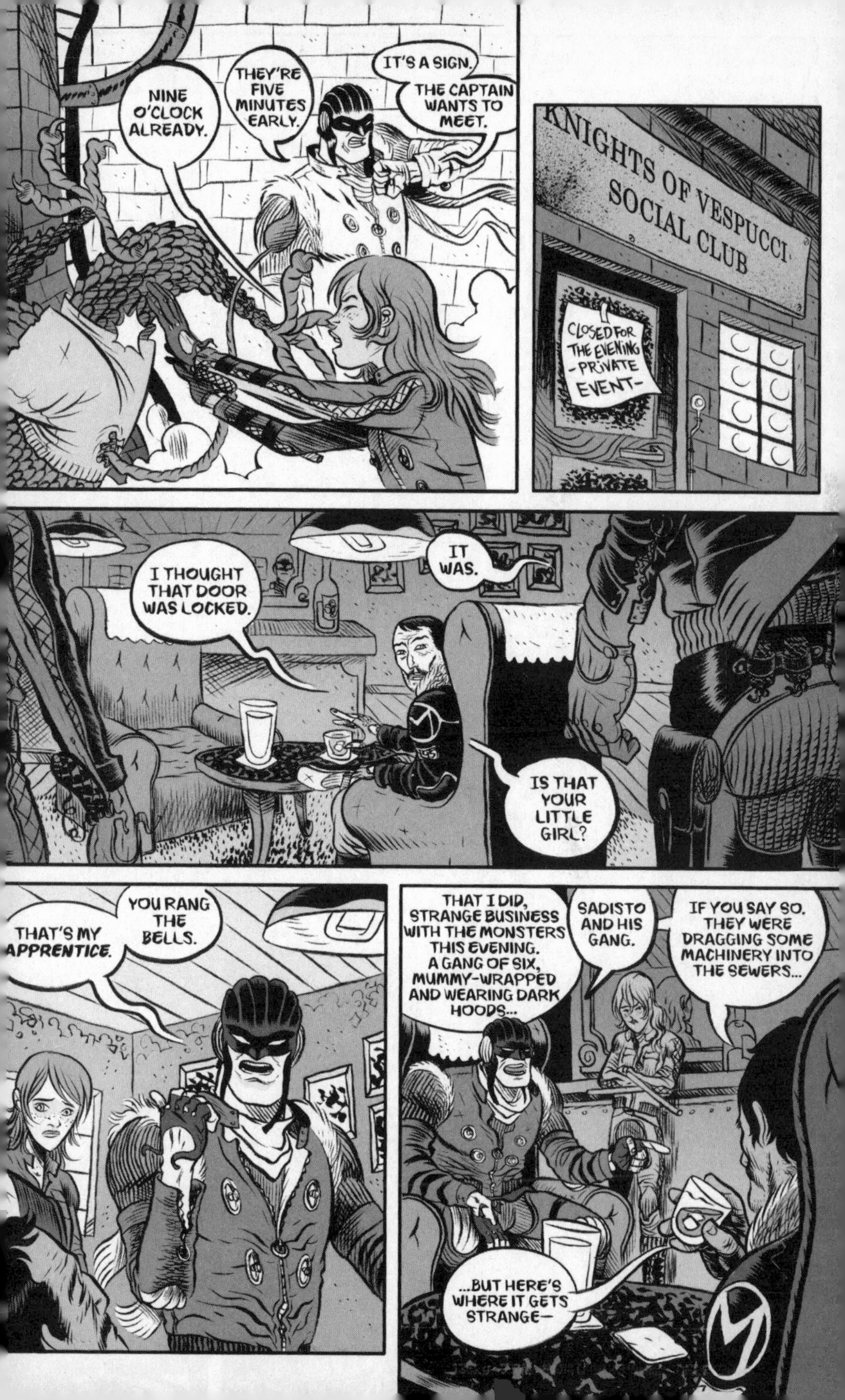
NINE O'CLOCK ALREADY.
THEY'RE FIVE MINUTES EARLY.
IT'S A SIGN.
THE CAPTAIN WANTS TO MEET.
KNIGHTS OF VESPUCCI SOCIAL CLUB
CLOSED FOR THE EVENING -PRIVATE EVENT-
I THOUGHT THAT DOOR WAS LOCKED.
IT WAS.
IS THAT YOUR LITTLE GIRL?
THAT'S MY APPRENTICE.
YOU RANG THE BELLS.
THAT I DID, STRANGE BUSINESS WITH THE MONSTERS THIS EVENING. A GANG OF SIX, MUMMY-WRAPPED AND WEARING DARK HOODS...
SADISTO AND HIS GANG.
IF YOU SAY SO. THEY WERE DRAGGING SOME MACHINERY INTO THE SEWERS...
...BUT HERE'S WHERE IT GETS STRANGE—

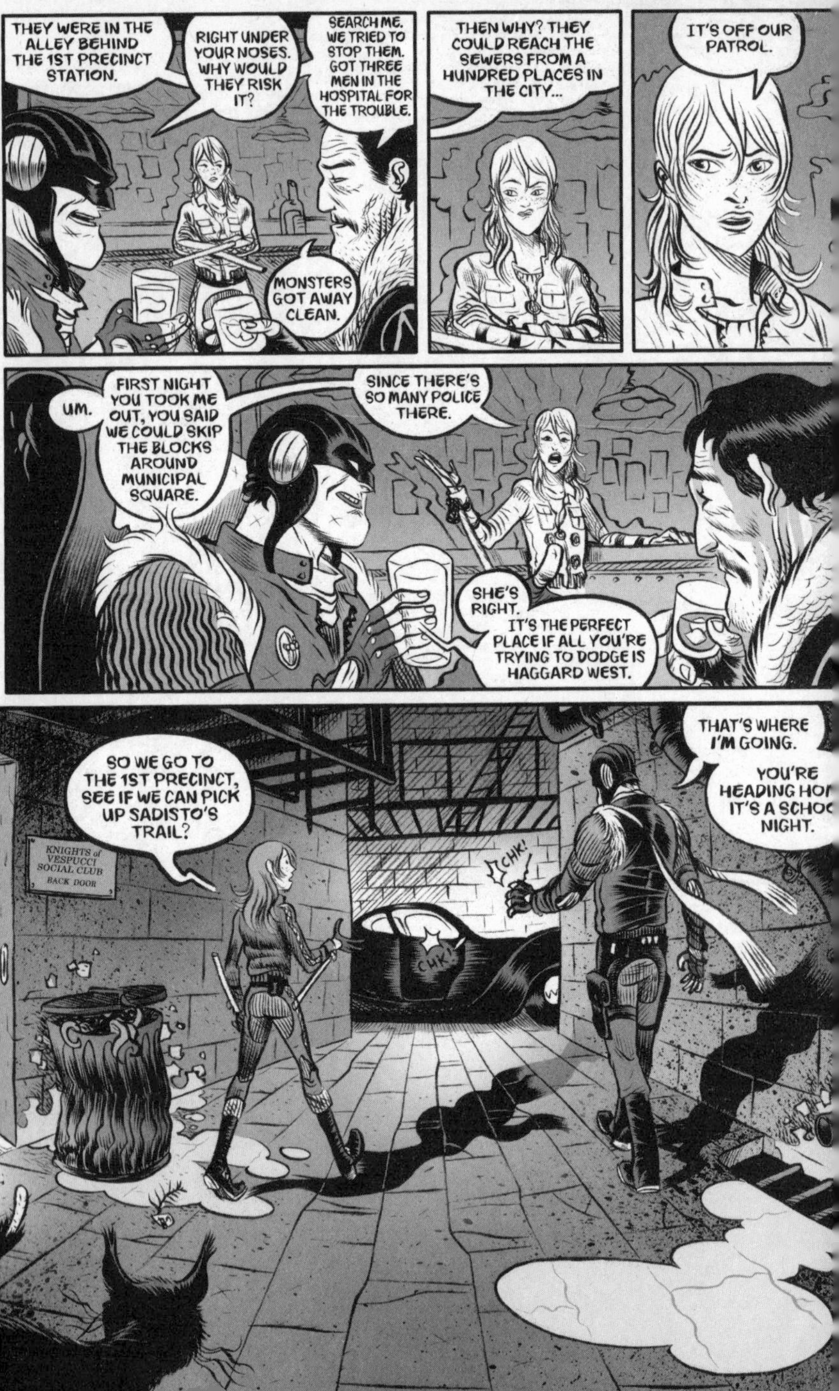
THEY WERE IN THE ALLEY BEHIND THE 1ST PRECINCT STATION.
RIGHT UNDER YOUR NOSES. WHY WOULD THEY RISK IT?
SEARCH ME. WE TRIED TO STOP THEM. GOT THREE MEN IN THE HOSPITAL FOR THE TROUBLE.
MONSTERS GOT AWAY CLEAN.
THEN WHY? THEY COULD REACH THE SEWERS FROM A HUNDRED PLACES IN THE CITY...
IT'S OFF OUR PATROL.
UM.
FIRST NIGHT YOU TOOK ME OUT, YOU SAID WE COULD SKIP THE BLOCKS AROUND MUNICIPAL SQUARE.
SINCE THERE'S SO MANY POLICE THERE.
SHE'S RIGHT.
IT'S THE PERFECT PLACE IF ALL YOU'RE TRYING TO DODGE IS HAGGARD WEST.
KNIGHTS of VESPUCCI SOCIAL CLUB BACK DOOR
SO WE GO TO THE 1ST PRECINCT, SEE IF WE CAN PICK UP SADISTO'S TRAIL?
CHK!
CHK!
THAT'S WHERE I'M GOING.
YOU'RE HEADING HO
IT'S A SCHO
NIGHT.

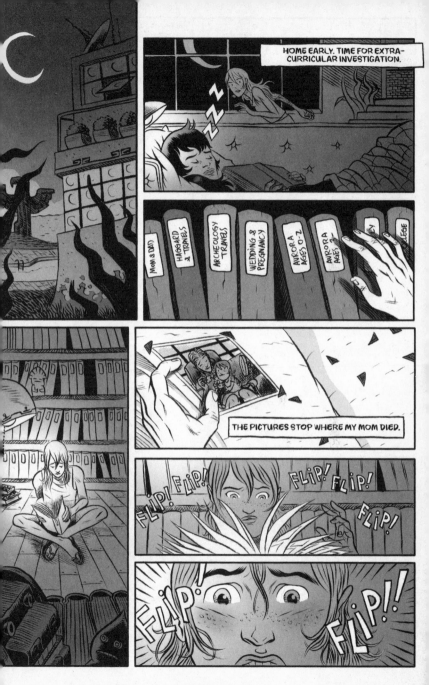

HOME EARLY. TIME FOR EXTRA-CURRICULAR INVESTIGATION.

MOM & DAD

HAGGARD & TRAVELS

ARCHEOLOGY TRAVELS

WEDDING & PREGNANCY

AURORA AGES 0-2

AURORA AGE 2

COLLEGE

THE PICTURES STOP WHERE MY MOM DIED.

FLIP! FLIP! FLIP! FLIP! FLIP!

FLIP! FLIP!!

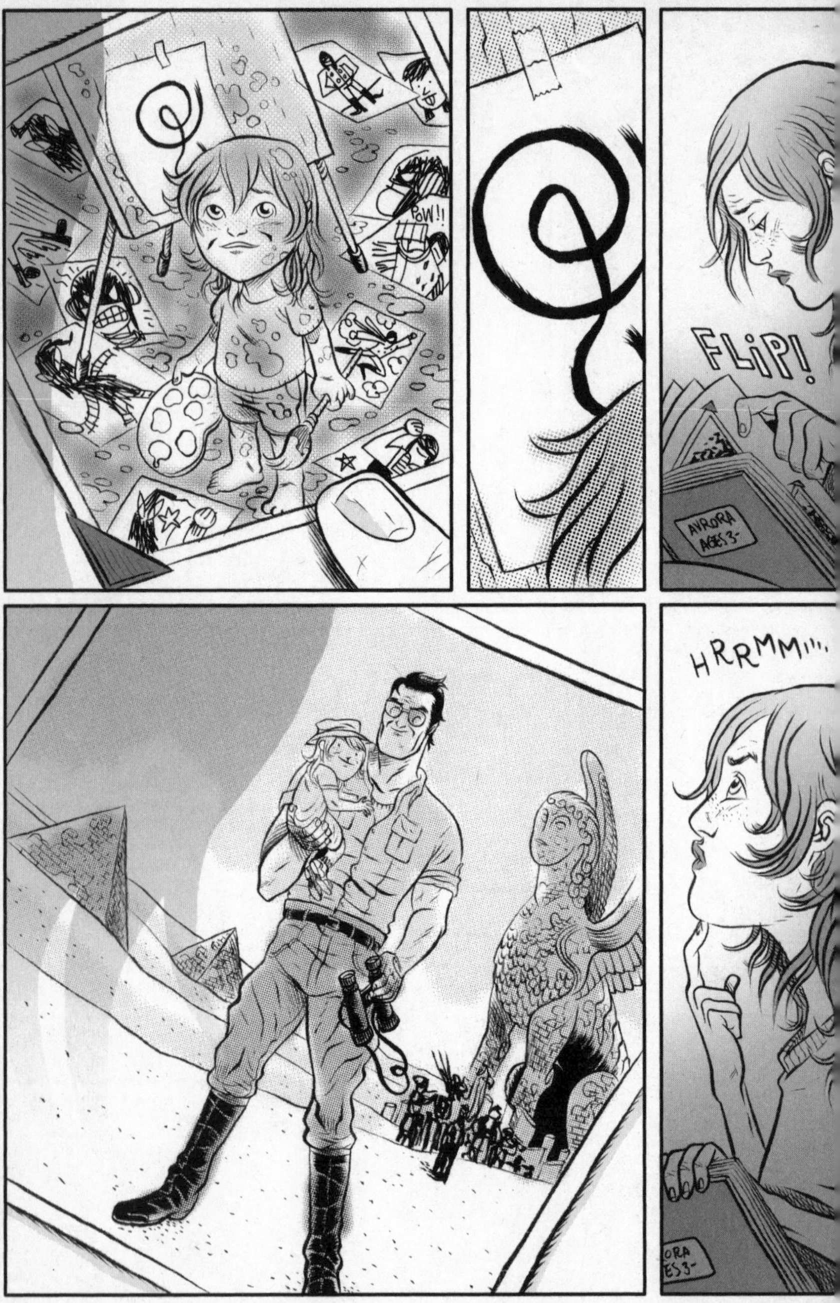
POW!!
FLIP!
AVRORA
AGES 3-
HRRMM...

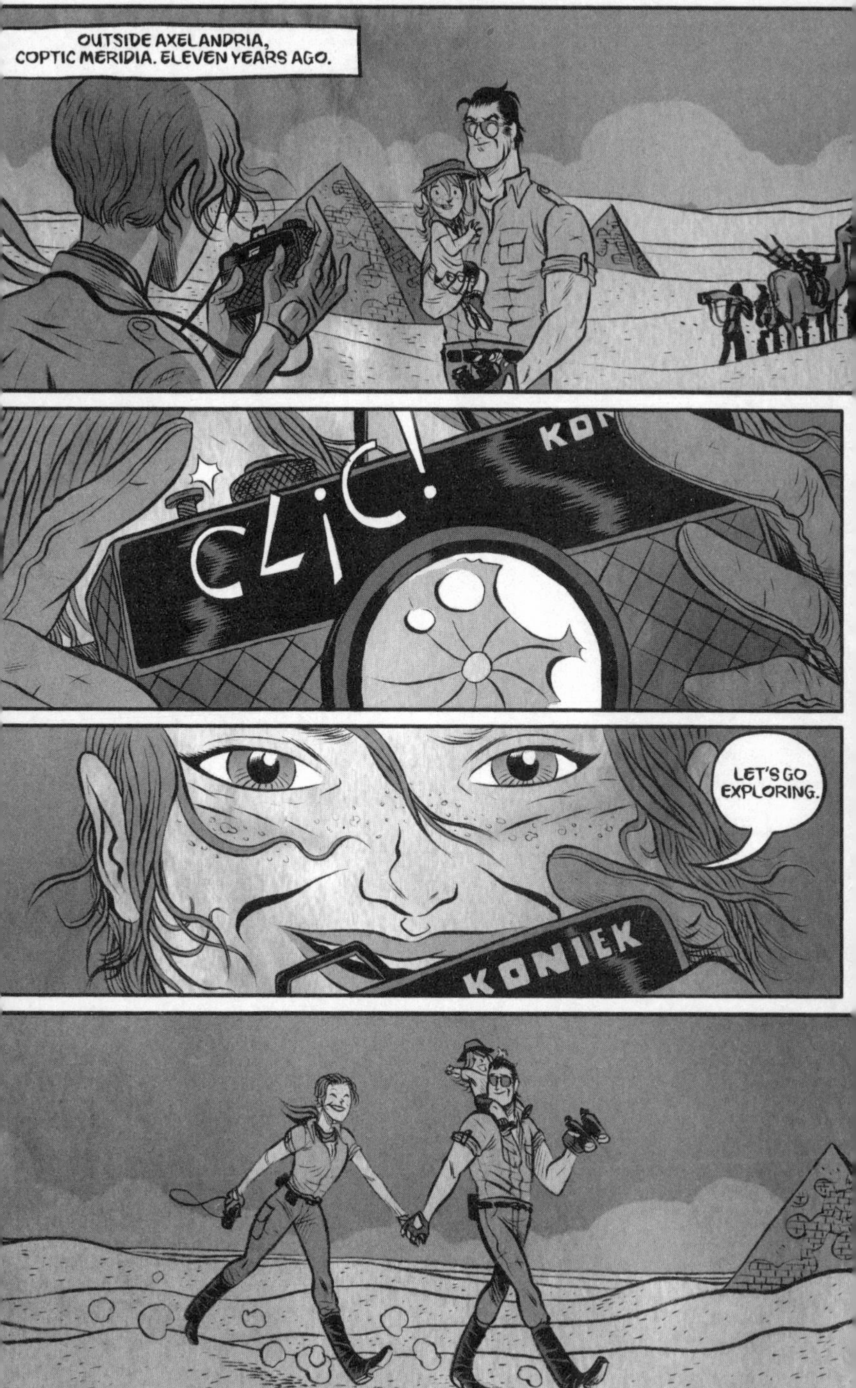
OUTSIDE AXELANDRIA, COPTIC MERIDIA. ELEVEN YEARS AGO.
KON
CLIC!
LET'S GO EXPLORING.
KONIEK

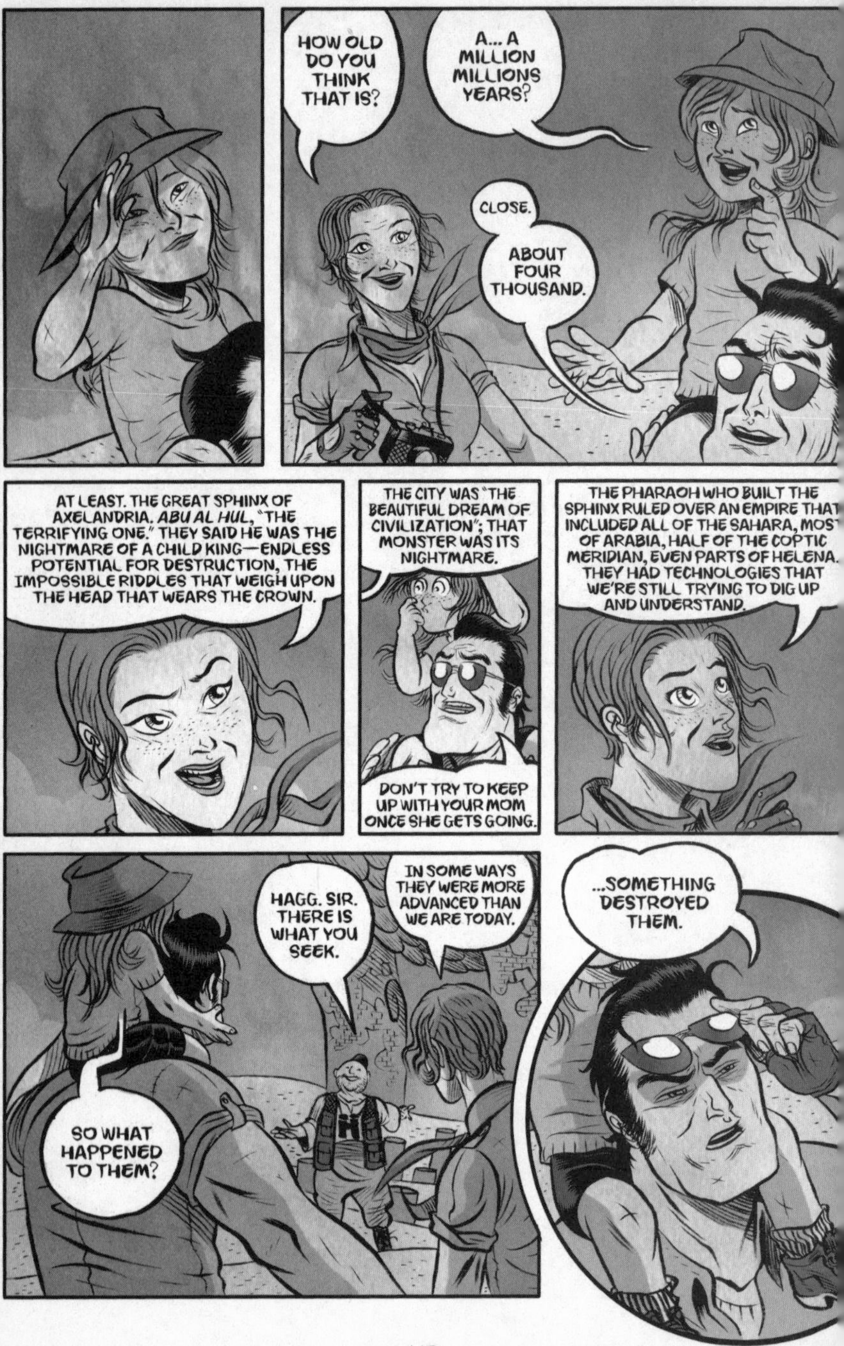
HOW OLD DO YOU THINK THAT IS?
A... A MILLION MILLIONS YEARS?
CLOSE.
ABOUT FOUR THOUSAND.
AT LEAST. THE GREAT SPHINX OF AXELANDRIA. *ABU AL HUL*, "THE TERRIFYING ONE." THEY SAID HE WAS THE NIGHTMARE OF A CHILD KING—ENDLESS POTENTIAL FOR DESTRUCTION, THE IMPOSSIBLE RIDDLES THAT WEIGH UPON THE HEAD THAT WEARS THE CROWN.
THE CITY WAS "THE BEAUTIFUL DREAM OF CIVILIZATION"; THAT MONSTER WAS ITS NIGHTMARE.
DON'T TRY TO KEEP UP WITH YOUR MOM ONCE SHE GETS GOING.
THE PHARAOH WHO BUILT THE SPHINX RULED OVER AN EMPIRE THAT INCLUDED ALL OF THE SAHARA, MOST OF ARABIA, HALF OF THE COPTIC MERIDIAN, EVEN PARTS OF HELENA. THEY HAD TECHNOLOGIES THAT WE'RE STILL TRYING TO DIG UP AND UNDERSTAND.
HAGG. SIR. THERE IS WHAT YOU SEEK.
IN SOME WAYS THEY WERE MORE ADVANCED THAN WE ARE TODAY.
SO WHAT HAPPENED TO THEM?
...SOMETHING DESTROYED THEM.

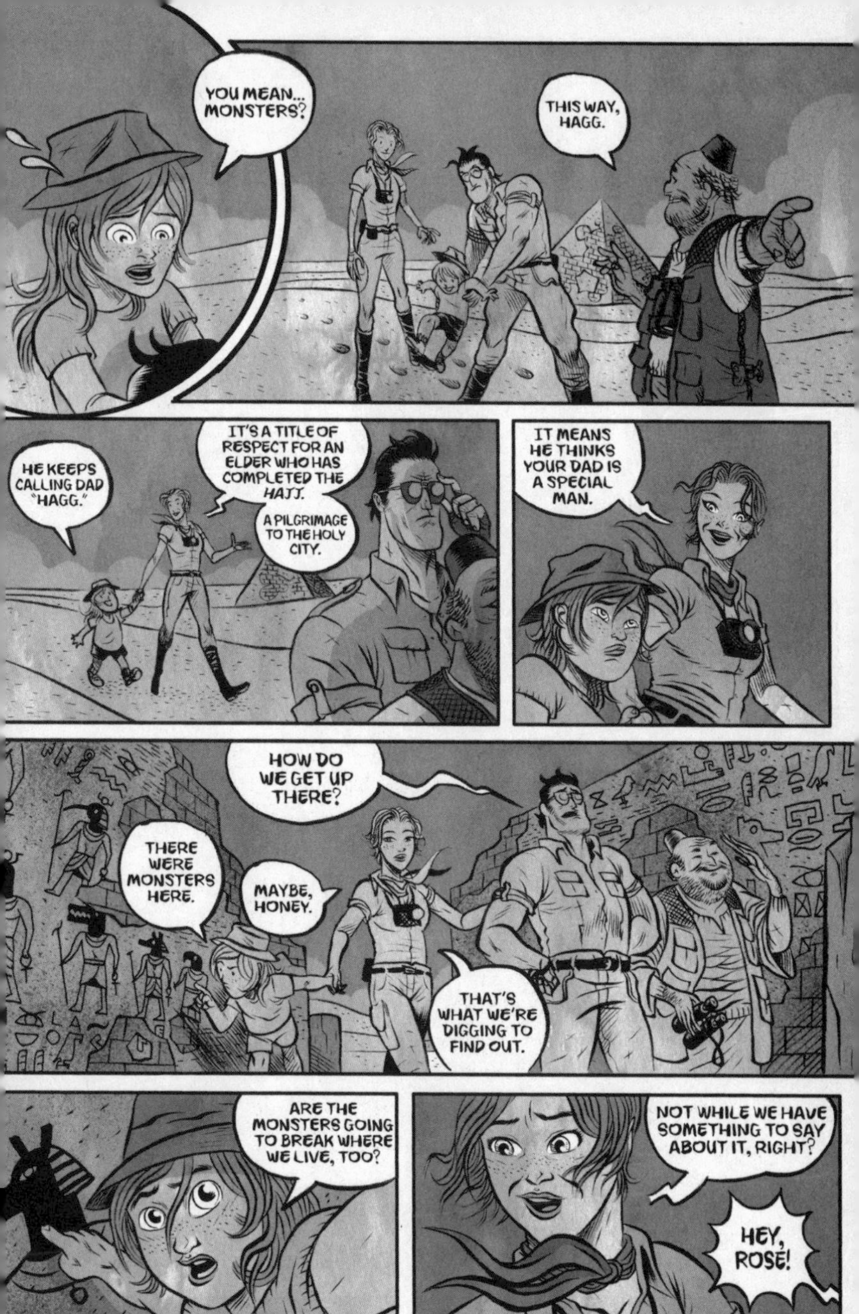
YOU MEAN... MONSTERS?
THIS WAY, HAGG.
HE KEEPS CALLING DAD "HAGG."
IT'S A TITLE OF RESPECT FOR AN ELDER WHO HAS COMPLETED THE *HAJJ.*
A PILGRIMAGE TO THE HOLY CITY.
IT MEANS HE THINKS YOUR DAD IS A SPECIAL MAN.
HOW DO WE GET UP THERE?
THERE WERE MONSTERS HERE.
MAYBE, HONEY.
THAT'S WHAT WE'RE DIGGING TO FIND OUT.
ARE THE MONSTERS GOING TO BREAK WHERE WE LIVE, TOO?
NOT WHILE WE HAVE SOMETHING TO SAY ABOUT IT, RIGHT?
HEY, ROSE!

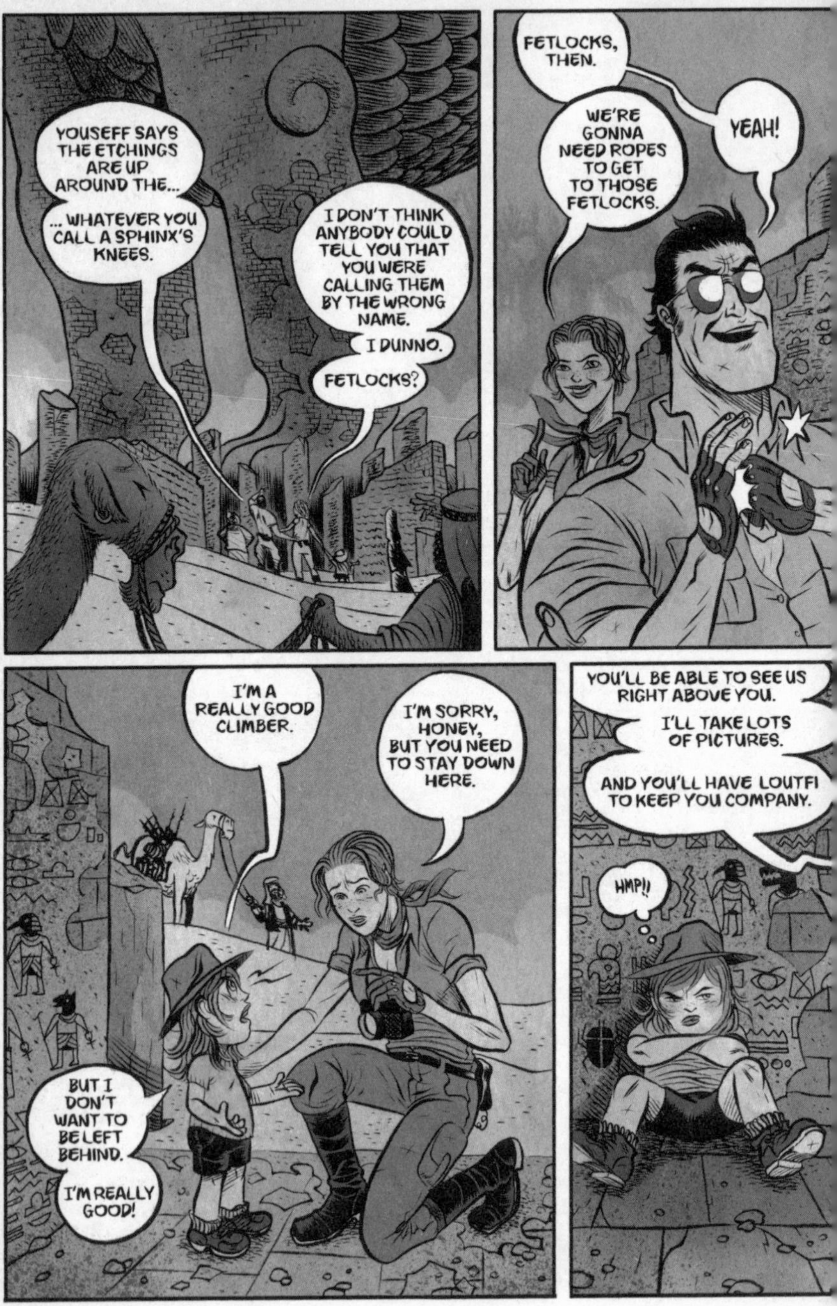
YOUSEFF SAYS THE ETCHINGS ARE UP AROUND THE...
... WHATEVER YOU CALL A SPHINX'S KNEES.
I DON'T THINK ANYBODY COULD TELL YOU THAT YOU WERE CALLING THEM BY THE WRONG NAME.
I DUNNO.
FETLOCKS?
FETLOCKS, THEN.
WE'RE GONNA NEED ROPES TO GET TO THOSE FETLOCKS.
YEAH!
I'M A REALLY GOOD CLIMBER.
I'M SORRY, HONEY, BUT YOU NEED TO STAY DOWN HERE.
BUT I DON'T WANT TO BE LEFT BEHIND.
I'M REALLY GOOD!
YOU'LL BE ABLE TO SEE US RIGHT ABOVE YOU.
I'LL TAKE LOTS OF PICTURES.
AND YOU'LL HAVE LOUTFI TO KEEP YOU COMPANY.
HMP!!

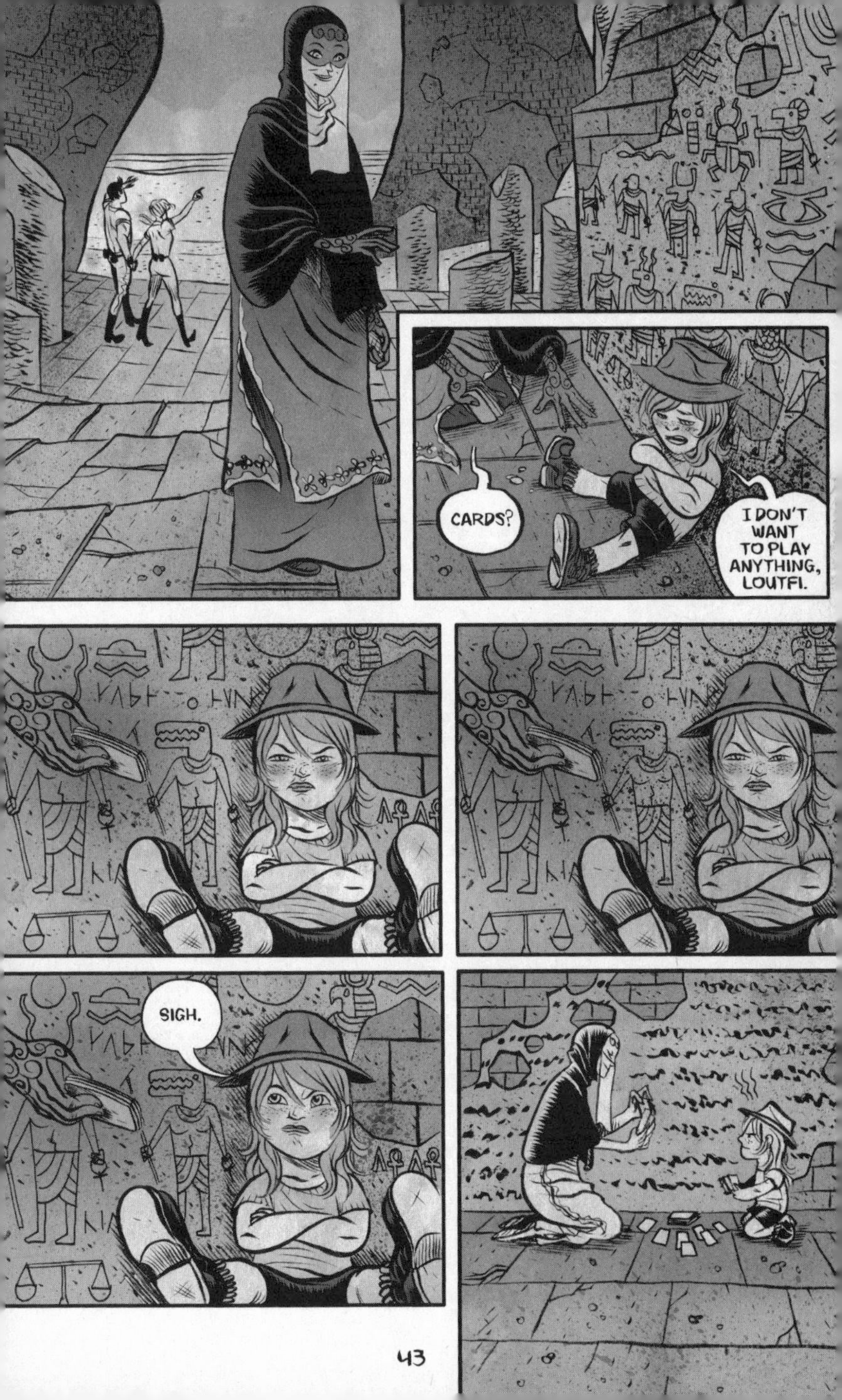
CARDS?
I DON'T WANT TO PLAY ANYTHING, LOUTFI.
SIGH.

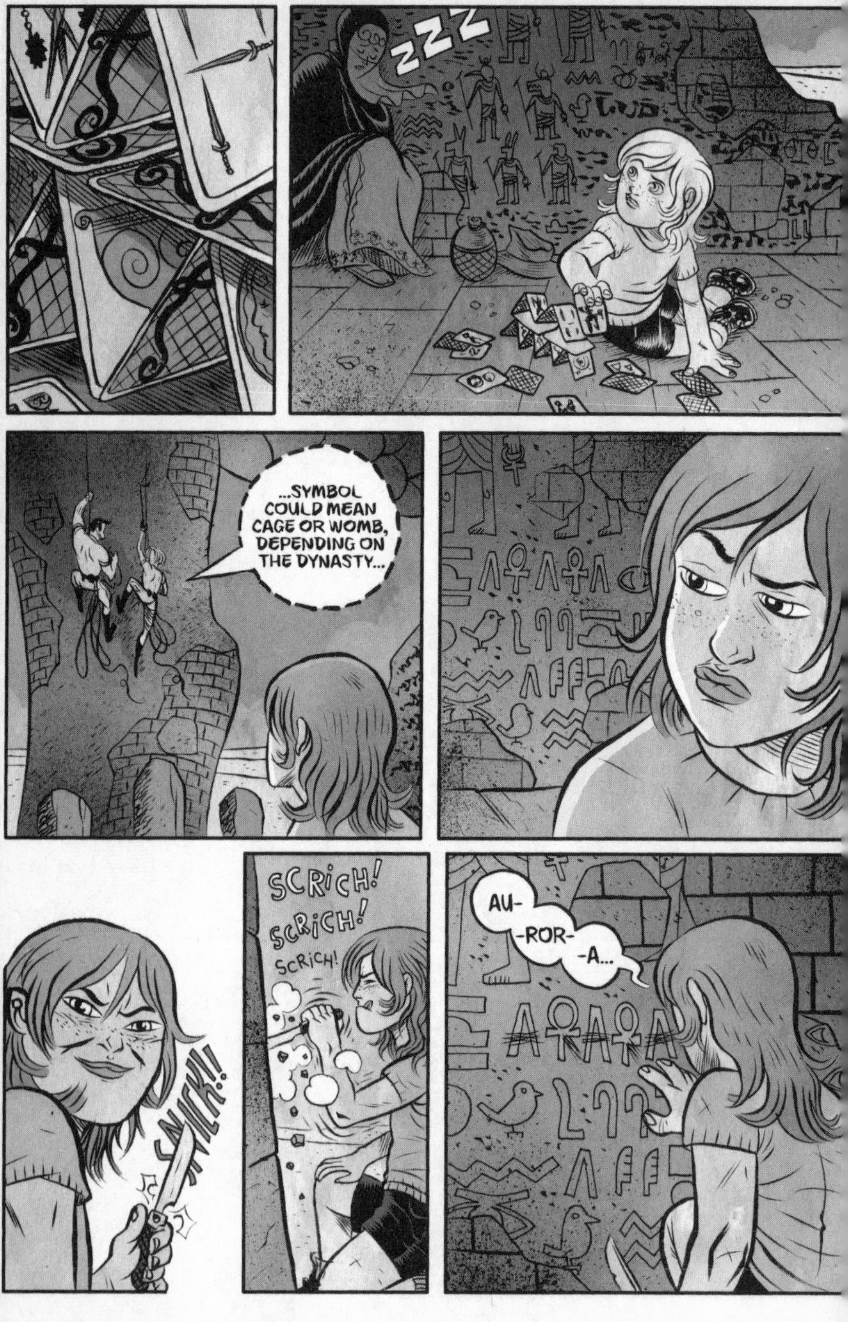
ZZZ
...SYMBOL COULD MEAN CAGE OR WOMB, DEPENDING ON THE DYNASTY...
SNICK!!
SCRICH!
SCRICH!
SCRICH!
AU-
-ROR-
-A...

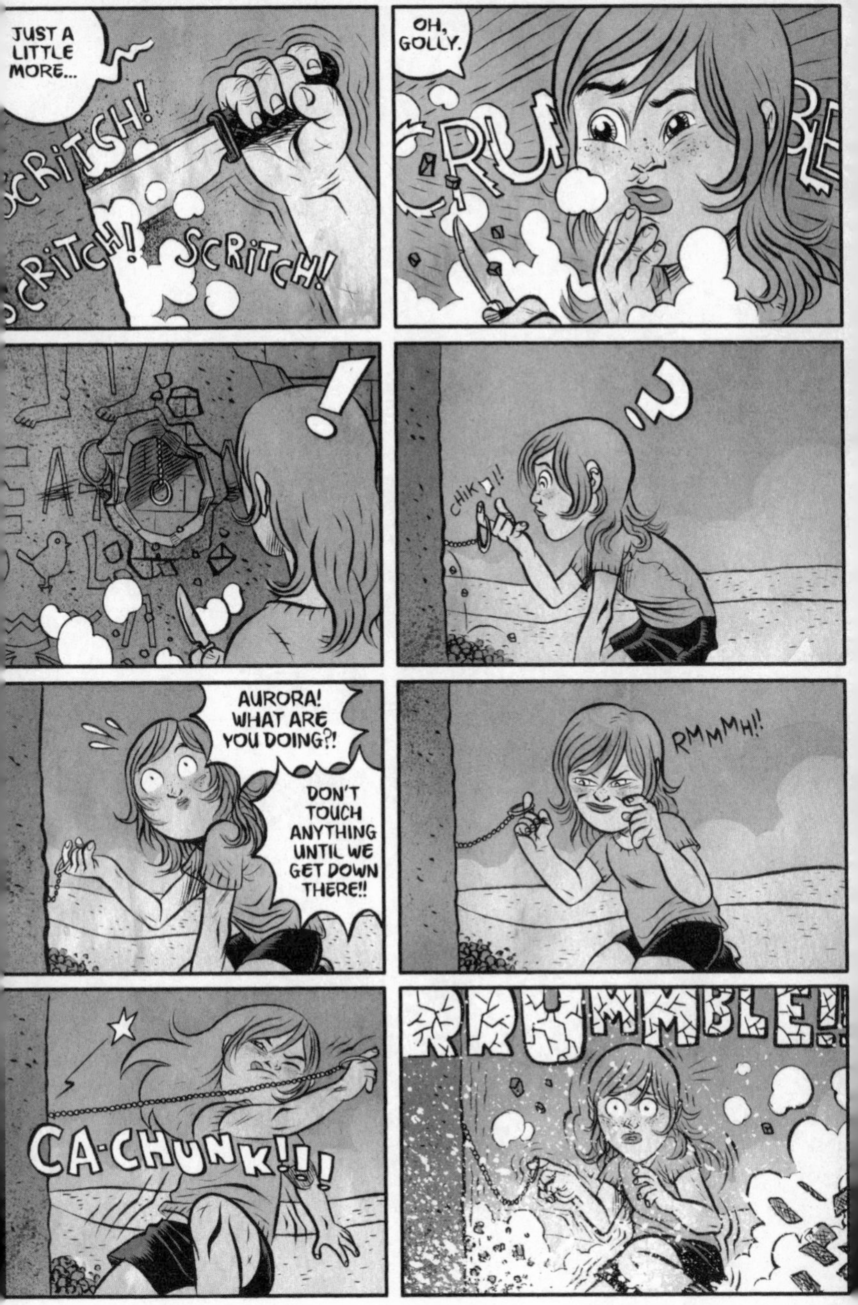
JUST A LITTLE MORE...
SCRITCH!
SCRITCH!
SCRITCH!
OH, GOLLY.
CRUMBLE
!
?
CHIK!!
AURORA! WHAT ARE YOU DOING?!
DON'T TOUCH ANYTHING UNTIL WE GET DOWN THERE!!
RMMMH!!
CA-CHUNK!!!
RRUMMBLE!!

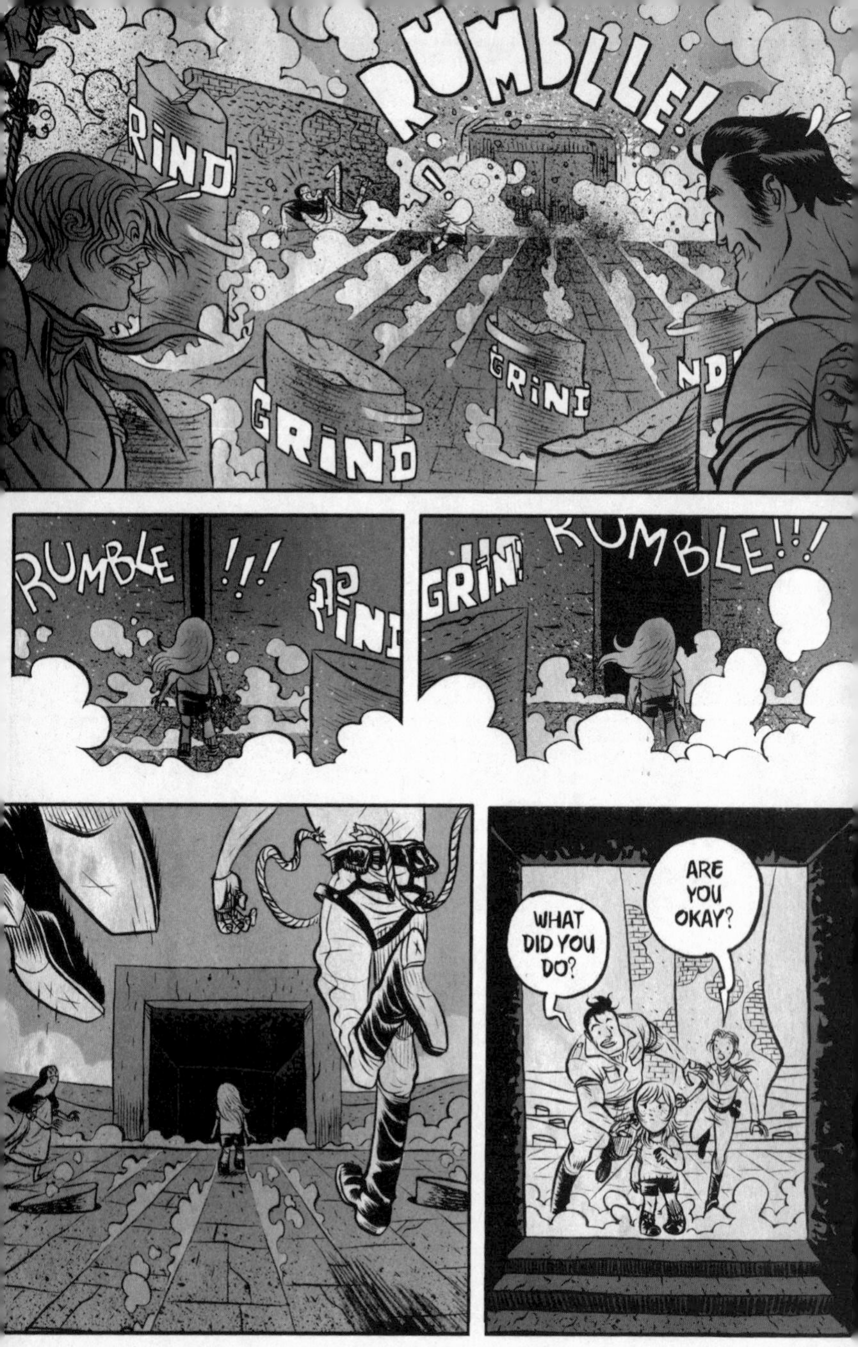
RUMBLLE!
RIND
!
GRIND
GRINI
NDI
RUMBLE !!!
RINI
GRIN
RUMBLE!!!
WHAT DID YOU DO?
ARE YOU OKAY?

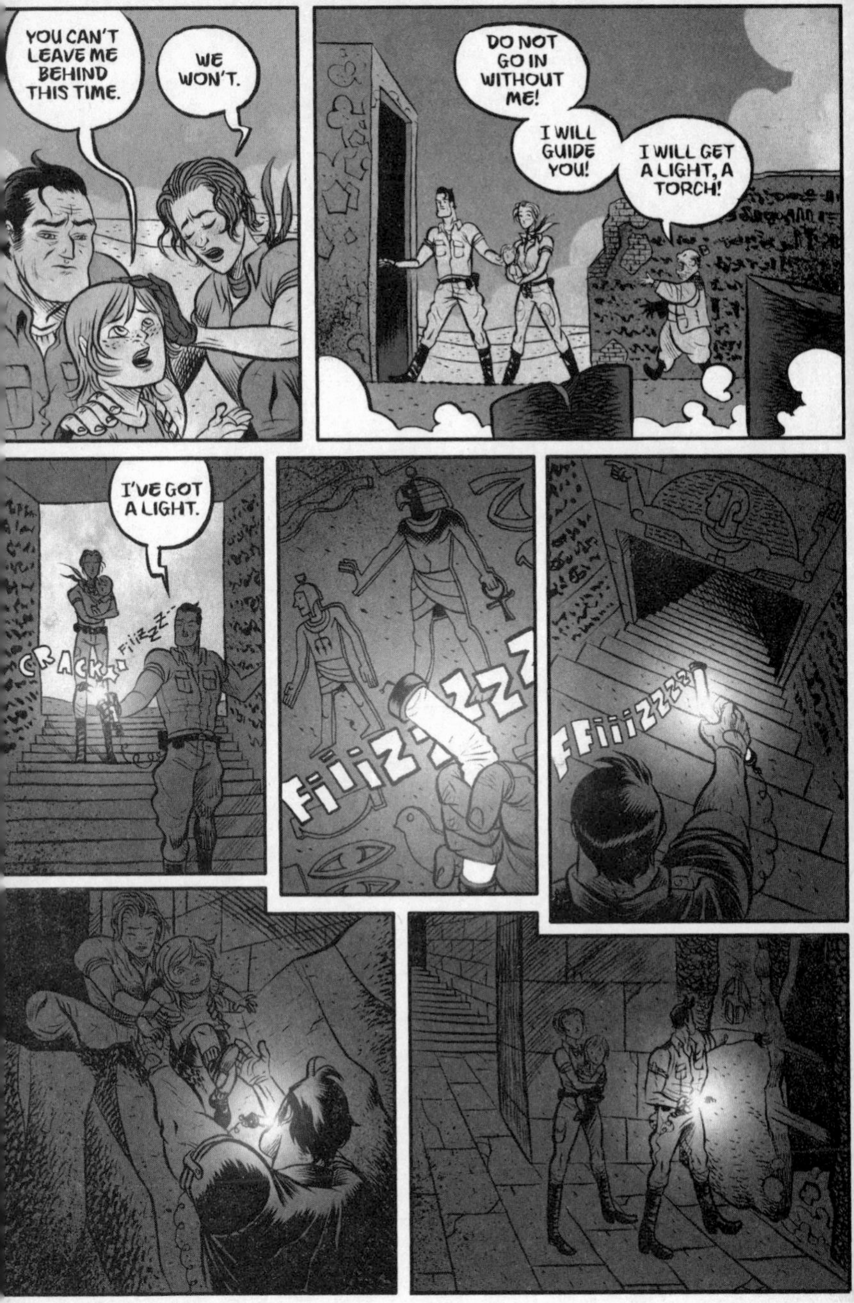
YOU CAN'T LEAVE ME BEHIND THIS TIME.
WE WON'T.
DO NOT GO IN WITHOUT ME!
I WILL GUIDE YOU!
I WILL GET A LIGHT, A TORCH!
I'VE GOT A LIGHT.
CRACK!
FIIIZZZ
FIIIZZZ
FFIIIZZZZ

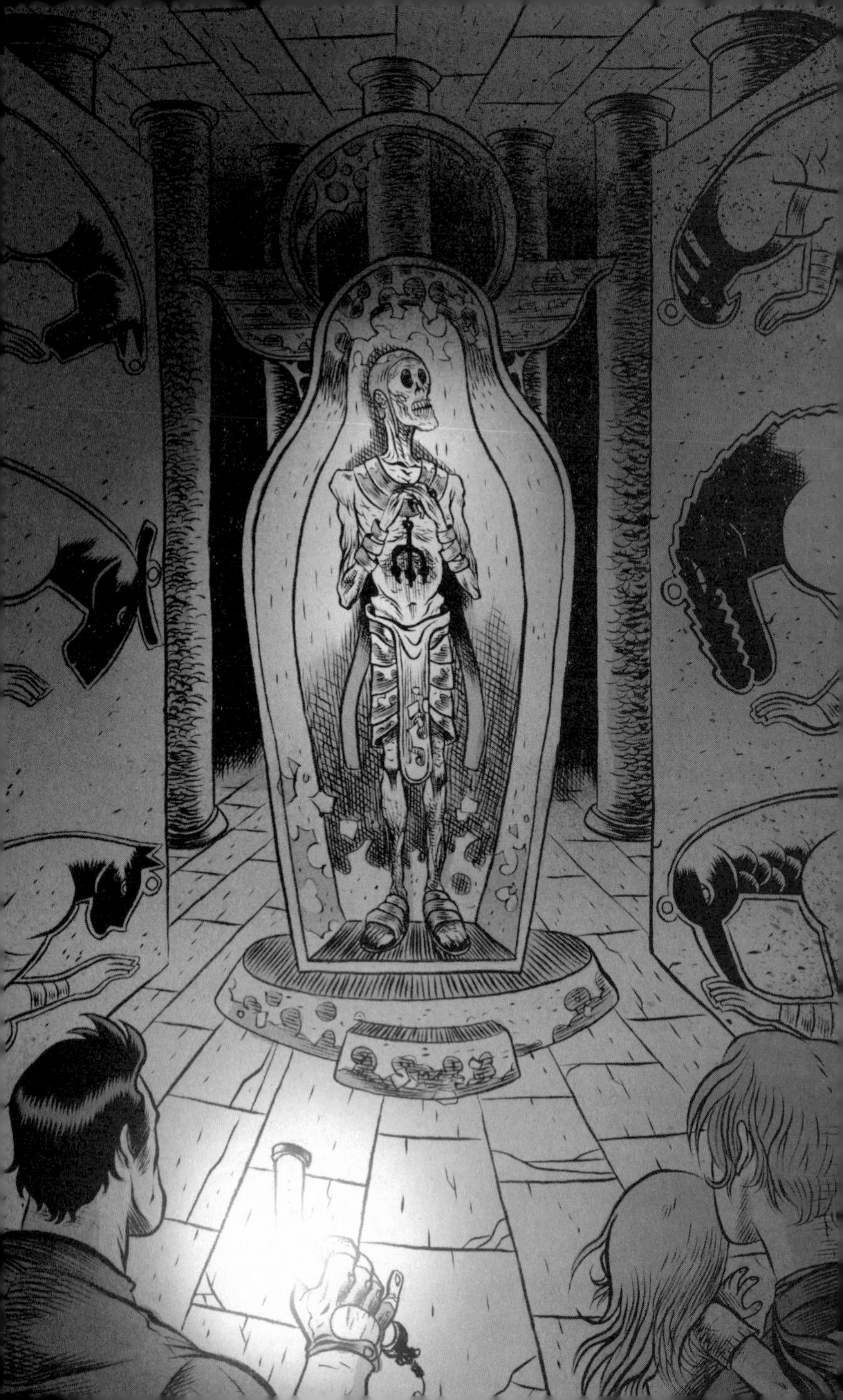

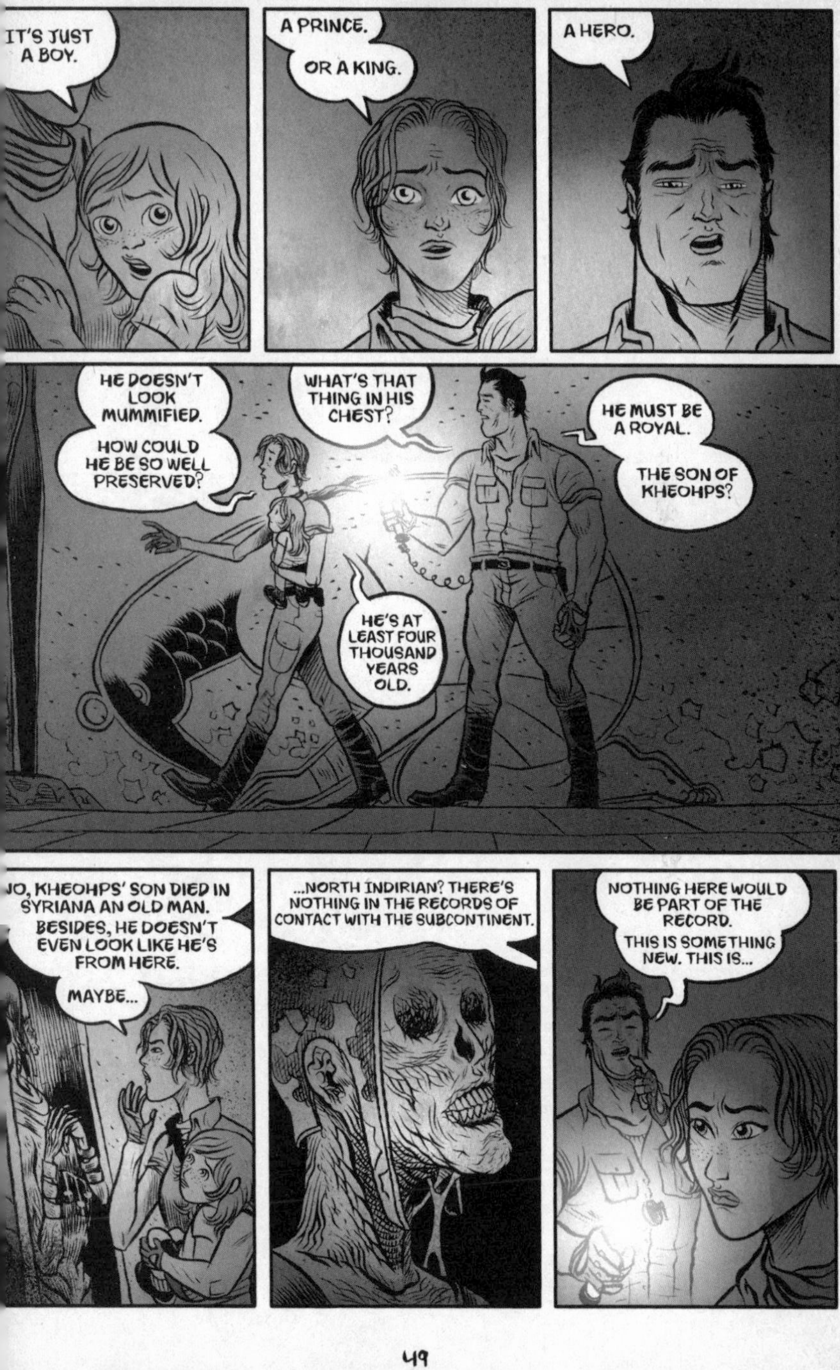
IT'S JUST A BOY.
A PRINCE.
OR A KING.
A HERO.
HE DOESN'T LOOK MUMMIFIED.
HOW COULD HE BE SO WELL PRESERVED?
WHAT'S THAT THING IN HIS CHEST?
HE MUST BE A ROYAL.
THE SON OF KHEOHPS?
HE'S AT LEAST FOUR THOUSAND YEARS OLD.
NO, KHEOHPS' SON DIED IN SYRIANA AN OLD MAN.
BESIDES, HE DOESN'T EVEN LOOK LIKE HE'S FROM HERE.
MAYBE...
...NORTH INDIRIAN? THERE'S NOTHING IN THE RECORDS OF CONTACT WITH THE SUBCONTINENT.
NOTHING HERE WOULD BE PART OF THE RECORD.
THIS IS SOMETHING NEW. THIS IS...

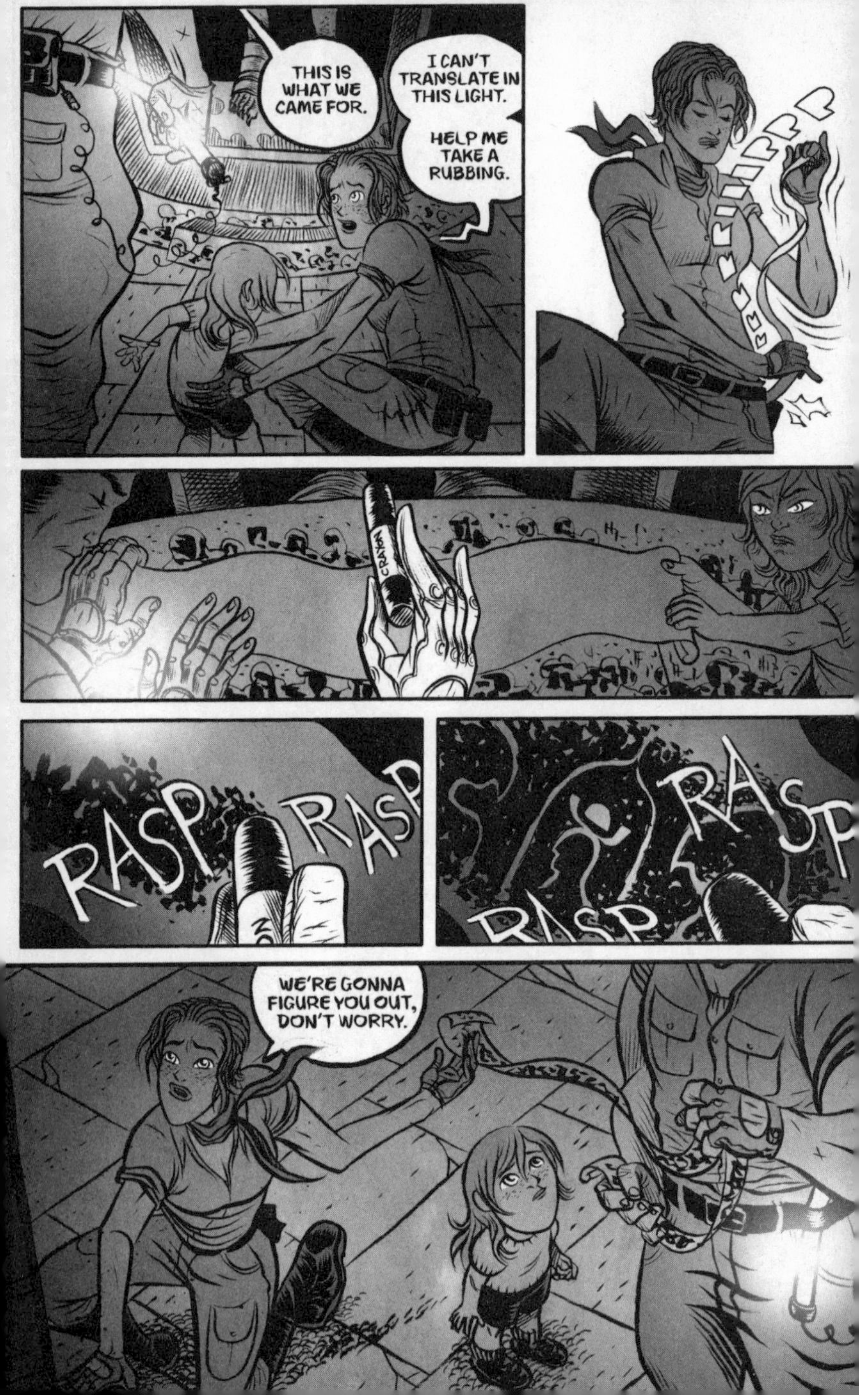
THIS IS WHAT WE CAME FOR.
I CAN'T TRANSLATE IN THIS LIGHT.
HELP ME TAKE A RUBBING.
CRAYON
RASP RASP
RASP RASP
WE'RE GONNA FIGURE YOU OUT, DON'T WORRY.

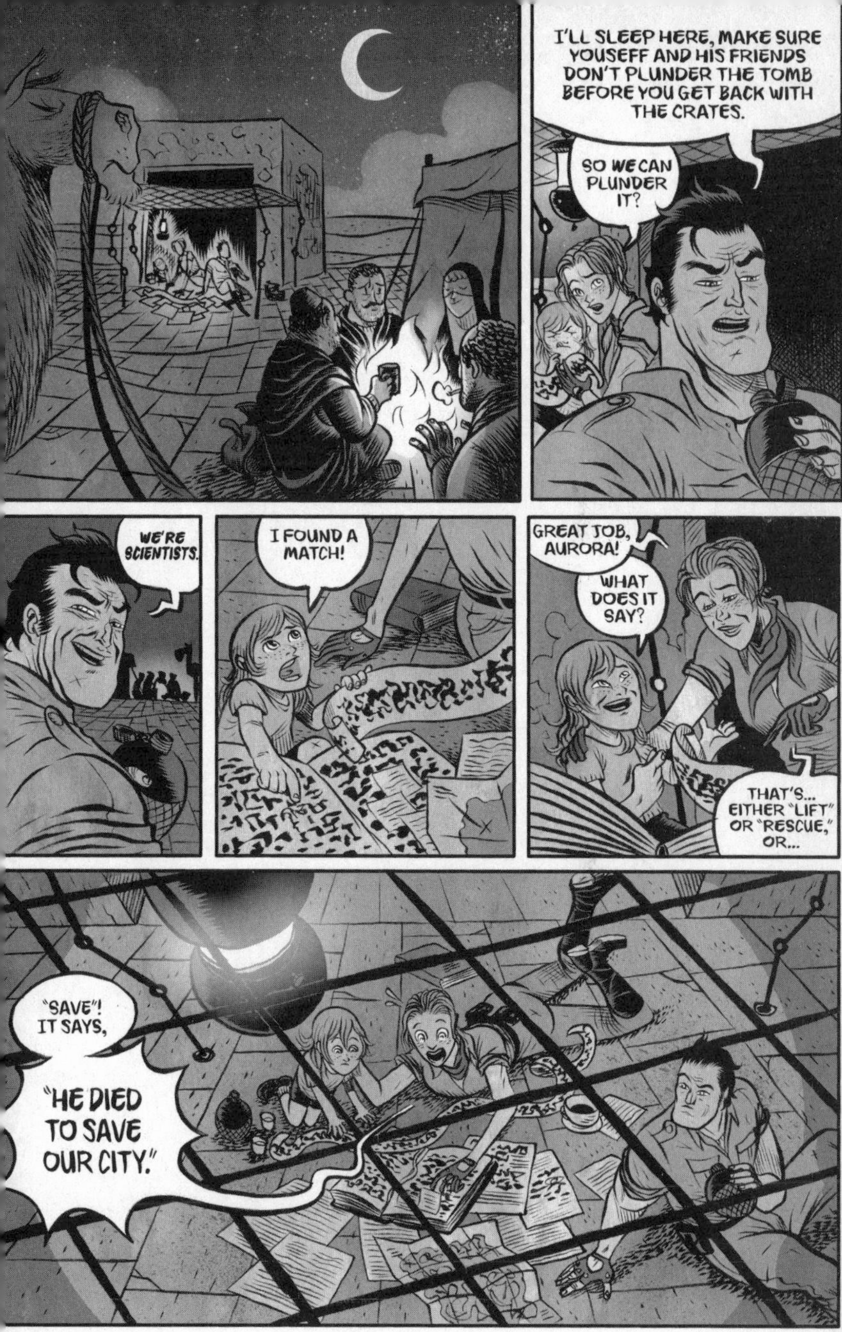
I'LL SLEEP HERE, MAKE SURE YOUSEFF AND HIS FRIENDS DON'T PLUNDER THE TOMB BEFORE YOU GET BACK WITH THE CRATES.
SO WE CAN PLUNDER IT?
WE'RE SCIENTISTS.
I FOUND A MATCH!
GREAT JOB, AURORA!
WHAT DOES IT SAY?
THAT'S... EITHER "LIFT" OR "RESCUE," OR...
"SAVE"! IT SAYS,
"HE DIED TO SAVE OUR CITY."

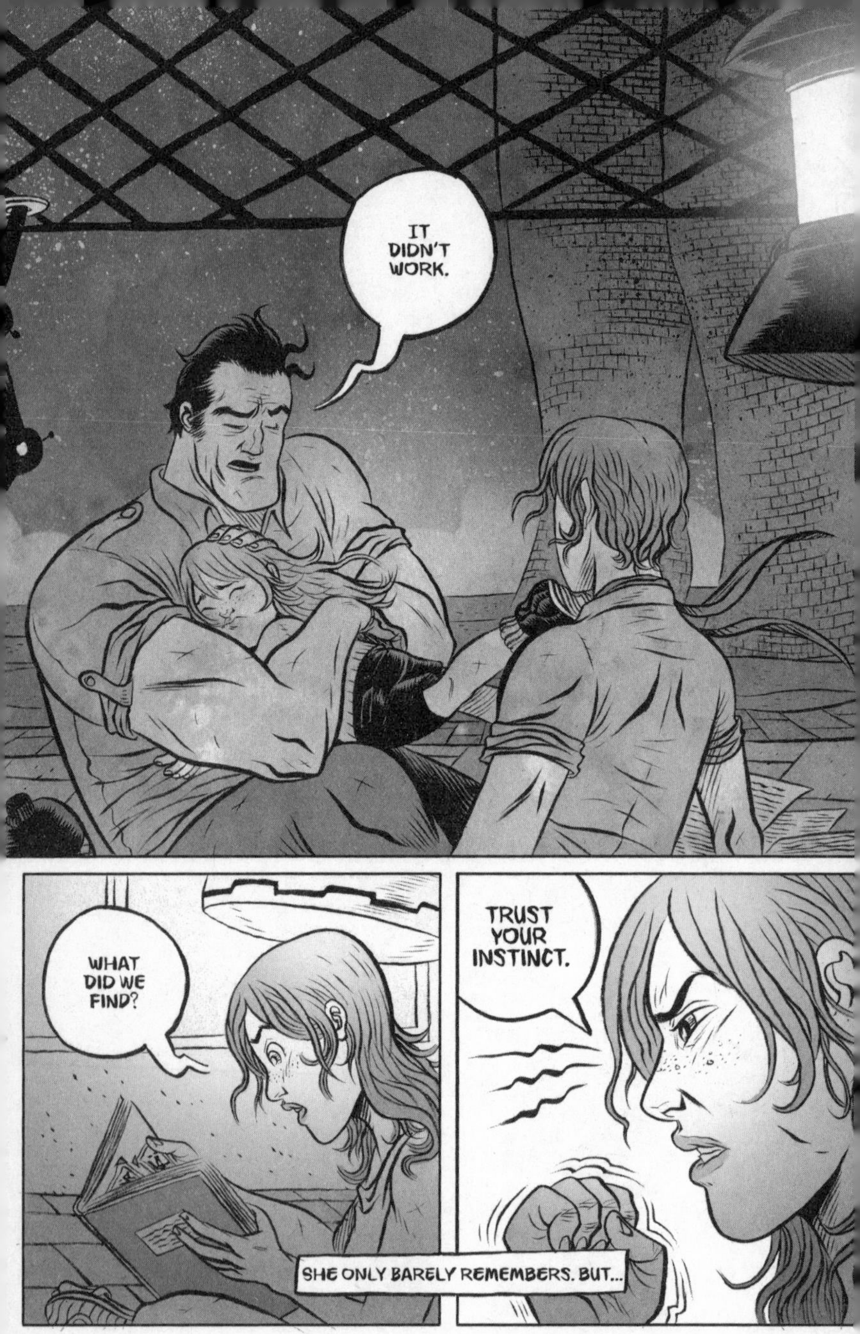
IT DIDN'T WORK.
WHAT DID WE FIND?
TRUST YOUR INSTINCT.
SHE ONLY BARELY REMEMBERS. BUT...

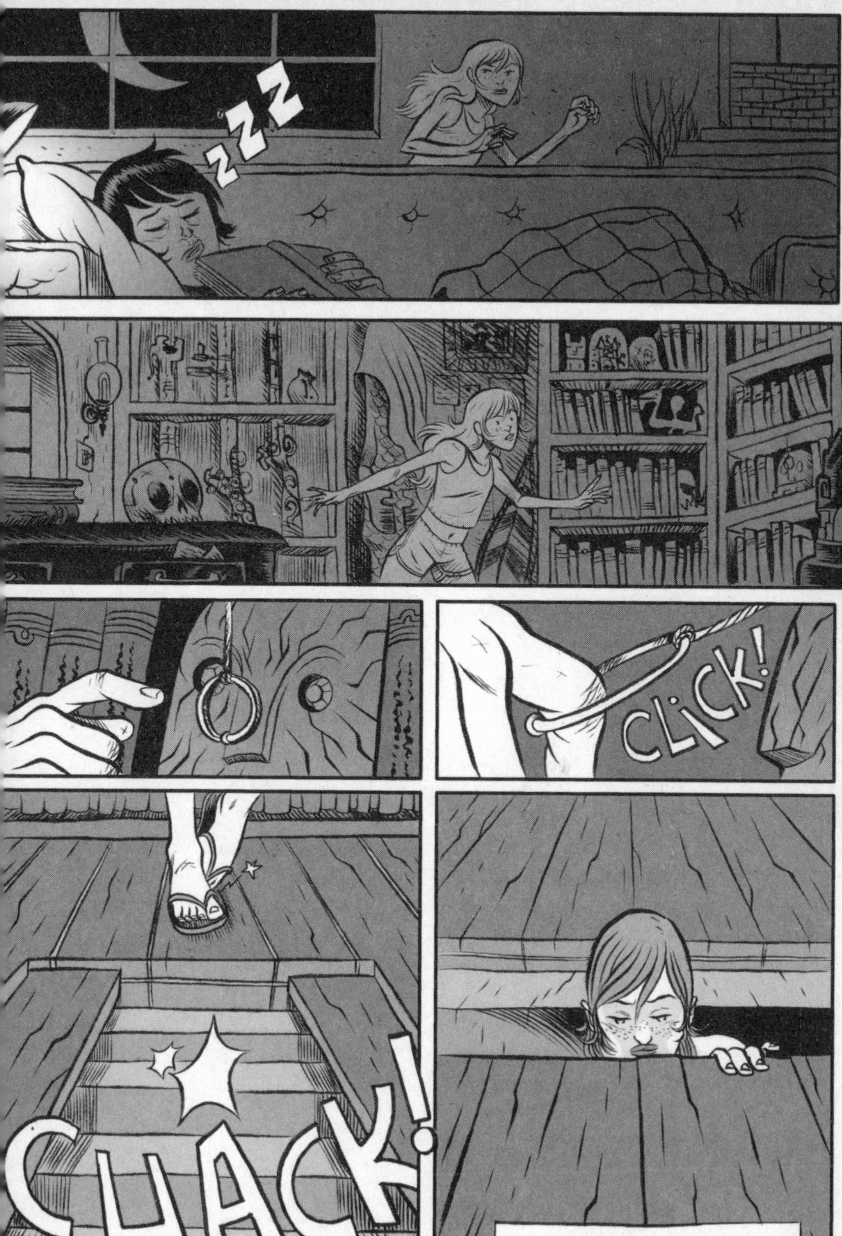
ZZZ
CLICK!
CHACK!
THE SECRET FILES OF HAGGARD WEST.

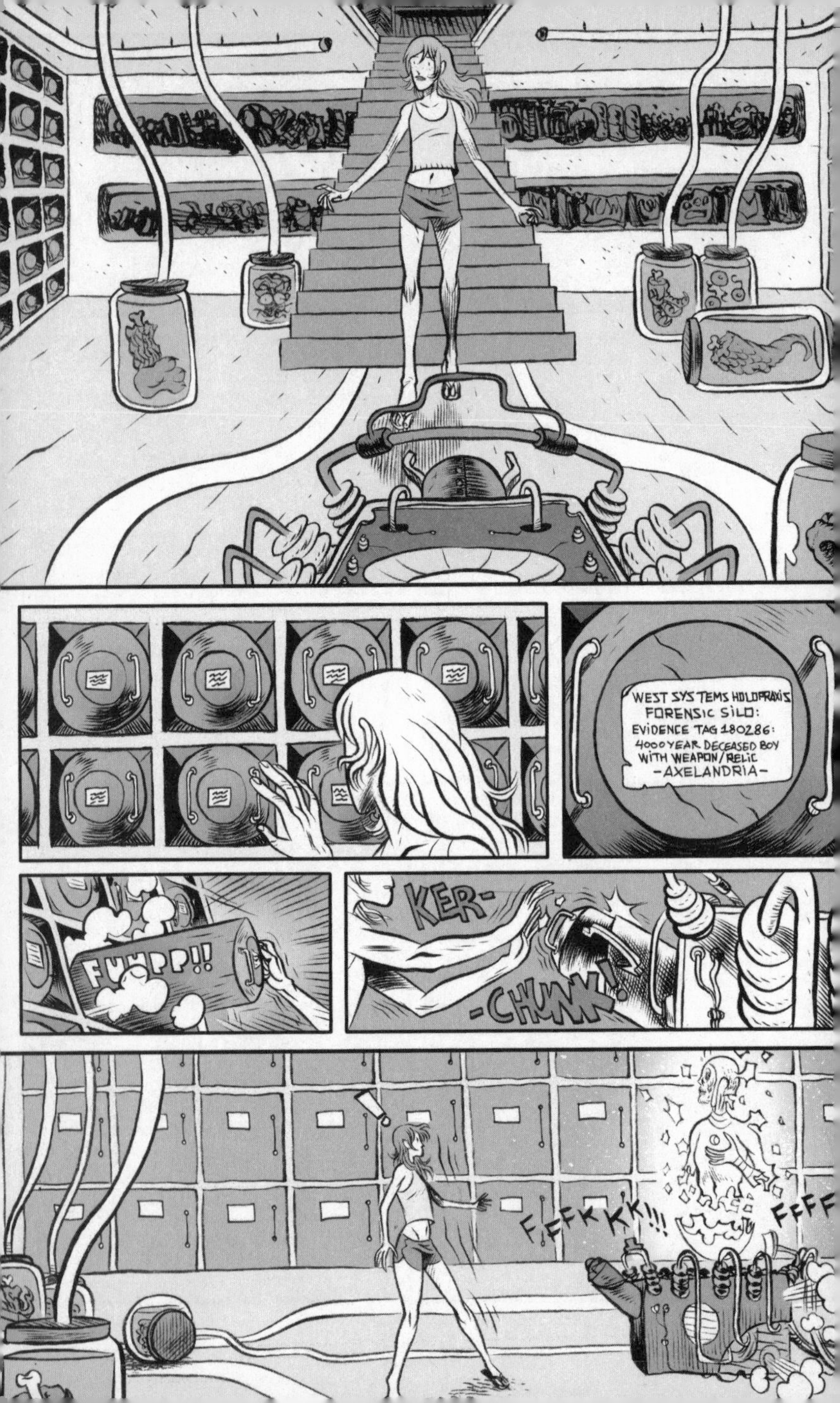
WEST SYSTEMS HOLOPRAXIS
FORENSIC SILO:
EVIDENCE TAG 180286:
4000 YEAR DECEASED BOY
WITH WEAPON/RELIC
-AXELANDRIA-
FUHPP!!
KER-
-CHUNK!
!
FFFKKK!!!
FFFF

56

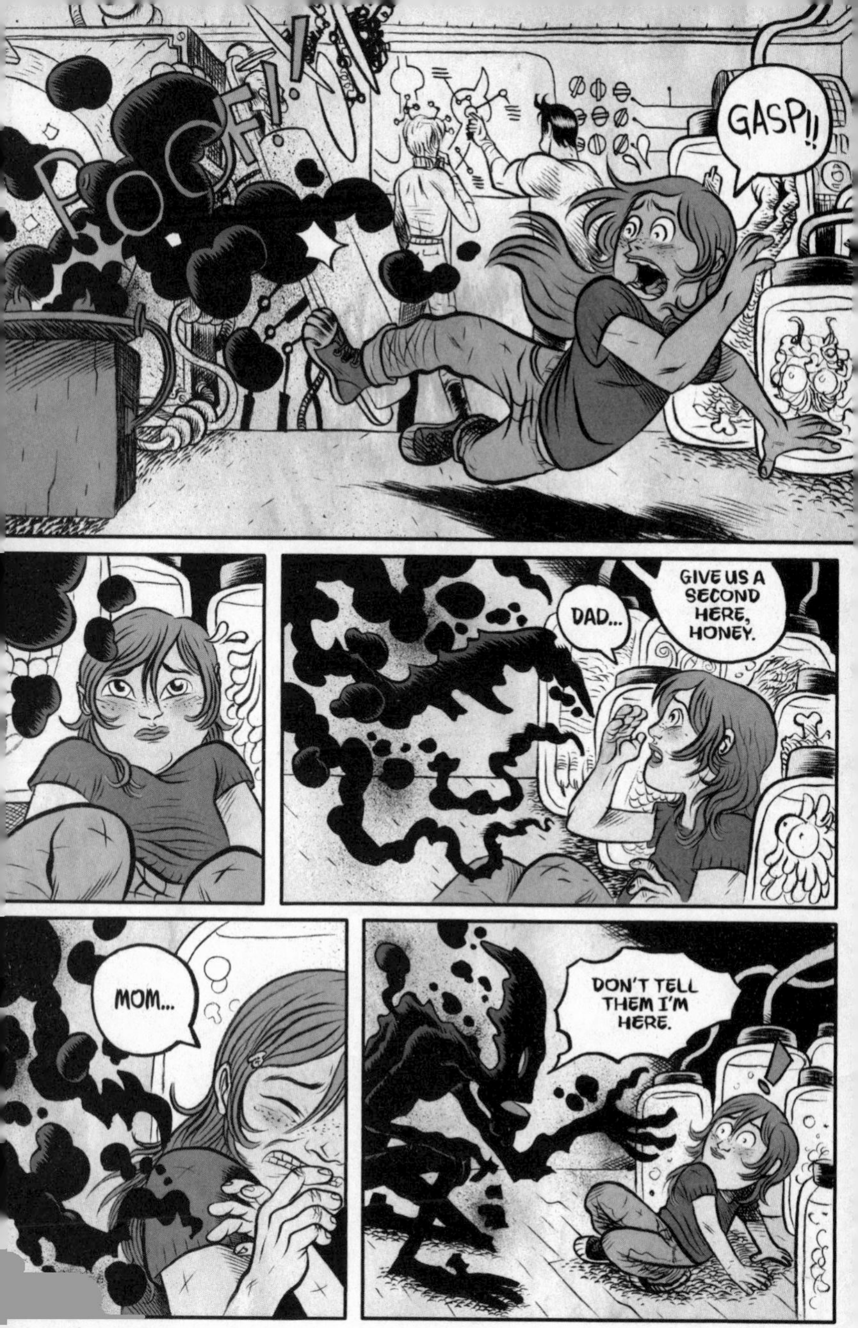
POOOF!!
GASP!!
DAD...
GIVE US A SECOND HERE, HONEY.
MOM...
DON'T TELL THEM I'M HERE.

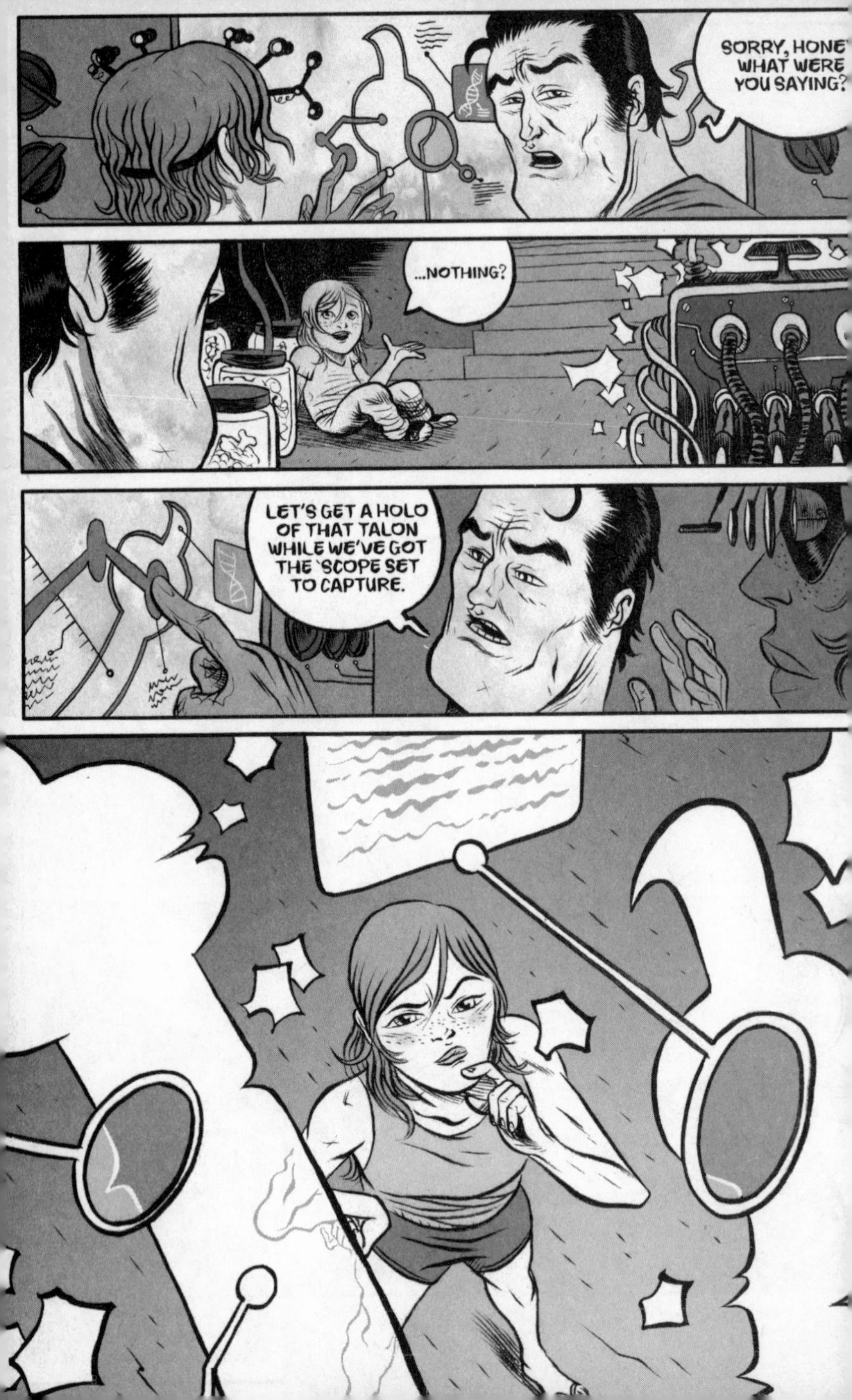
SORRY, HONE
WHAT WERE
YOU SAYING?
...NOTHING?
LET'S GET A HOLO OF THAT TALON WHILE WE'VE GOT THE 'SCOPE SET TO CAPTURE.

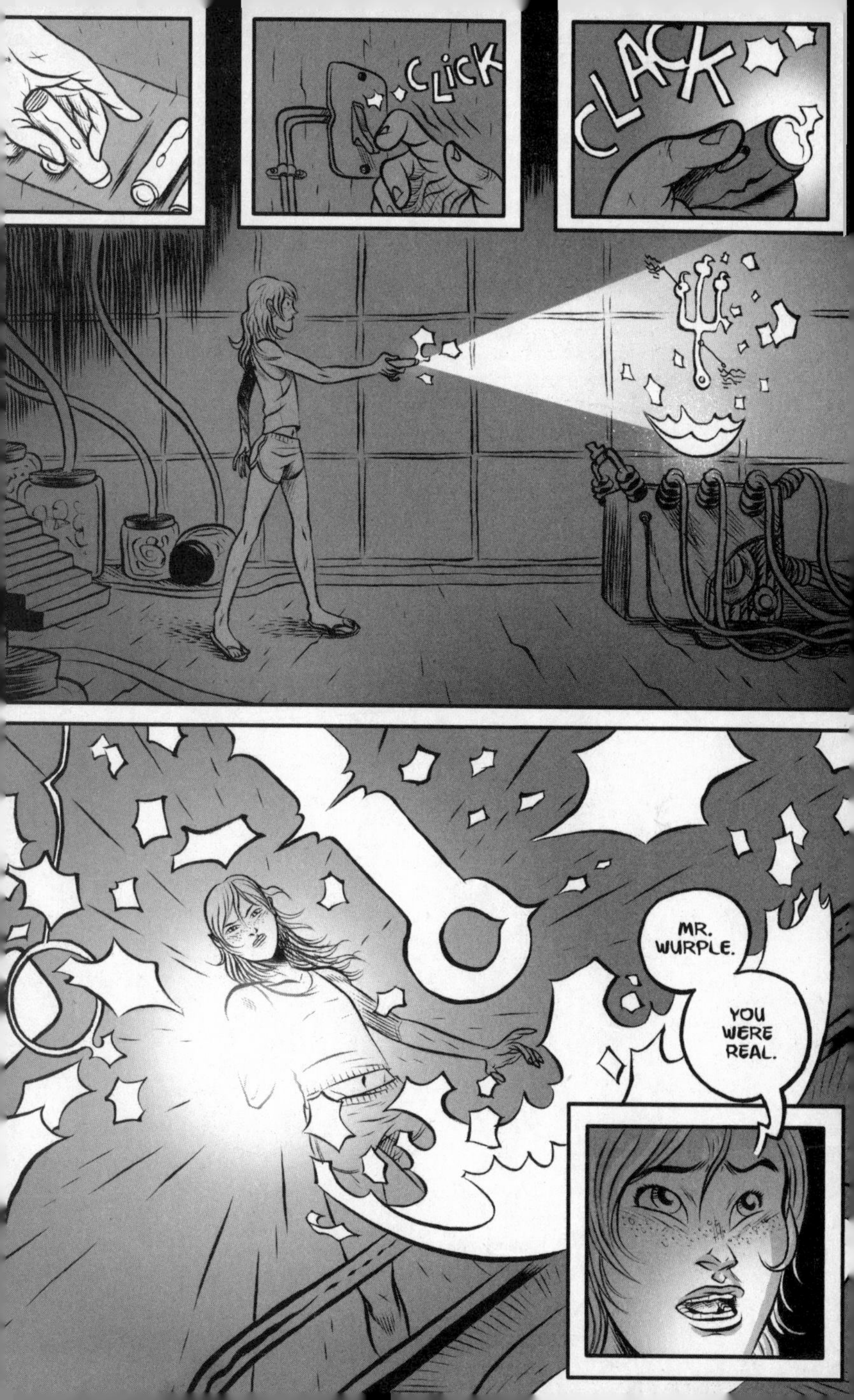
CLICK
CLACK
MR. WURPLE.
YOU WERE REAL.

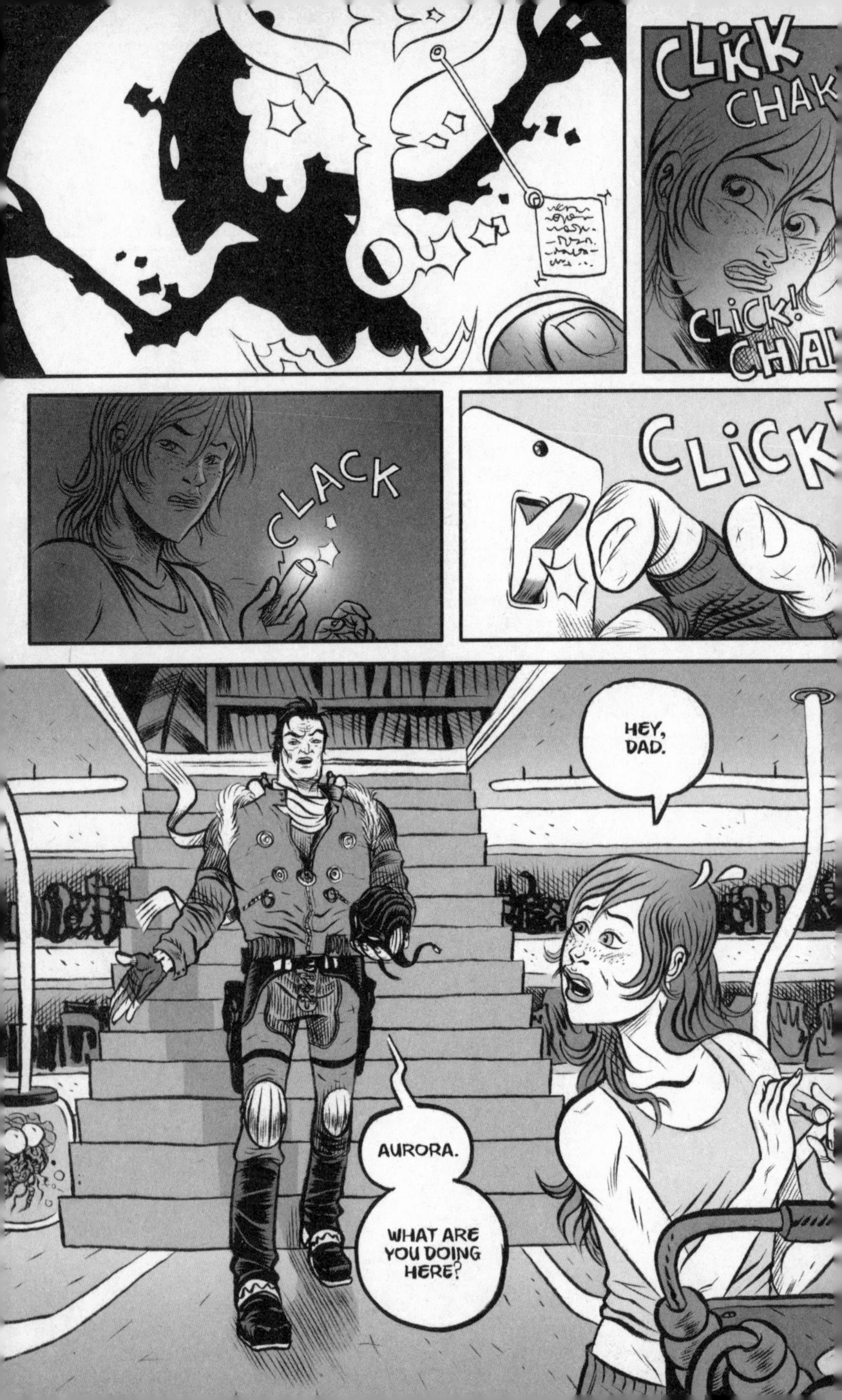

CLICK
CHAK
CLICK!
CHA
CLACK
CLICK
HEY, DAD.
AURORA.
WHAT ARE YOU DOING HERE?

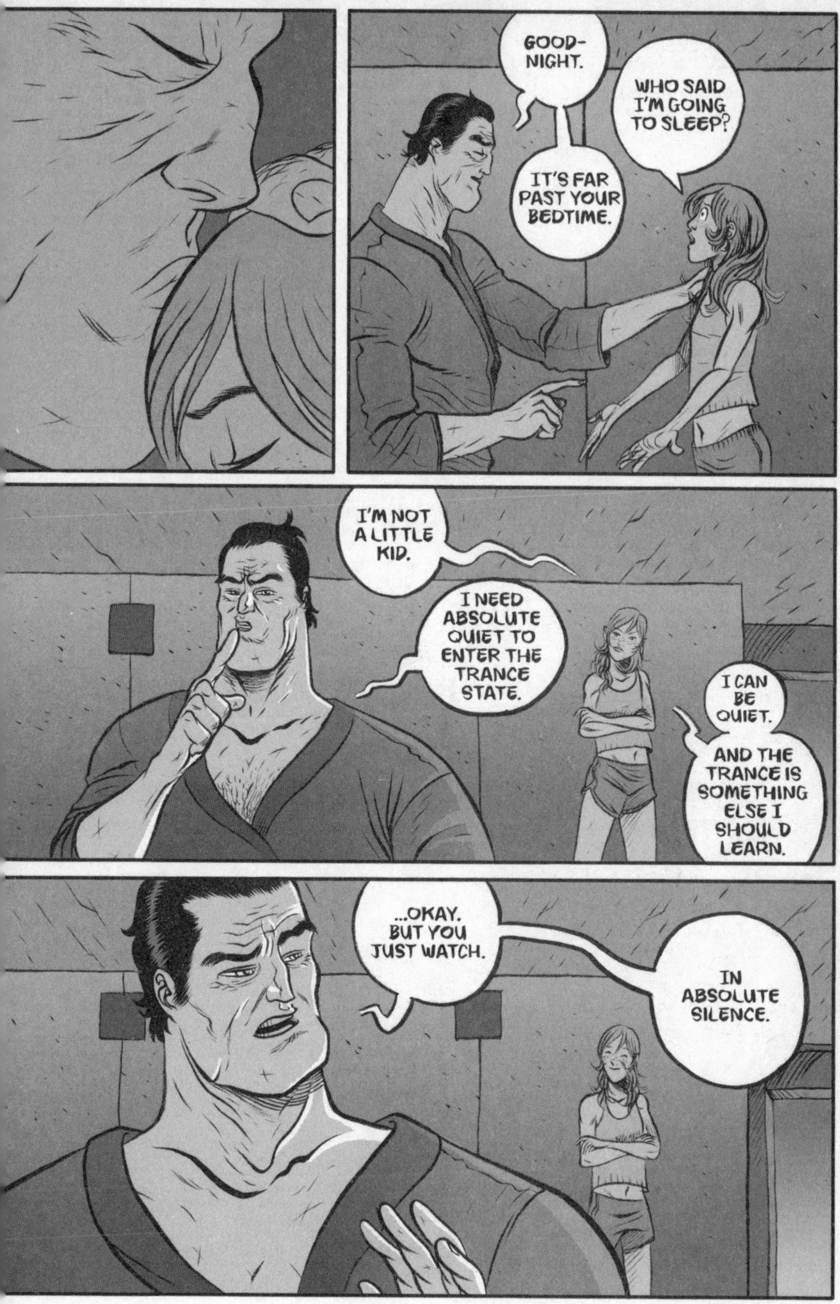
GOOD-NIGHT.
IT'S FAR PAST YOUR BEDTIME.
WHO SAID I'M GOING TO SLEEP?
I'M NOT A LITTLE KID.
I NEED ABSOLUTE QUIET TO ENTER THE TRANCE STATE.
I CAN BE QUIET.
AND THE TRANCE IS SOMETHING ELSE I SHOULD LEARN.
...OKAY. BUT YOU JUST WATCH.
IN ABSOLUTE SILENCE.

I LEARNED TUATARA MEDITATION FROM A BLIND MONK TWENTY YEARS AGO IN A SHI-FAN TEMPLE IN AL-LHASA.

WITH ENOUGH DISCIPLINE, HE COULD REGAIN SIGHT THROUGH HIS INNER EYE, BUT ONLY IN THE PAST.

THE TECHNIQUE EXPLOITS THE ENORMOUS AMOUNT OF INFORMATION YOUR SENSES ABSORB THAT DON'T NECESSARILY FIND PURCHASE IN YOUR MIND.

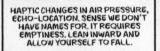

HAPTIC CHANGES IN AIR PRESSURE, ECHO-LOCATION. SENSE WE DON'T HAVE NAMES FOR. IT REQUIRES EMPTINESS. LEAN INWARD AND ALLOW YOURSELF TO FALL.

BONG- -OOOMMM-

BONG- -OOMMM

BONG- -ZZZZ- -OOMM

THE BELLS PROVIDE THE MANTRA. EVERYTHING ELSE... ABSOLUTE SILENCE FROM HERE ON OUT.

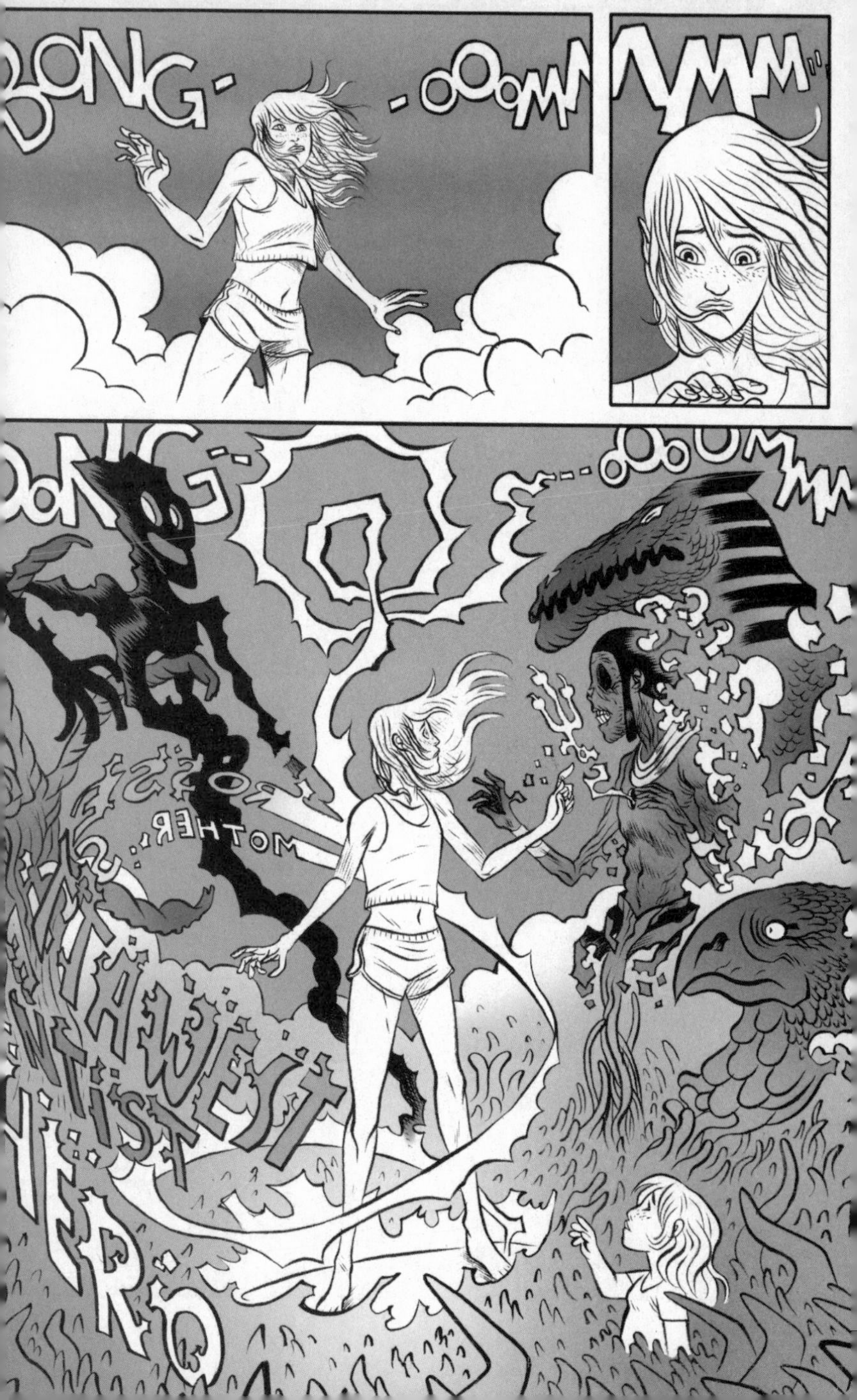
BONG-
-OOoMMMMM
BONG--
--OOoOOMM
ROSE'S
MOTHER...

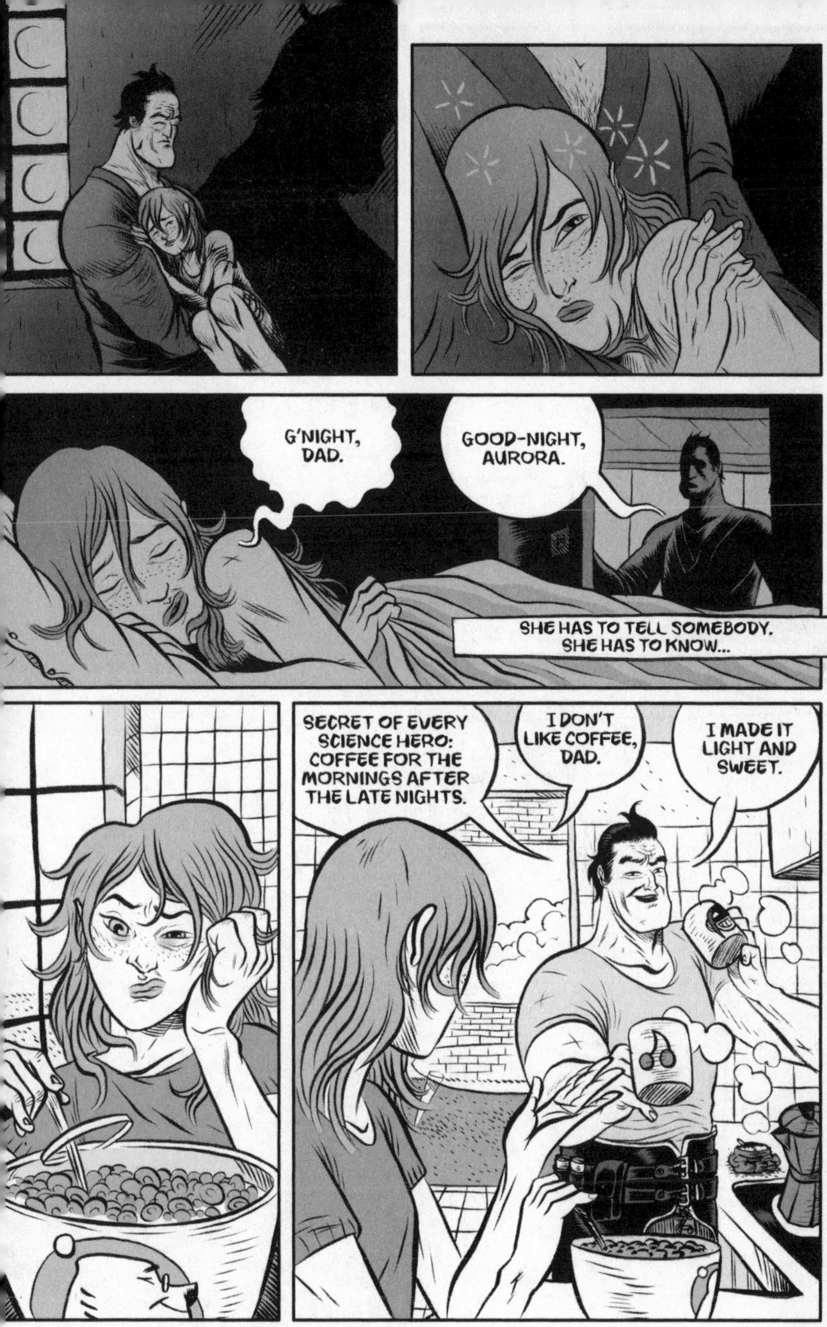
G'NIGHT, DAD.
GOOD-NIGHT, AURORA.
SHE HAS TO TELL SOMEBODY. SHE HAS TO KNOW...
SECRET OF EVERY SCIENCE HERO: COFFEE FOR THE MORNINGS AFTER THE LATE NIGHTS.
I DON'T LIKE COFFEE, DAD.
I MADE IT LIGHT AND SWEET.

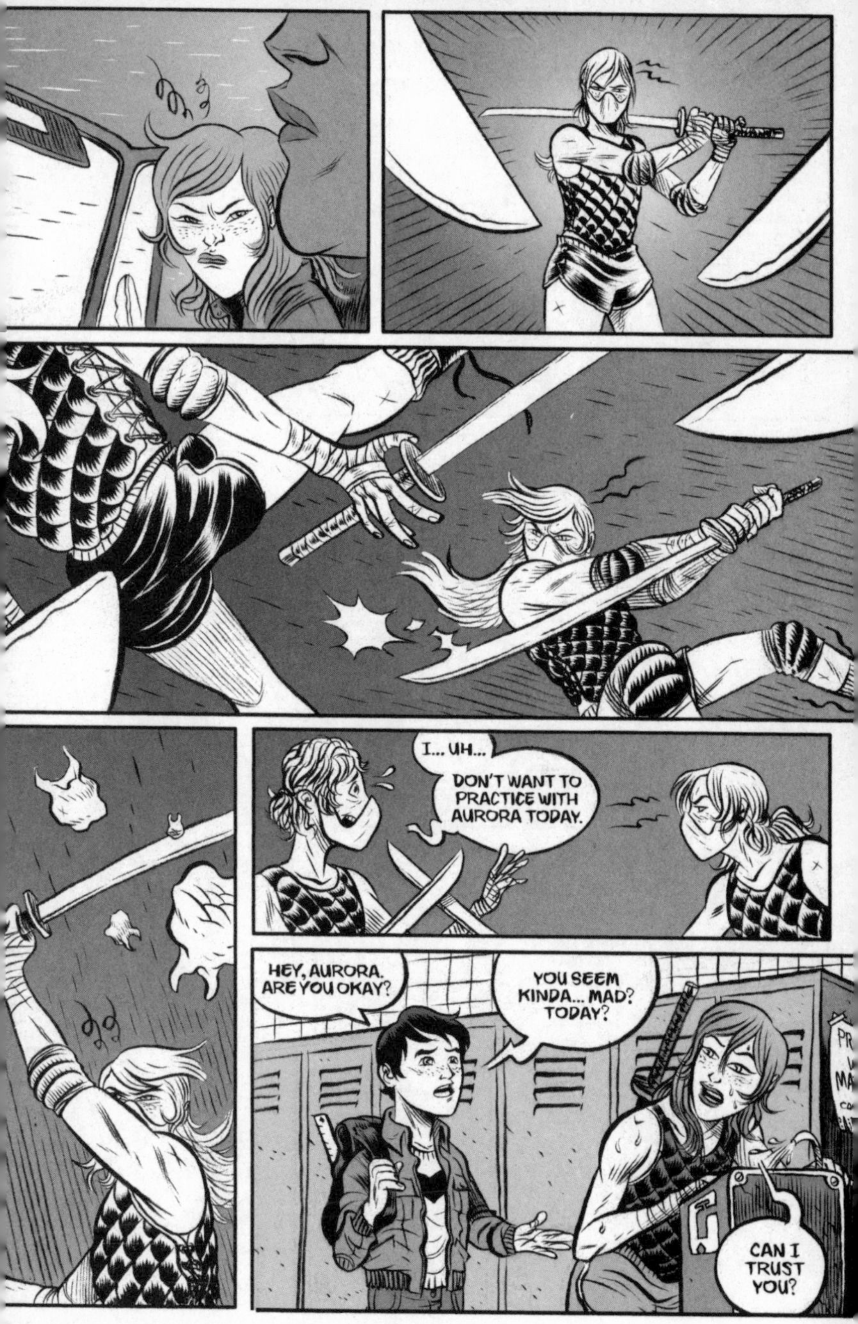
I... UH...
DON'T WANT TO PRACTICE WITH AURORA TODAY.
HEY, AURORA. ARE YOU OKAY?
YOU SEEM KINDA... MAD? TODAY?
CAN I TRUST YOU?

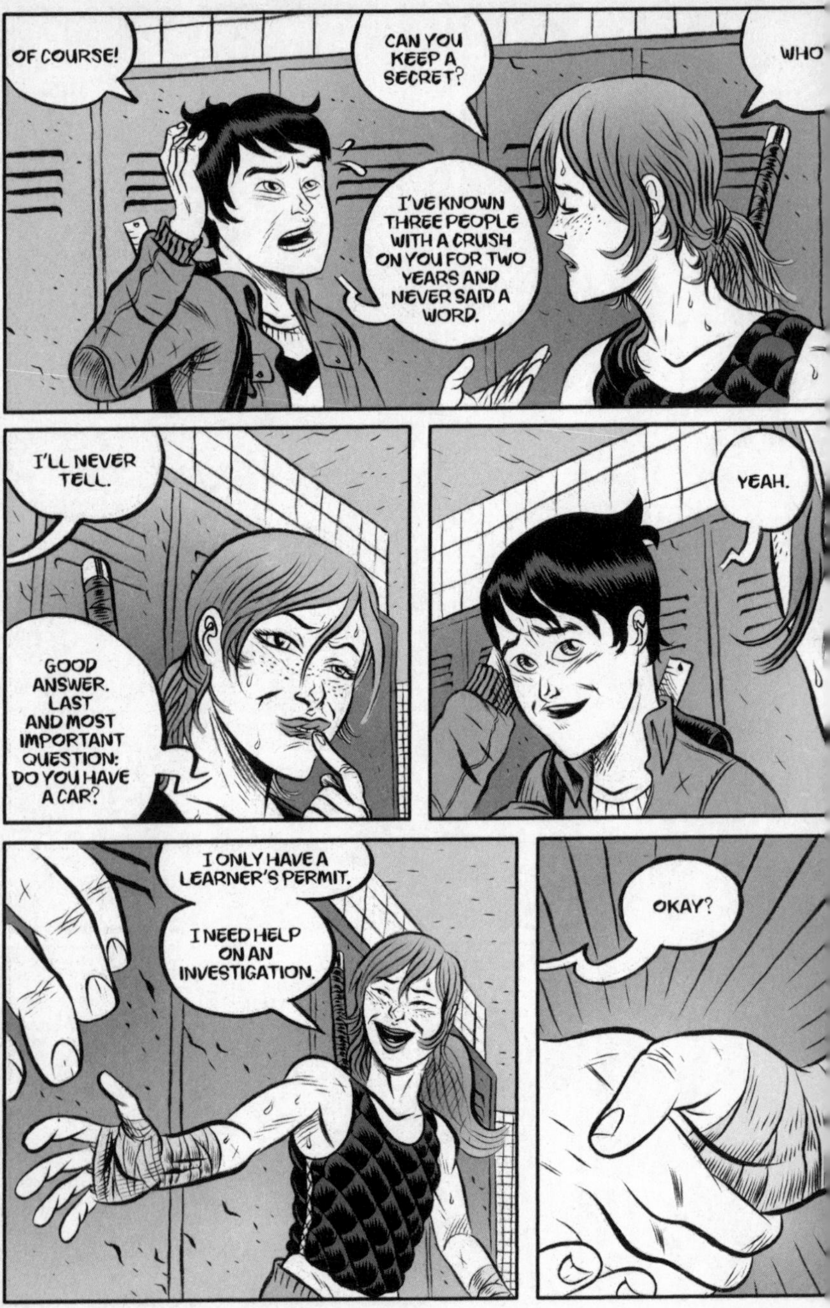

OF COURSE!
CAN YOU KEEP A SECRET?
WHO
I'VE KNOWN THREE PEOPLE WITH A CRUSH ON YOU FOR TWO YEARS AND NEVER SAID A WORD.
I'LL NEVER TELL.
GOOD ANSWER. LAST AND MOST IMPORTANT QUESTION: DO YOU HAVE A CAR?
YEAH.
I ONLY HAVE A LEARNER'S PERMIT.
I NEED HELP ON AN INVESTIGATION.
OKAY?

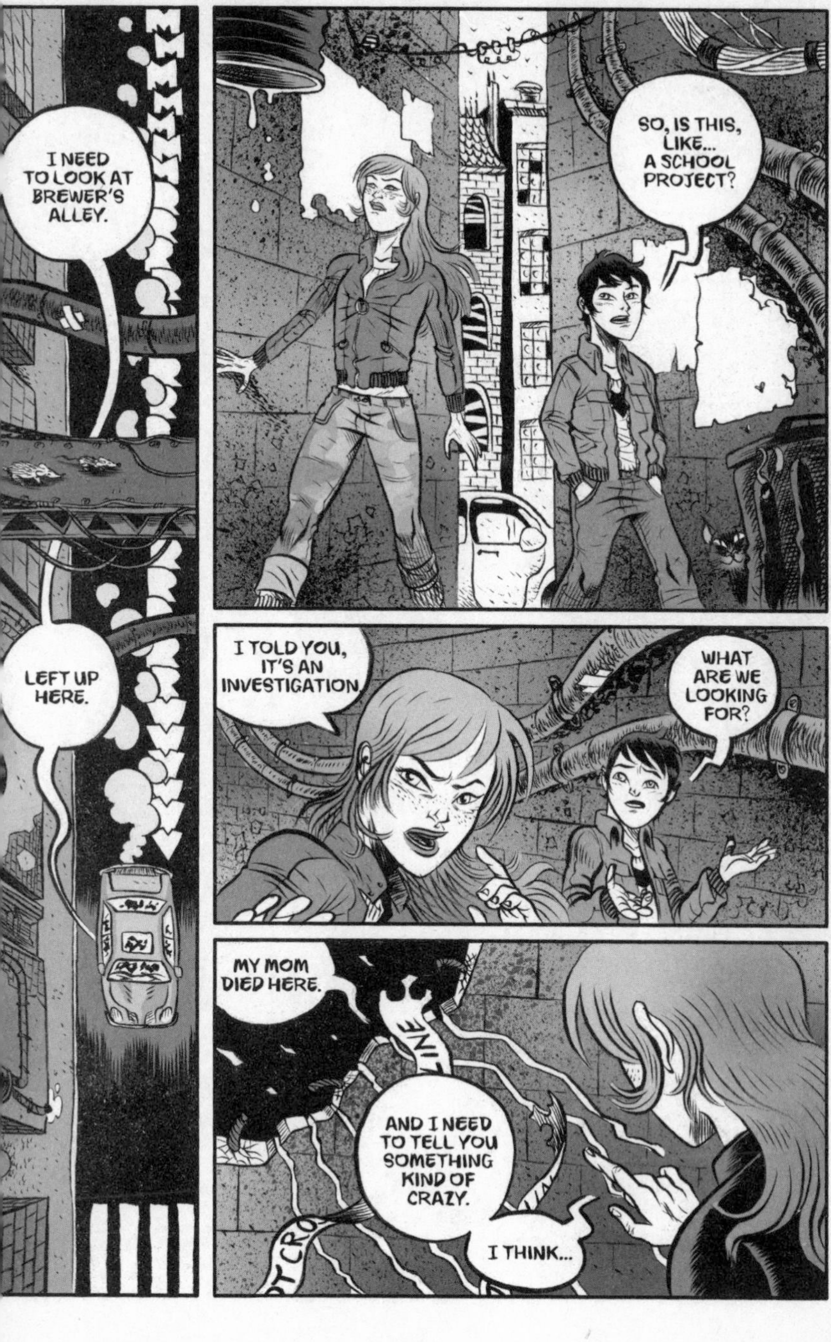
I NEED TO LOOK AT BREWER'S ALLEY.
LEFT UP HERE.
SO, IS THIS, LIKE... A SCHOOL PROJECT?
I TOLD YOU, IT'S AN INVESTIGATION.
WHAT ARE WE LOOKING FOR?
MY MOM DIED HERE.
AND I NEED TO TELL YOU SOMETHING KIND OF CRAZY.
I THINK...

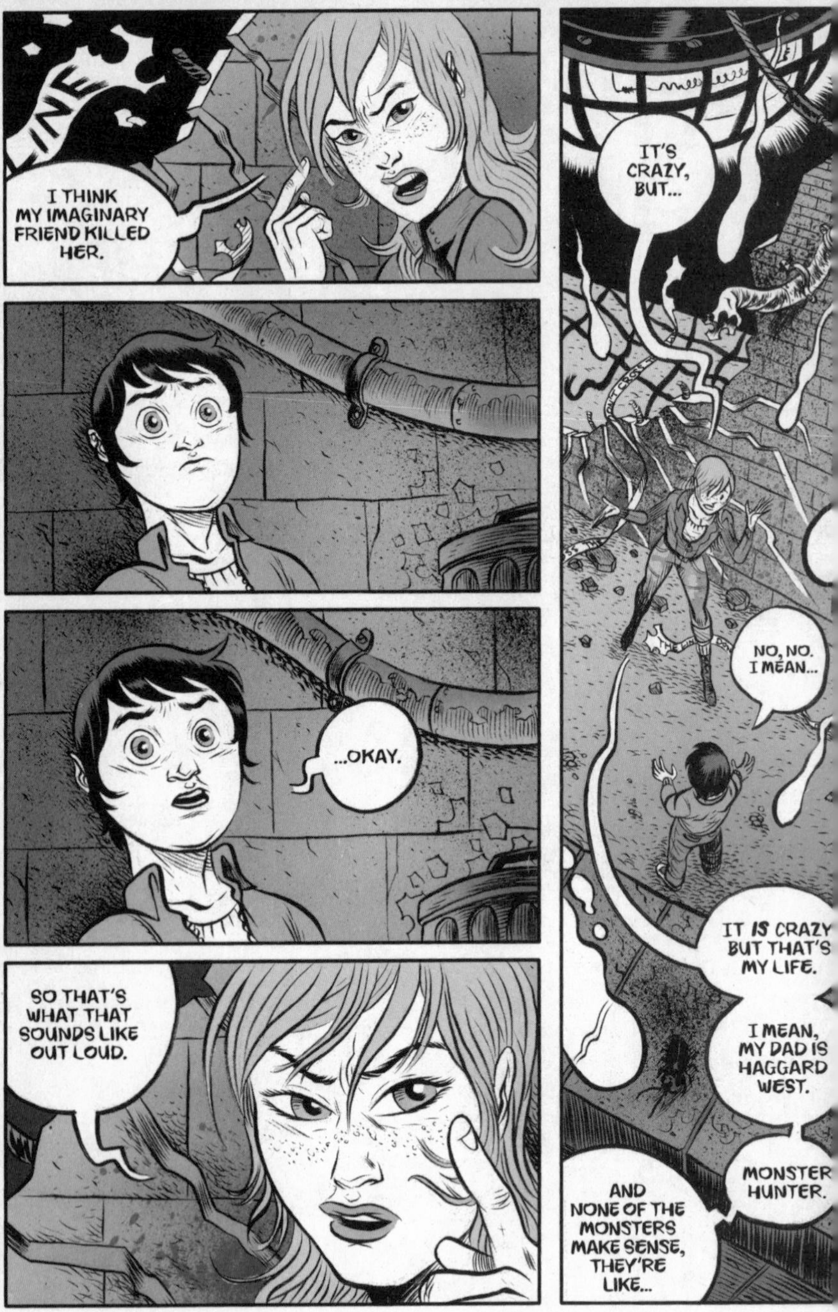
INE
I THINK MY IMAGINARY FRIEND KILLED HER.
...OKAY.
SO THAT'S WHAT THAT SOUNDS LIKE OUT LOUD.
IT'S CRAZY, BUT...
NO, NO. I MEAN...
IT IS CRAZY BUT THAT'S MY LIFE.
I MEAN, MY DAD IS HAGGARD WEST.
MONSTER HUNTER.
AND NONE OF THE MONSTERS MAKE SENSE, THEY'RE LIKE...

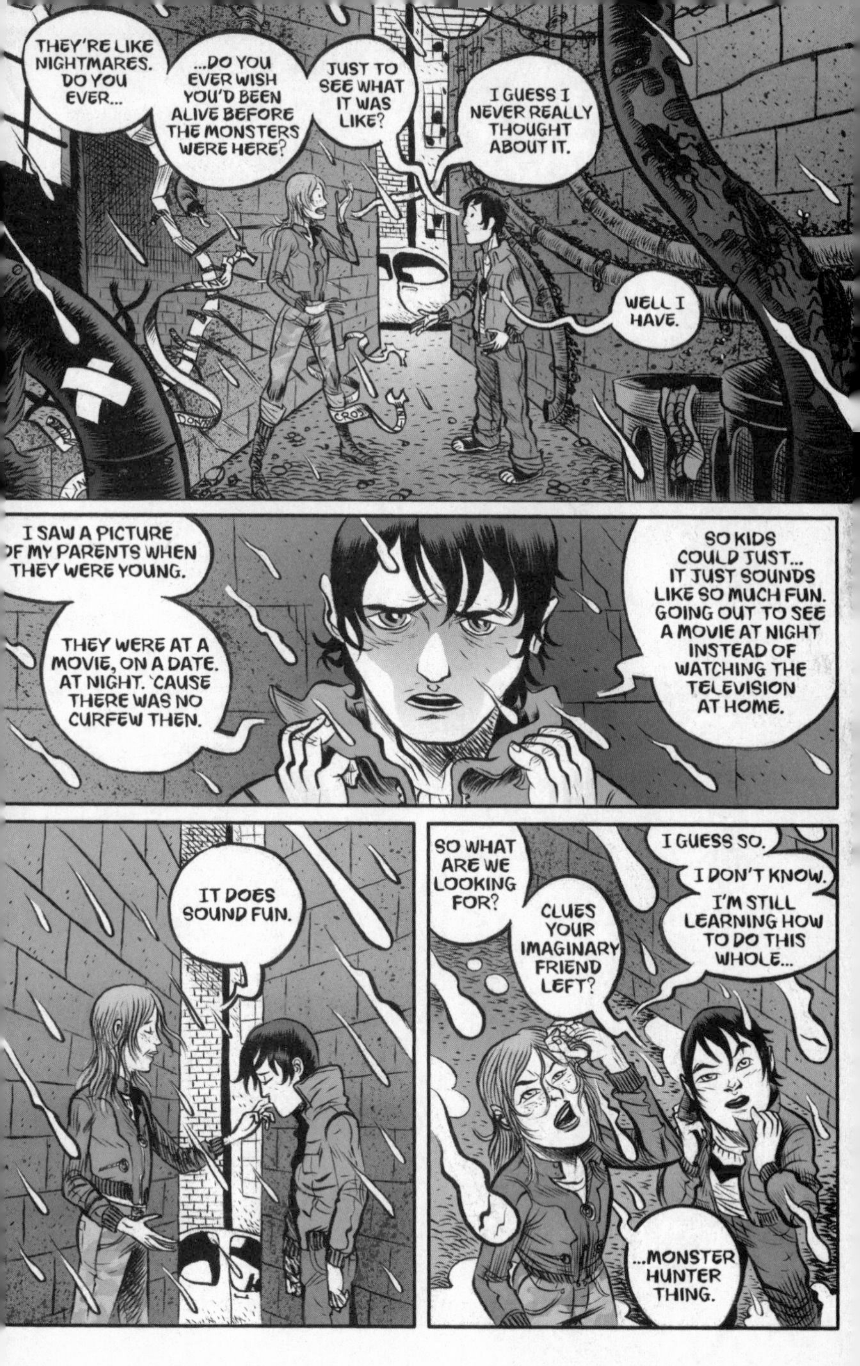
THEY'RE LIKE NIGHTMARES. DO YOU EVER...
...DO YOU EVER WISH YOU'D BEEN ALIVE BEFORE THE MONSTERS WERE HERE?
JUST TO SEE WHAT IT WAS LIKE?
I GUESS I NEVER REALLY THOUGHT ABOUT IT.
WELL I HAVE.
I SAW A PICTURE OF MY PARENTS WHEN THEY WERE YOUNG.
THEY WERE AT A MOVIE, ON A DATE. AT NIGHT. 'CAUSE THERE WAS NO CURFEW THEN.
SO KIDS COULD JUST... IT JUST SOUNDS LIKE SO MUCH FUN. GOING OUT TO SEE A MOVIE AT NIGHT INSTEAD OF WATCHING THE TELEVISION AT HOME.
IT DOES SOUND FUN.
SO WHAT ARE WE LOOKING FOR?
CLUES YOUR IMAGINARY FRIEND LEFT?
I GUESS SO.
I DON'T KNOW.
I'M STILL LEARNING HOW TO DO THIS WHOLE...
...MONSTER HUNTER THING.

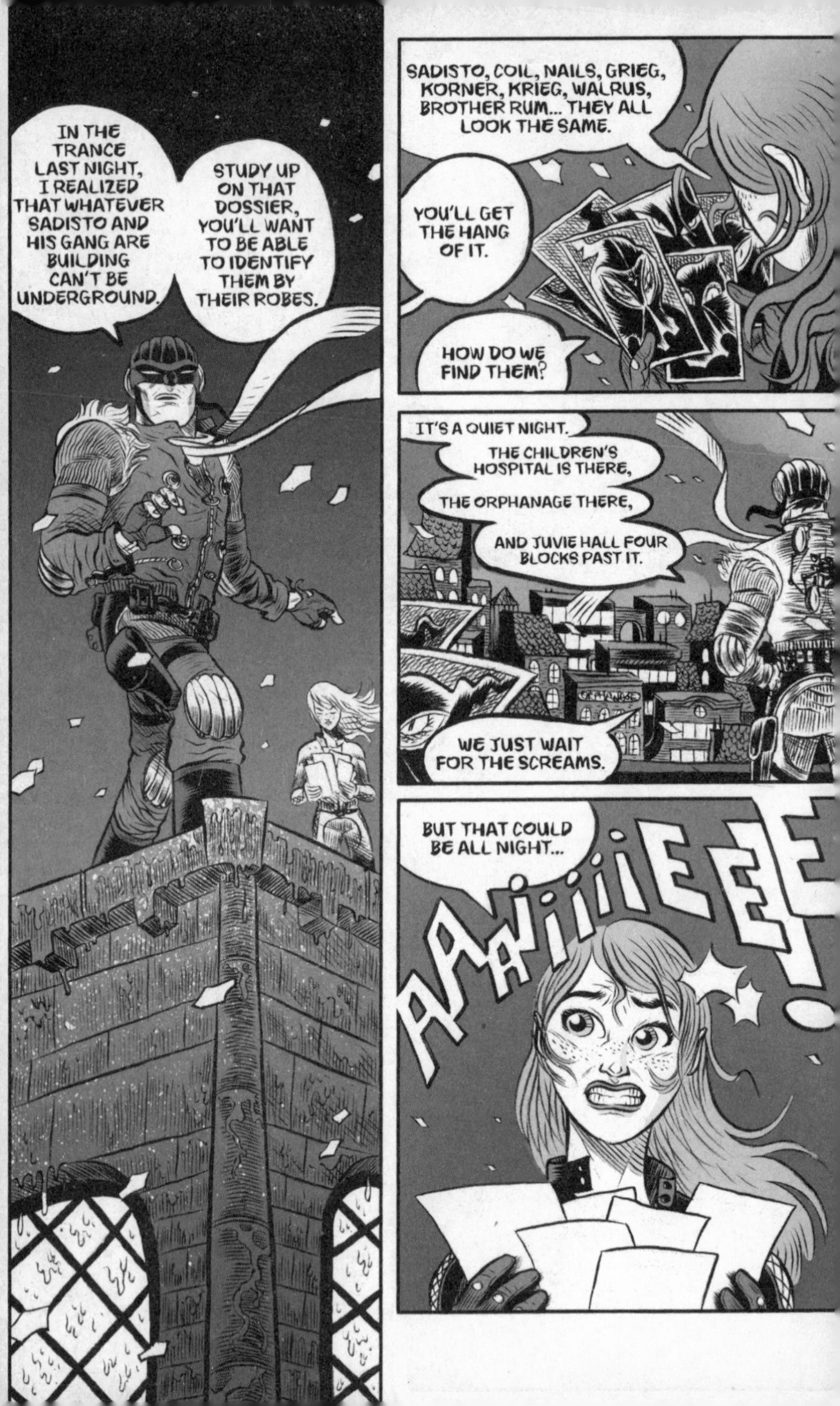
IN THE TRANCE LAST NIGHT, I REALIZED THAT WHATEVER SADISTO AND HIS GANG ARE BUILDING CAN'T BE UNDERGROUND.
STUDY UP ON THAT DOSSIER, YOU'LL WANT TO BE ABLE TO IDENTIFY THEM BY THEIR ROBES.
SADISTO, COIL, NAILS, GRIEG, KORNER, KRIEG, WALRUS, BROTHER RUM... THEY ALL LOOK THE SAME.
YOU'LL GET THE HANG OF IT.
HOW DO WE FIND THEM?
IT'S A QUIET NIGHT.
THE CHILDREN'S HOSPITAL IS THERE,
THE ORPHANAGE THERE,
AND JUVIE HALL FOUR BLOCKS PAST IT.
WE JUST WAIT FOR THE SCREAMS.
BUT THAT COULD BE ALL NIGHT...
AAAiiiiEEEE!

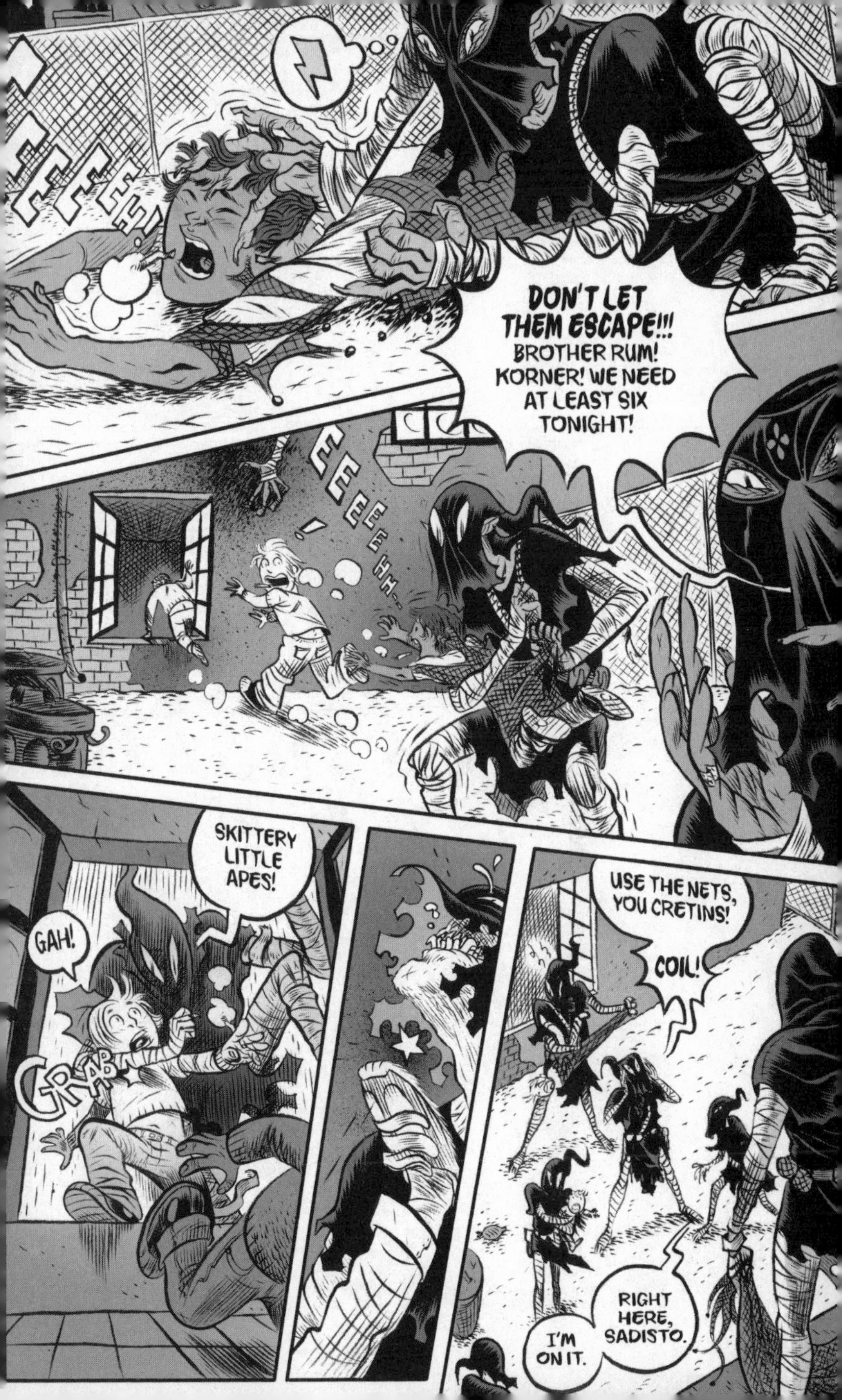
EEEE!
DON'T LET THEM ESCAPE!!! BROTHER RUM! KORNER! WE NEED AT LEAST SIX TONIGHT!
EEEEEEEHH...
SKITTERY LITTLE APES!
GAH!
GRAB
USE THE NETS, YOU CRETINS!
COIL!
RIGHT HERE, SADISTO.
I'M ON IT.

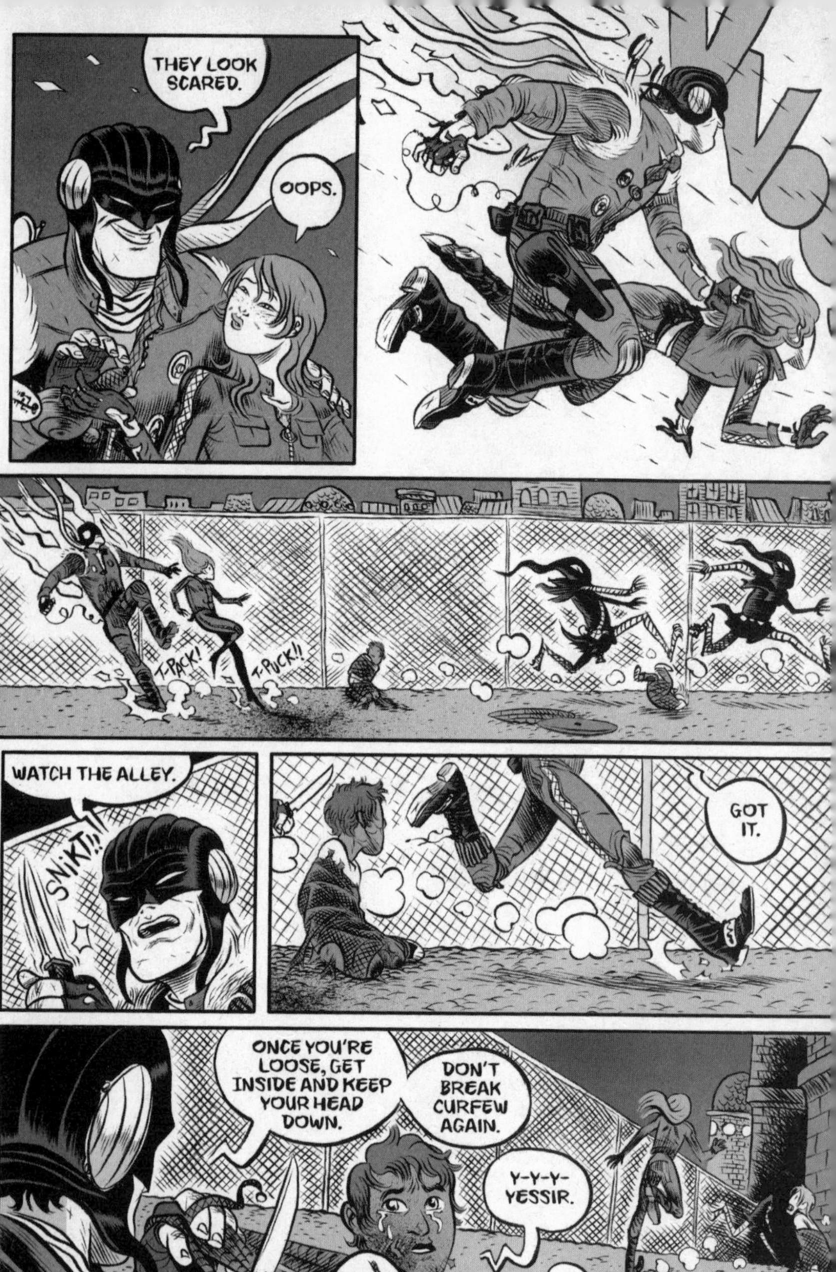
THEY LOOK SCARED.
OOPS.
T-PACK!
T-PUCK!!
WATCH THE ALLEY.
SNIKT!!
GOT IT.
ONCE YOU'RE LOOSE, GET INSIDE AND KEEP YOUR HEAD DOWN.
DON'T BREAK CURFEW AGAIN.
Y-Y-Y-YESSIR.

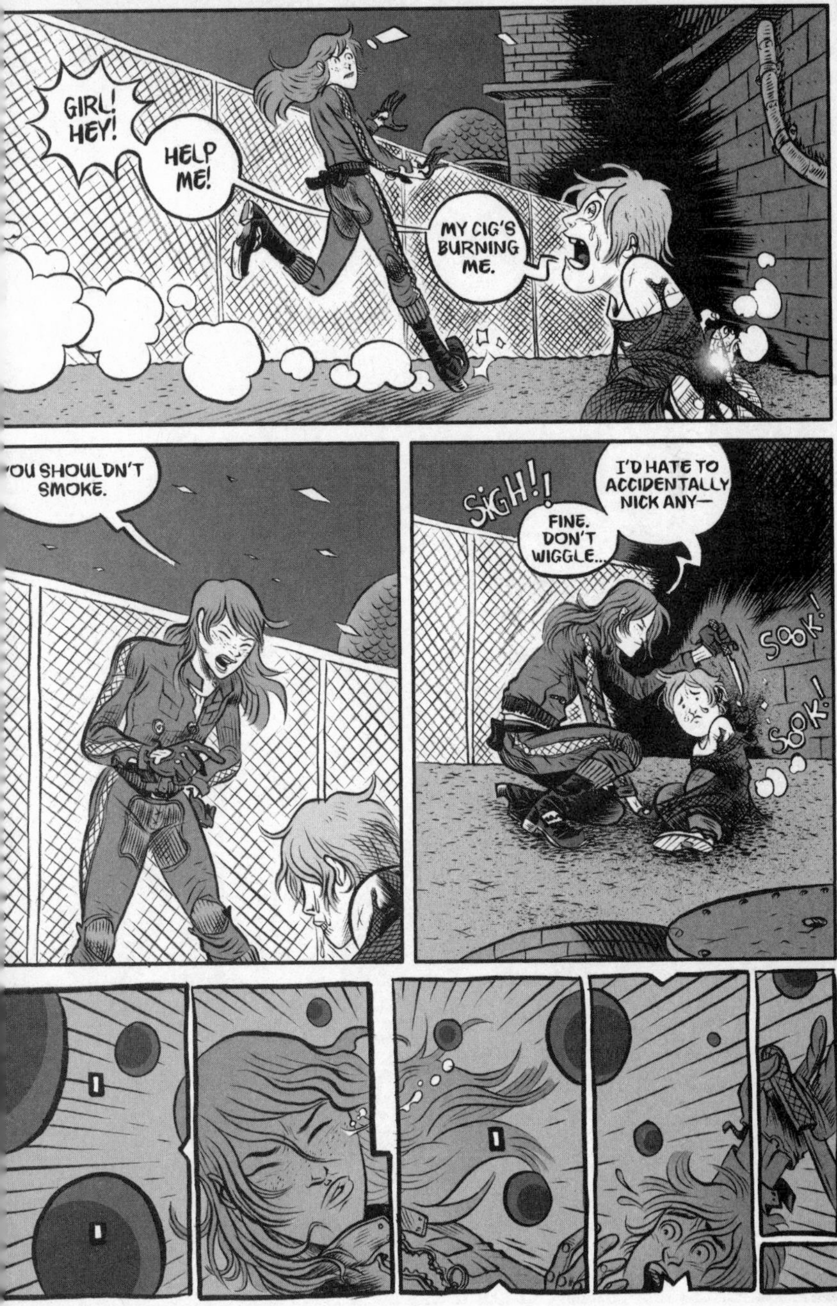
GIRL! HEY!
HELP ME!
MY CIG'S BURNING ME.
YOU SHOULDN'T SMOKE.
SIGH!
FINE. DON'T WIGGLE...
I'D HATE TO ACCIDENTALLY NICK ANY—
SOOK!
SOOK!

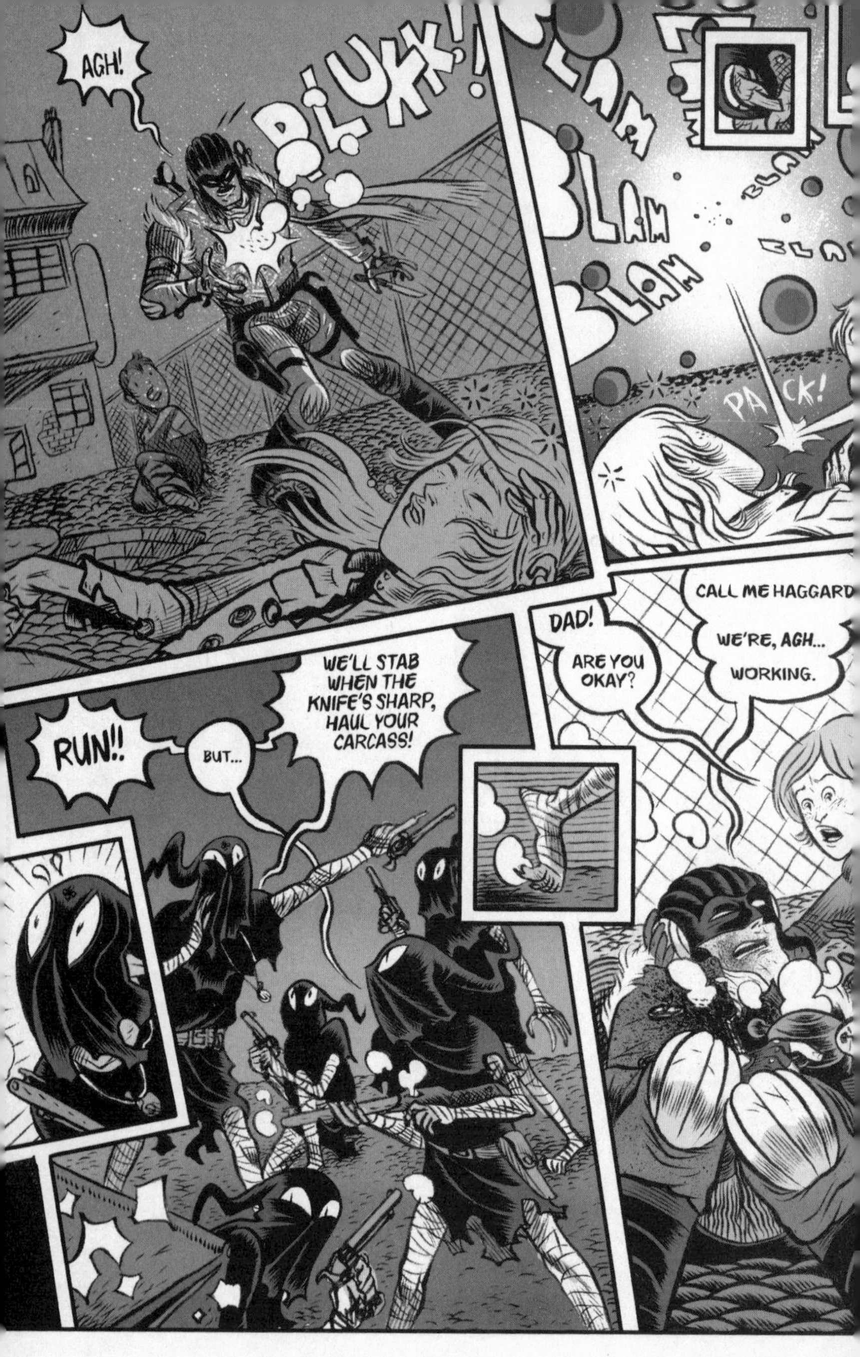
AGH!
BLUKK!
BLAM
BLAM
BLAM
BLAM
PACK!
DAD!
ARE YOU OKAY?
CALL ME HAGGARD
WE'RE, AGH...
WORKING.
RUN!!
BUT...
WE'LL STAB WHEN THE KNIFE'S SHARP, HAUL YOUR CARCASS!

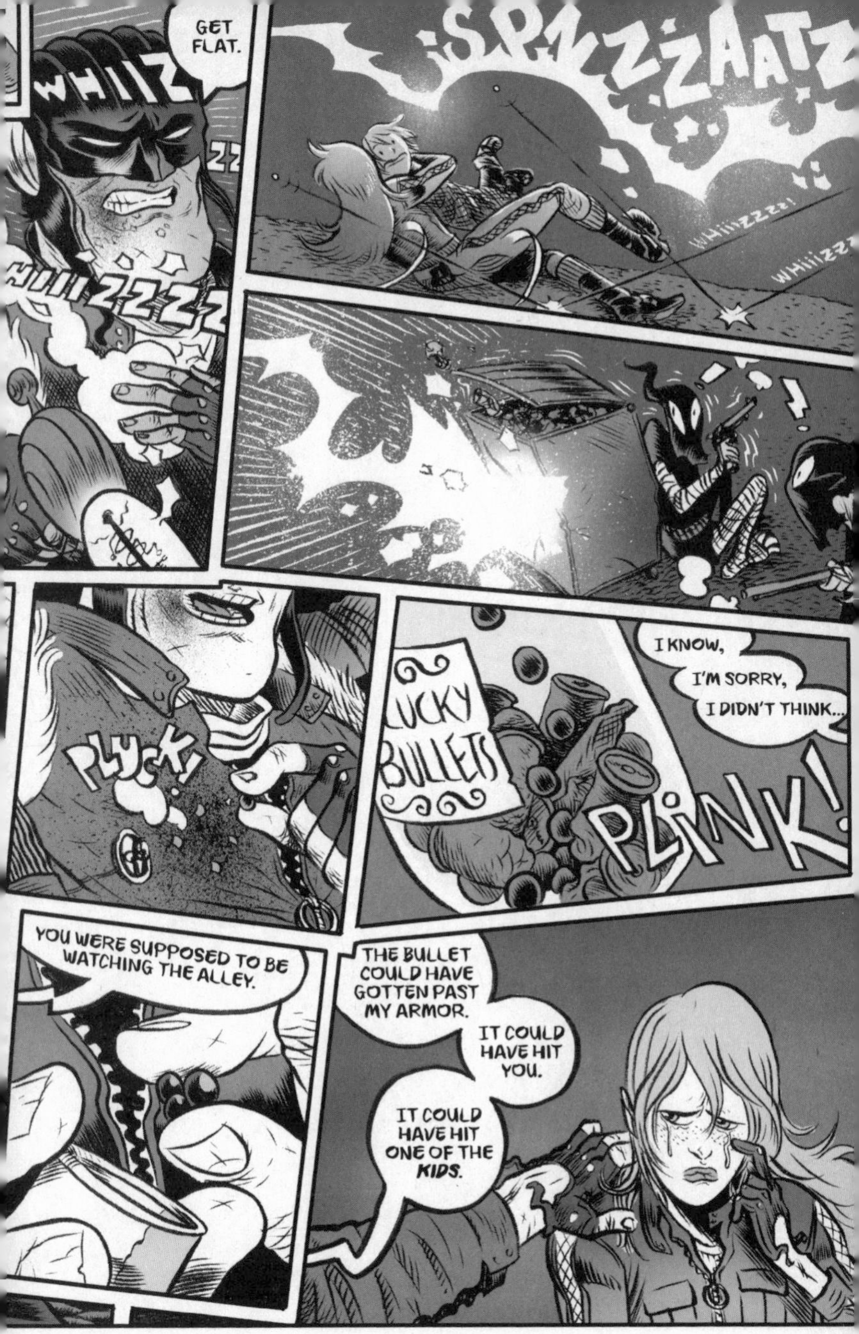
GET FLAT.
WHIIZ
ZZ
SPAZZAATZ
WHIIIZZZZ!
WHIIIZZZ
HUIIZZZZ
PLUCK!
LUCKY BULLETS
I KNOW,
I'M SORRY,
I DIDN'T THINK...
PLINK!
YOU WERE SUPPOSED TO BE WATCHING THE ALLEY.
THE BULLET COULD HAVE GOTTEN PAST MY ARMOR.
IT COULD HAVE HIT YOU.
IT COULD HAVE HIT ONE OF THE *KIDS*.

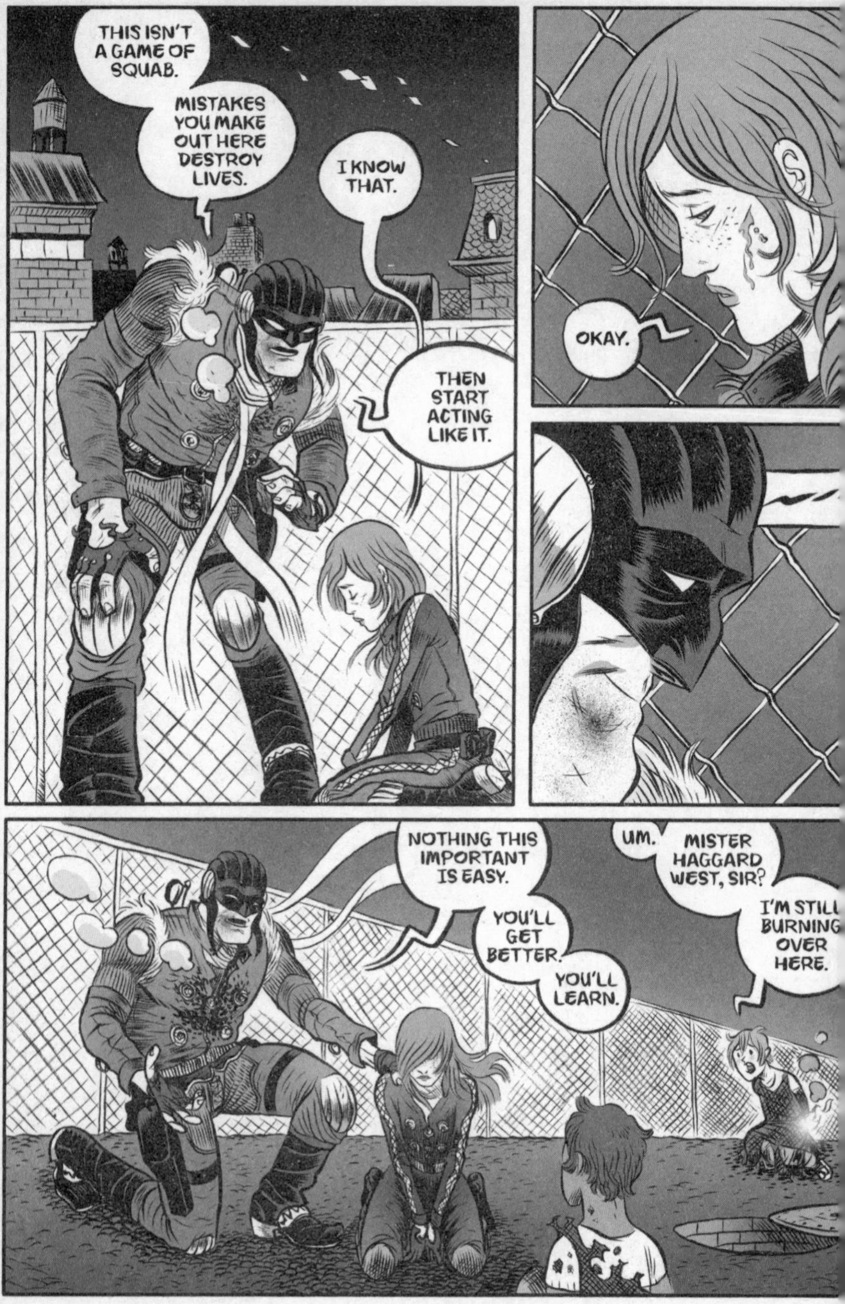
THIS ISN'T A GAME OF SQUAB.
MISTAKES YOU MAKE OUT HERE DESTROY LIVES.
I KNOW THAT.
THEN START ACTING LIKE IT.
OKAY.
NOTHING THIS IMPORTANT IS EASY.
YOU'LL GET BETTER.
YOU'LL LEARN.
UM.
MISTER HAGGARD WEST, SIR?
I'M STILL BURNING OVER HERE.

83

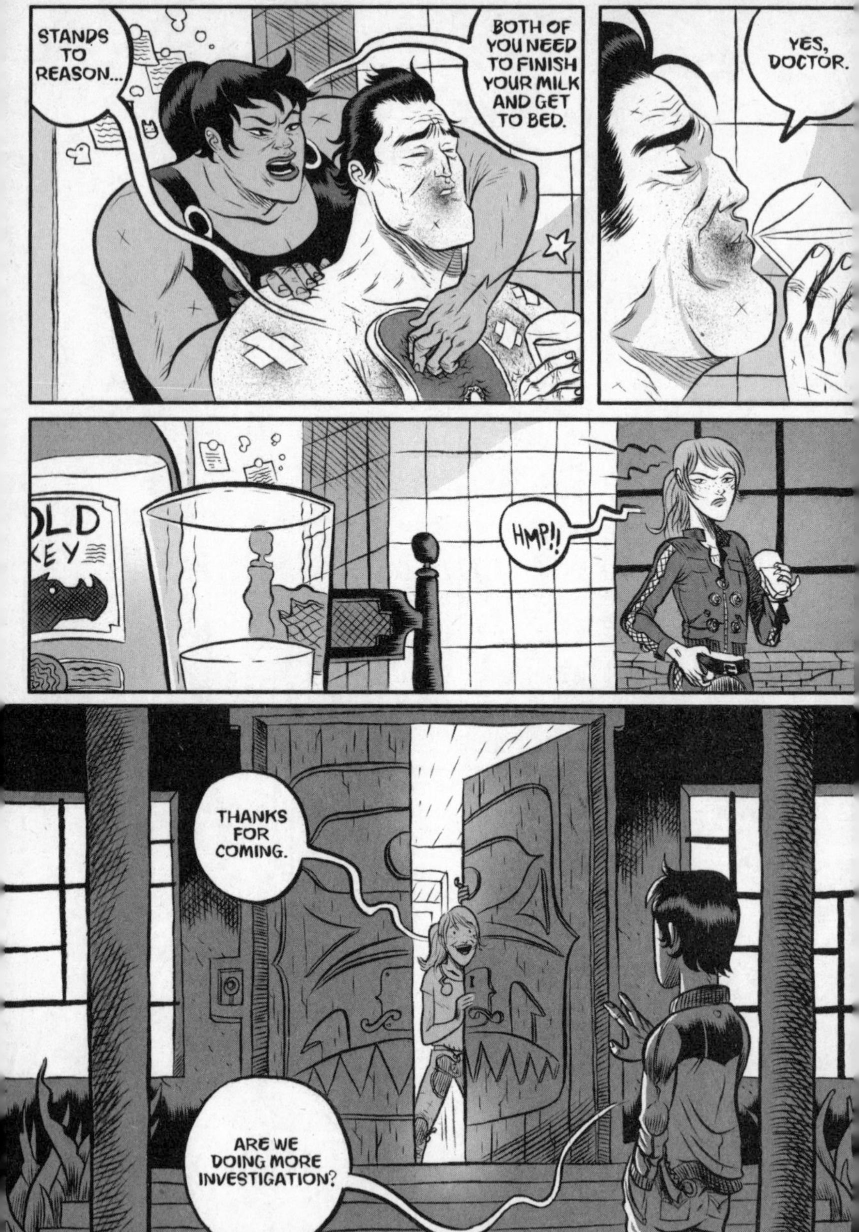
STANDS TO REASON...
BOTH OF YOU NEED TO FINISH YOUR MILK AND GET TO BED.
YES, DOCTOR.
HMP!!
THANKS FOR COMING.
ARE WE DOING MORE INVESTIGATION?

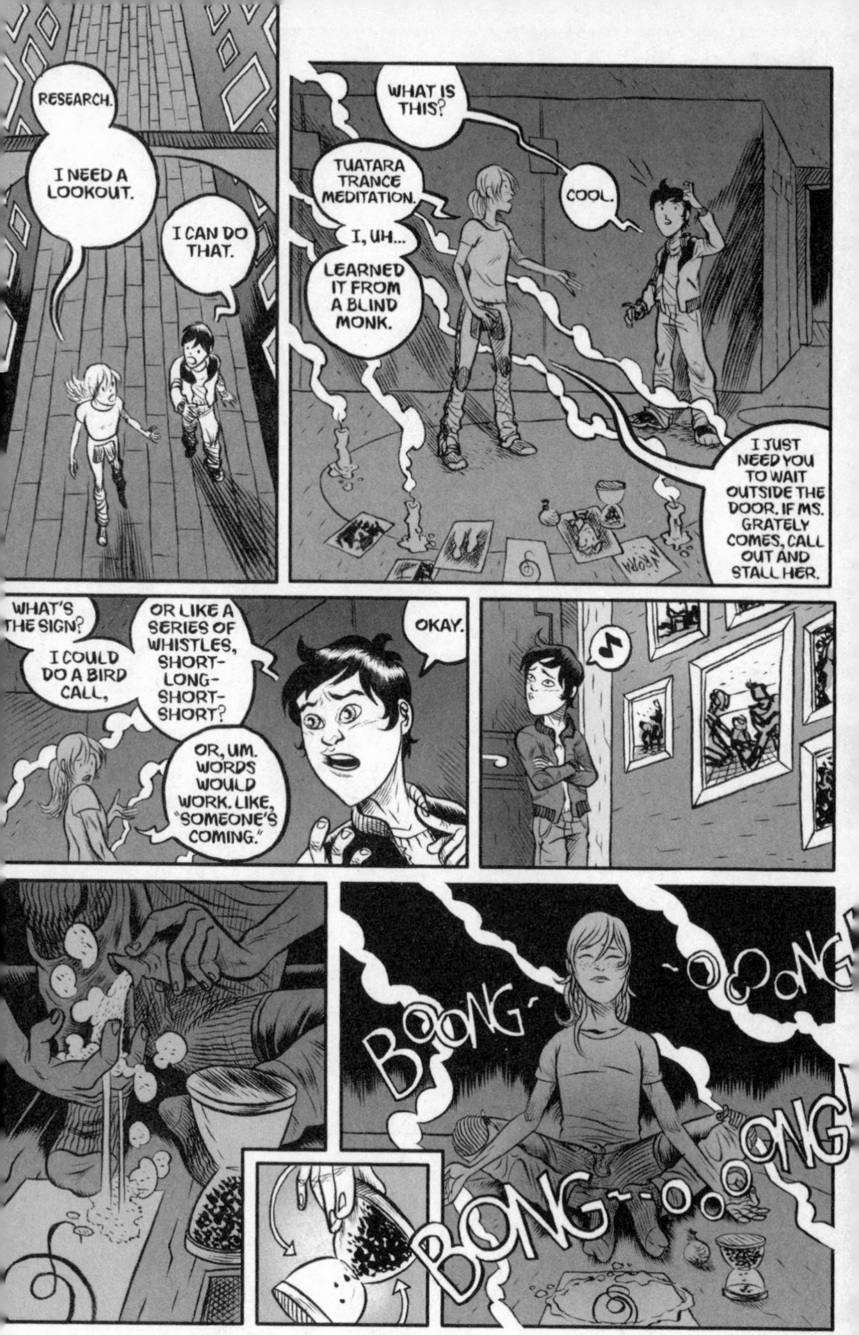
RESEARCH.
I NEED A LOOKOUT.
I CAN DO THAT.
WHAT IS THIS?
TUATARA TRANCE MEDITATION.
COOL.
I, UH...
LEARNED IT FROM A BLIND MONK.
I JUST NEED YOU TO WAIT OUTSIDE THE DOOR. IF MS. GRATELY COMES, CALL OUT AND STALL HER.
WHAT'S THE SIGN?
I COULD DO A BIRD CALL,
OR LIKE A SERIES OF WHISTLES, SHORT-LONG-SHORT-SHORT?
OKAY.
OR, UM. WORDS WOULD WORK. LIKE, "SOMEONE'S COMING."
BOONG-OOONG
BONG-O-O-OONG

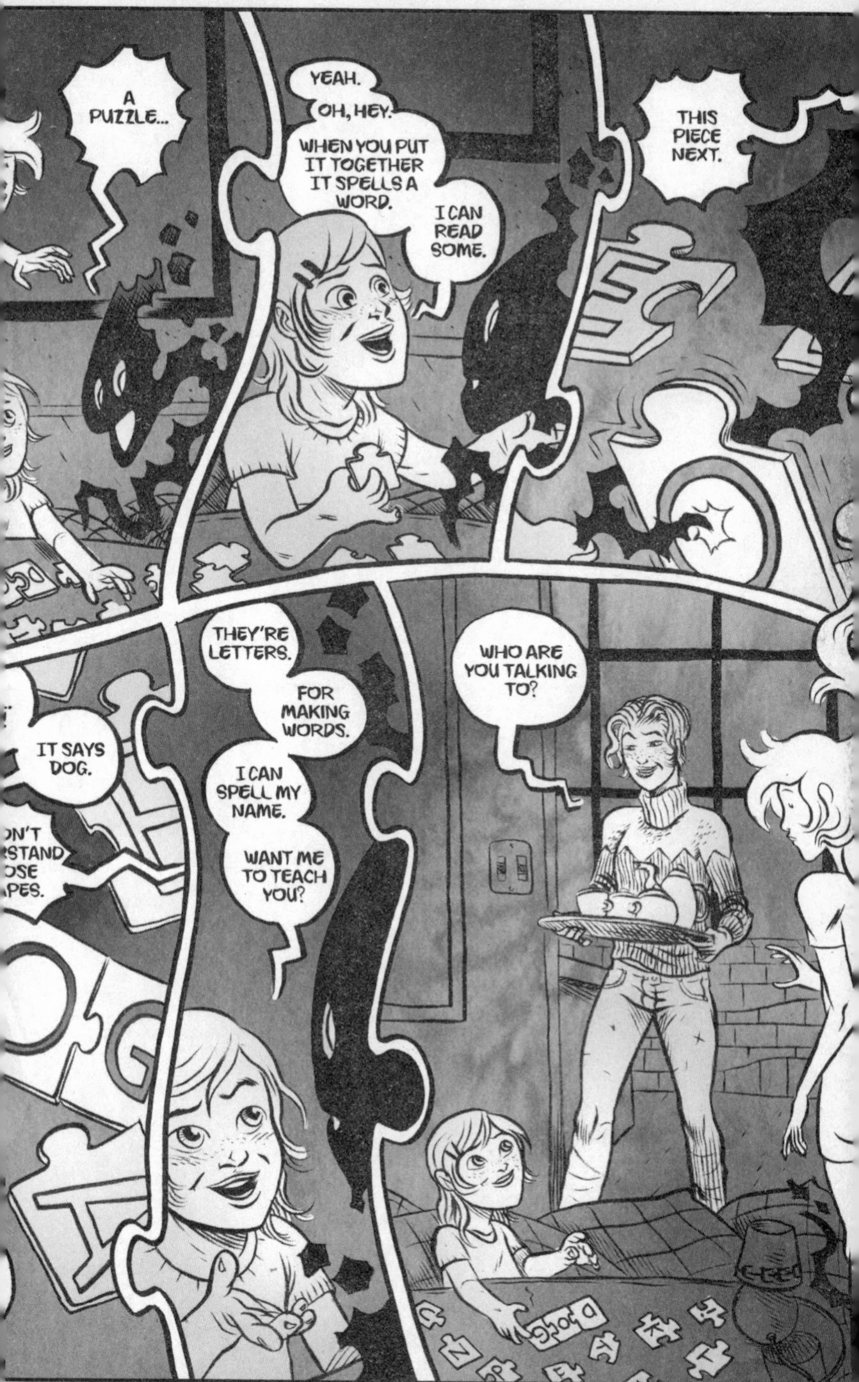

A PUZZLE...
YEAH.
OH, HEY.
WHEN YOU PUT IT TOGETHER IT SPELLS A WORD.
I CAN READ SOME.
THIS PIECE NEXT.
IT SAYS DOG.
THEY'RE LETTERS.
FOR MAKING WORDS.
I CAN SPELL MY NAME.
WANT ME TO TEACH YOU?
WHO ARE YOU TALKING TO?

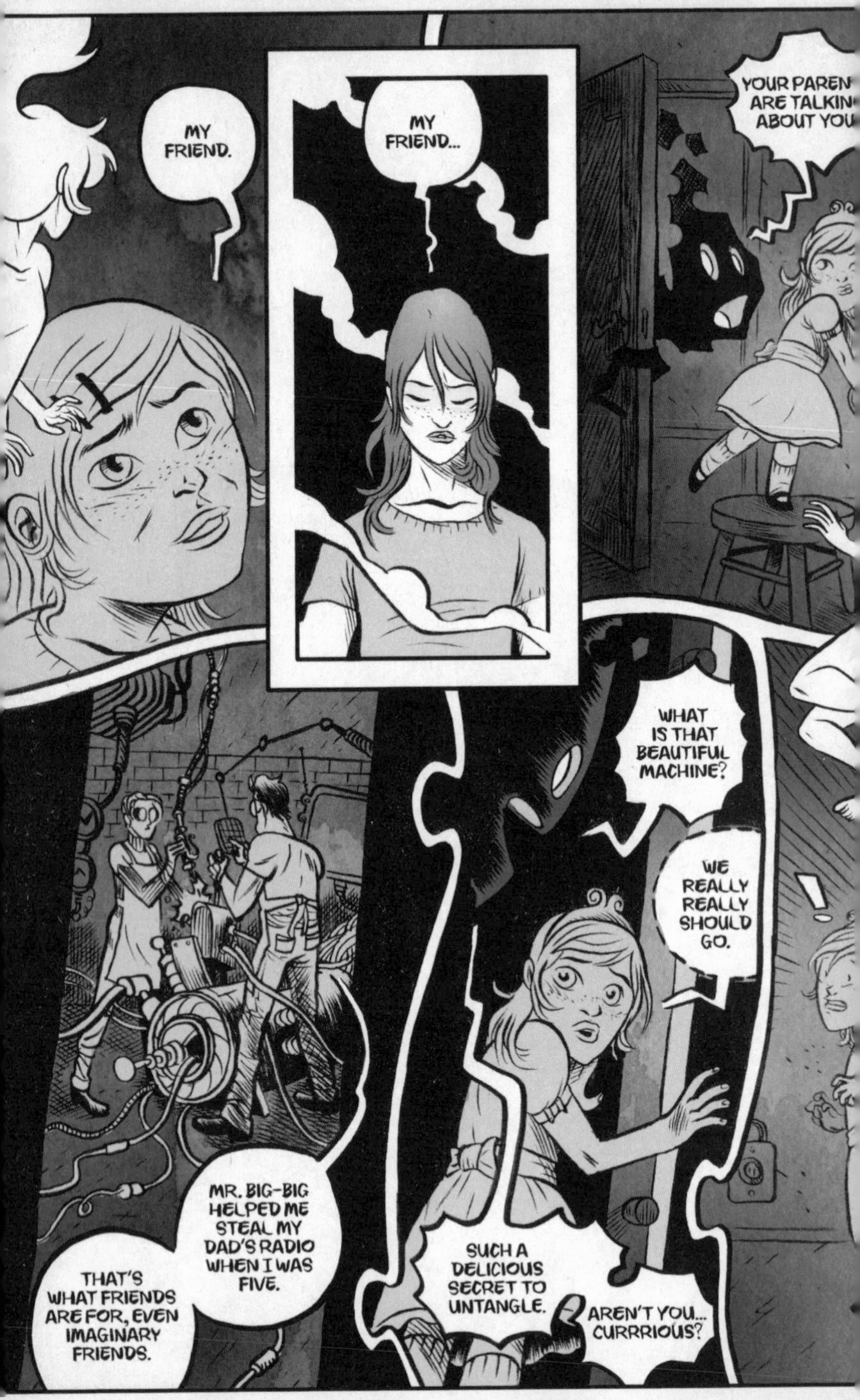
MY FRIEND.
MY FRIEND...
YOUR PAREN
ARE TALKIN
ABOUT YOU
WHAT IS THAT BEAUTIFUL MACHINE?
WE REALLY REALLY SHOULD GO.
MR. BIG-BIG HELPED ME STEAL MY DAD'S RADIO WHEN I WAS FIVE.
THAT'S WHAT FRIENDS ARE FOR, EVEN IMAGINARY FRIENDS.
SUCH A DELICIOUS SECRET TO UNTANGLE.
AREN'T YOU... CURRRIOUS?

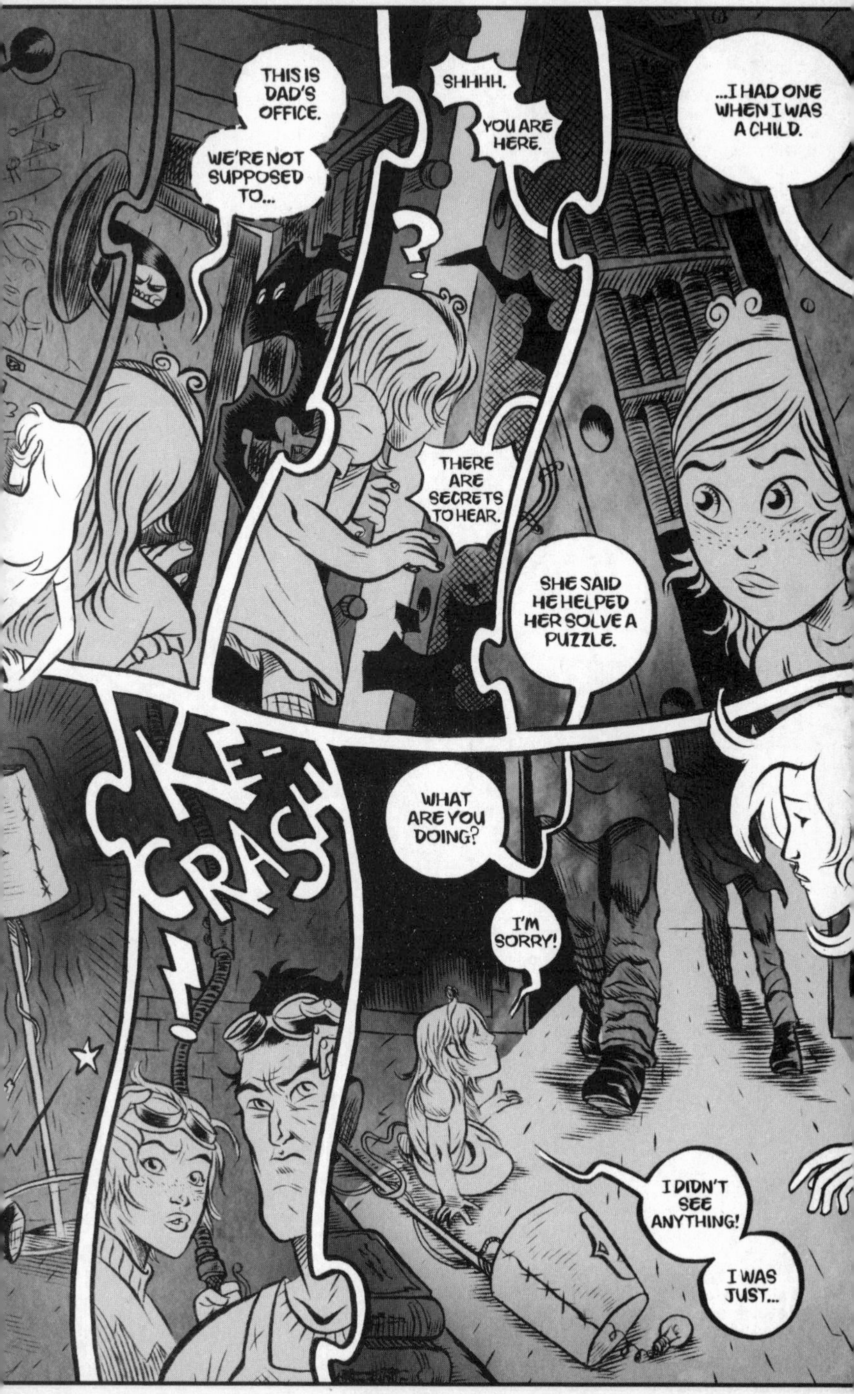
THIS IS DAD'S OFFICE.
WE'RE NOT SUPPOSED TO...
SHHHH.
YOU ARE HERE.
?
...I HAD ONE WHEN I WAS A CHILD.
THERE ARE SECRETS TO HEAR.
SHE SAID HE HELPED HER SOLVE A PUZZLE.
KE-CRASH
!
WHAT ARE YOU DOING?
I'M SORRY!
I DIDN'T SEE ANYTHING!
I WAS JUST...

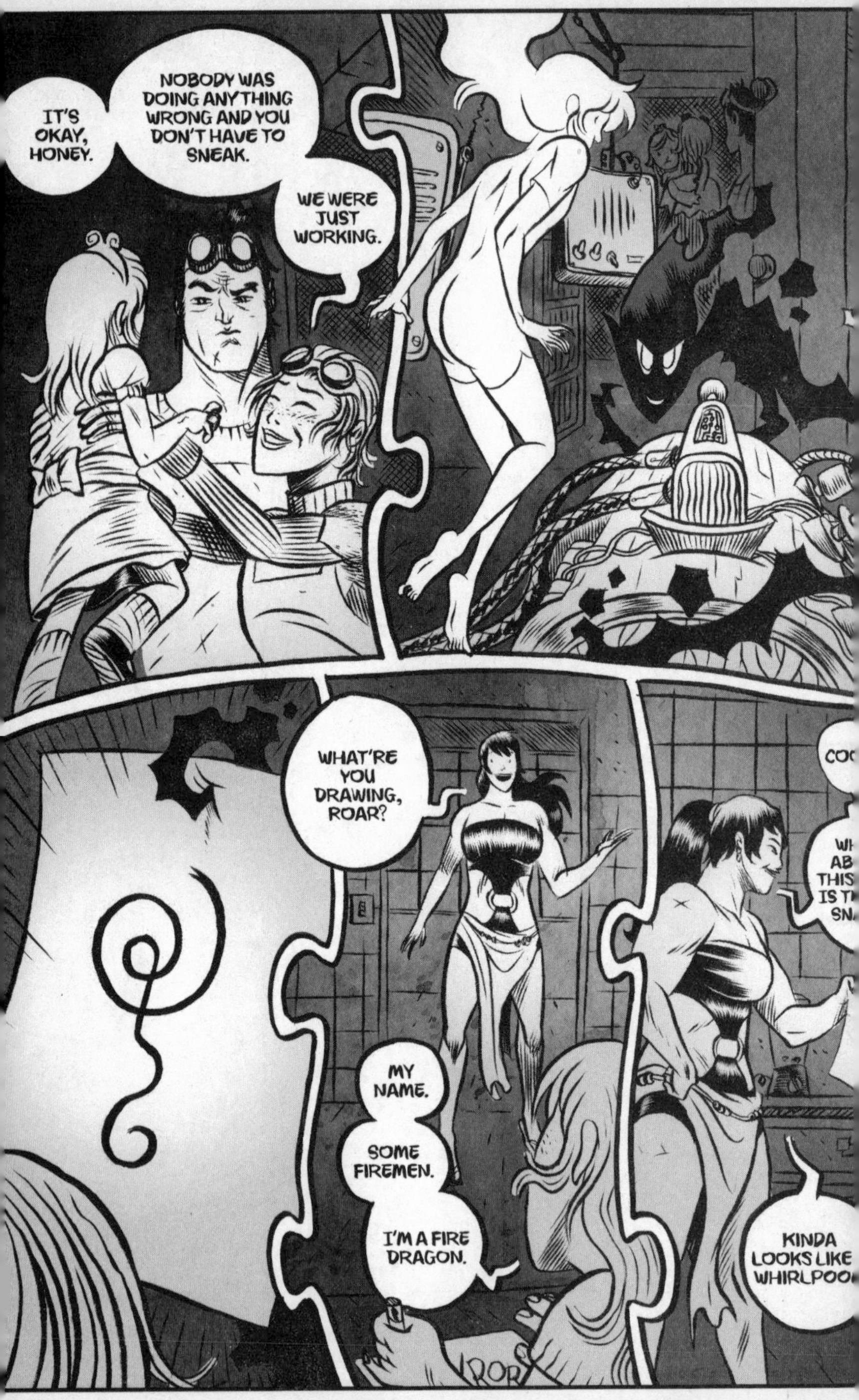

IT'S OKAY, HONEY.
NOBODY WAS DOING ANYTHING WRONG AND YOU DON'T HAVE TO SNEAK.
WE WERE JUST WORKING.
WHAT'RE YOU DRAWING, ROAR?
MY NAME.
SOME FIREMEN.
I'M A FIRE DRAGON.
KINDA LOOKS LIKE WHIRLPOO

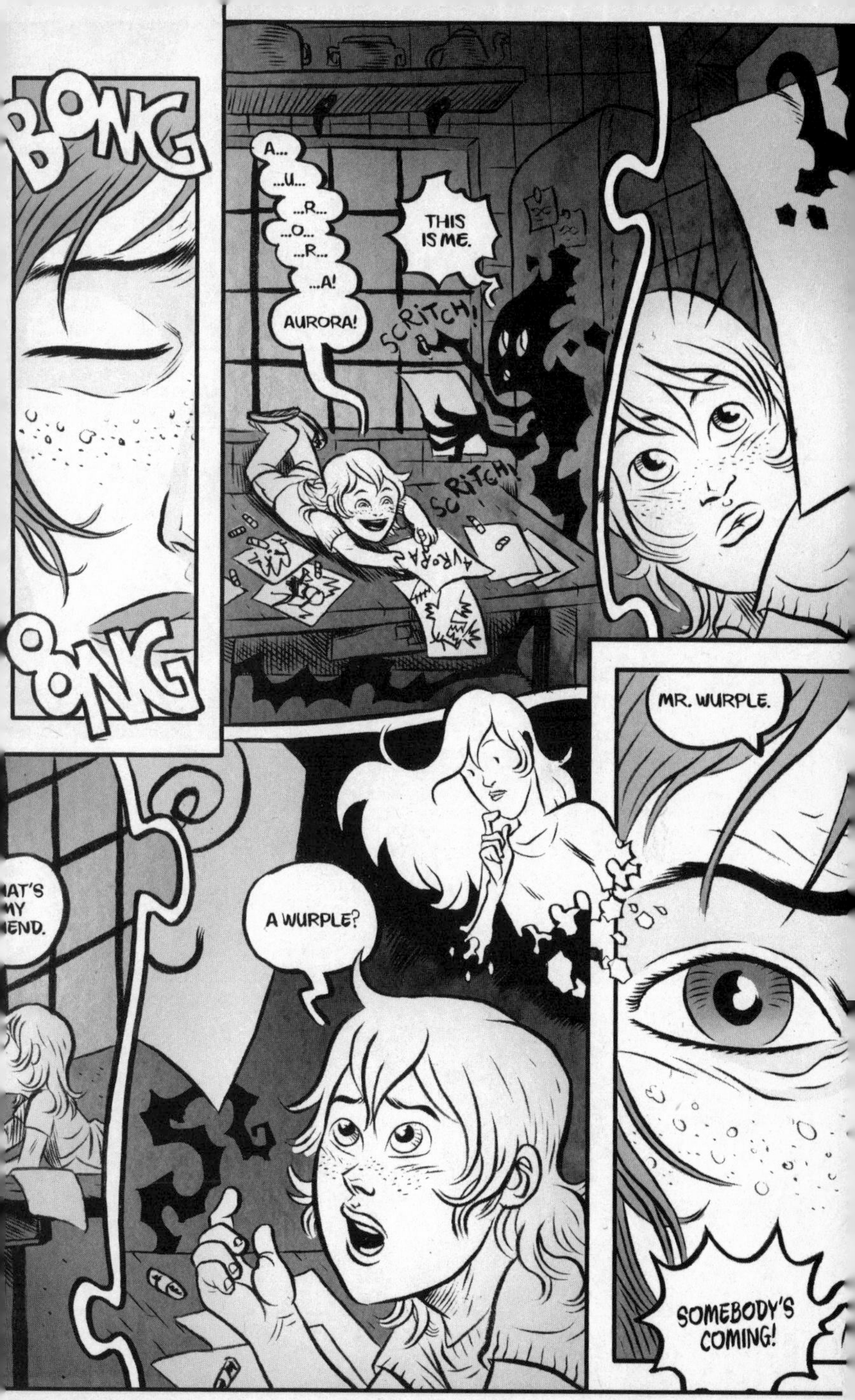
BONG
BONG
A...
...U...
...R...
...O...
...R...
...A!
AURORA!
THIS IS ME.
SCRITCH!
SCRITCH!
AURORA
MR. WURPLE.
AT'S
MY
IEND.
A WURPLE?
SOMEBODY'S COMING!

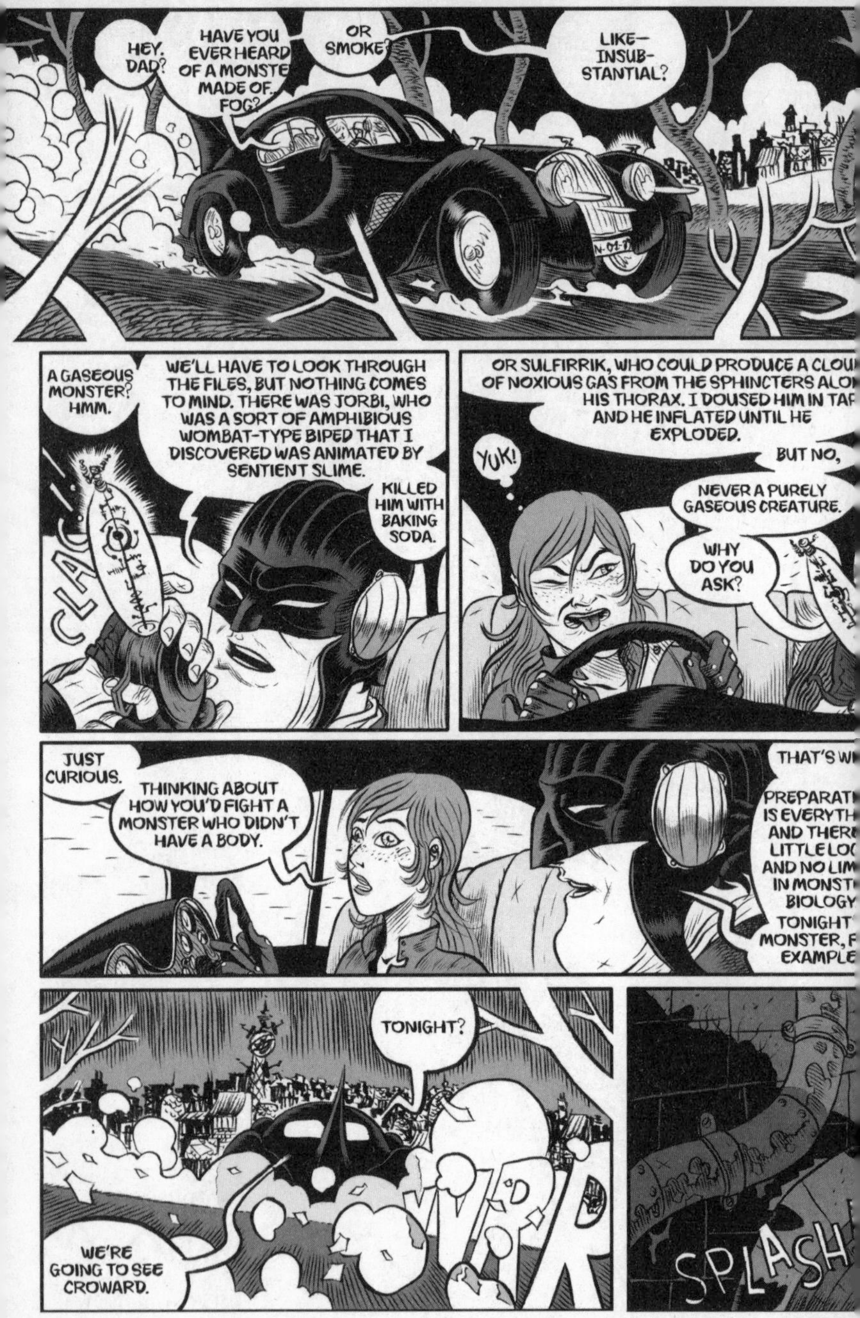
HEY, DAD?
HAVE YOU EVER HEARD OF A MONSTE MADE OF FOG?
OR SMOKE?
LIKE— INSUB-STANTIAL?
A GASEOUS MONSTER? HMM.
WE'LL HAVE TO LOOK THROUGH THE FILES, BUT NOTHING COMES TO MIND. THERE WAS JORBI, WHO WAS A SORT OF AMPHIBIOUS WOMBAT-TYPE BIPED THAT I DISCOVERED WAS ANIMATED BY SENTIENT SLIME.
KILLED HIM WITH BAKING SODA.
CLAC
OR SULFIRRIK, WHO COULD PRODUCE A CLOU OF NOXIOUS GAS FROM THE SPHINCTERS ALO HIS THORAX. I DOUSED HIM IN TA AND HE INFLATED UNTIL HE EXPLODED.
YUK!
BUT NO,
NEVER A PURELY GASEOUS CREATURE.
WHY DO YOU ASK?
JUST CURIOUS.
THINKING ABOUT HOW YOU'D FIGHT A MONSTER WHO DIDN'T HAVE A BODY.
THAT'S W
PREPARAT IS EVERYTH AND THER LITTLE LO AND NO LIM IN MONST BIOLOGY
TONIGHT MONSTER, F EXAMPLE
TONIGHT?
WE'RE GOING TO SEE CROWARD.
SPLASH

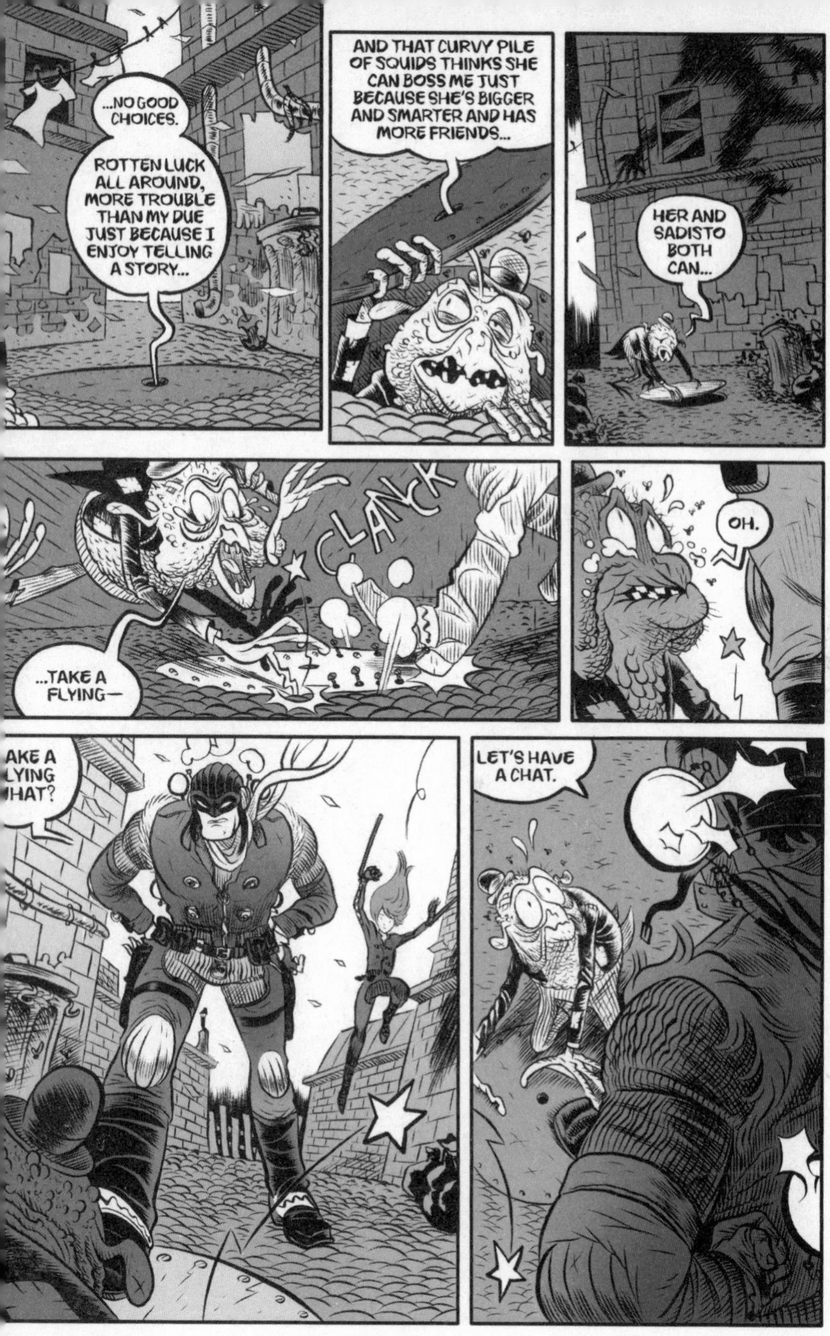
...NO GOOD CHOICES.
ROTTEN LUCK ALL AROUND, MORE TROUBLE THAN MY DUE JUST BECAUSE I ENJOY TELLING A STORY...
AND THAT CURVY PILE OF SQUIDS THINKS SHE CAN BOSS ME JUST BECAUSE SHE'S BIGGER AND SMARTER AND HAS MORE FRIENDS...
HER AND SADISTO BOTH CAN...
...TAKE A FLYING—
CLANCK
OH.
AKE A LYING HAT?
LET'S HAVE A CHAT.

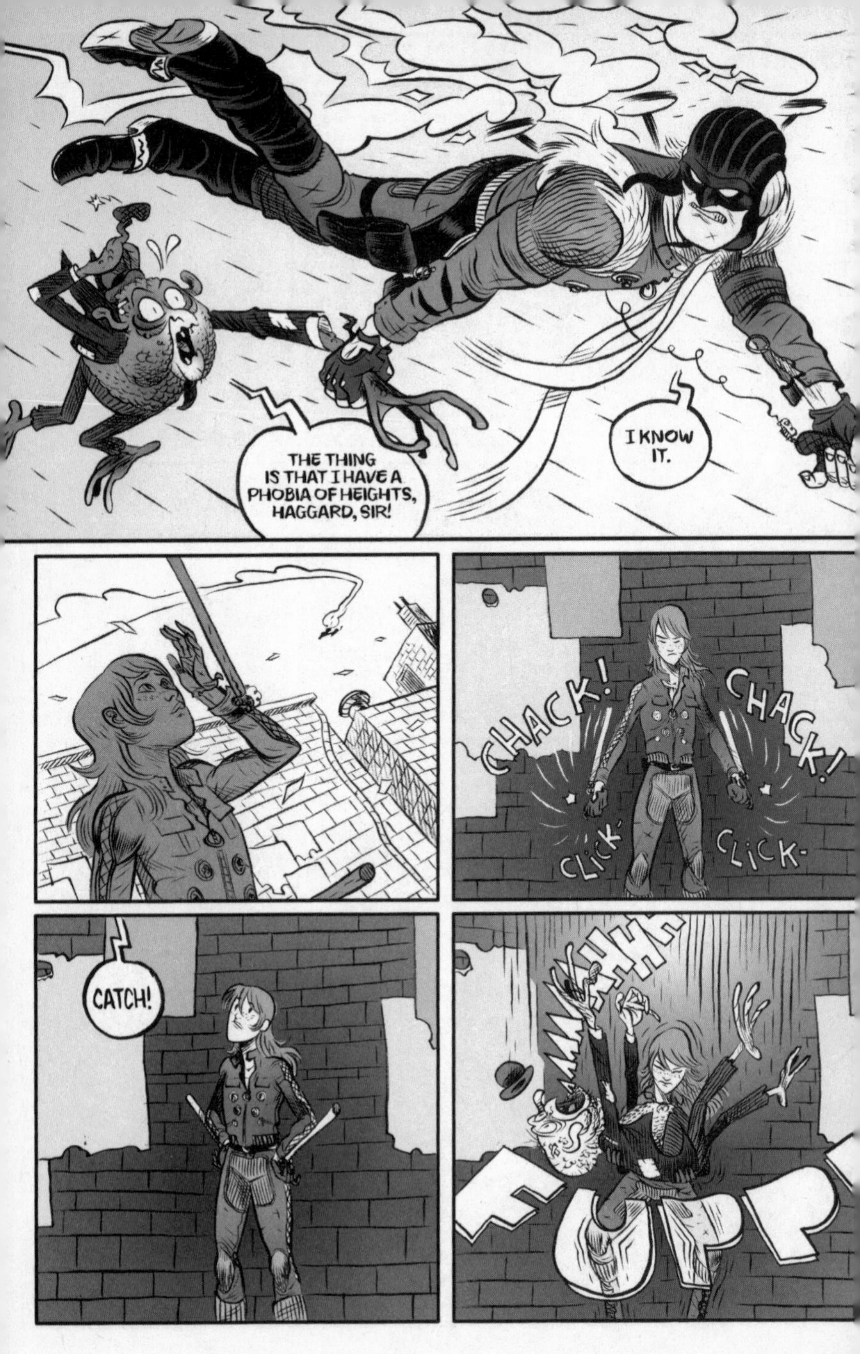
THE THING IS THAT I HAVE A PHOBIA OF HEIGHTS, HAGGARD, SIR!
I KNOW IT.
CHACK!
CHACK!
CLICK-
CLICK-
CATCH!

TOMORROW!

TOMORROW AT MIDNIGHT MEDULA DELIVERS THE LAST PIECE TO SADISTO'S GANG AND THEY FINISH THE MACHINE!

OVER EASY, THEY SAID.

LAST PIECE OF WHAT?

I DON'T KNOW, TOO COMPLEXICATED FOR MY HEAD. ALL TANGLY.

WHERE DOES THE DELIVERY HAPPEN?

I DON'T KNOW.

OVER EASY, THEY SAID IT WOULD BE OVER EASY.

DON'T FLY ME AGAIN.

IS THAT WHAT MONSTER PEE SMELLS LIKE?

WE'RE JUST GONNA LET HIM GO?

YEAH.

GROSS.

DROP HIM.

CROWARD'S TOO INCOMPETENT TO POSE ANY KIND OF REAL THREAT AND HE'S A GOOD SNITCH TO BOOT.

WE NEED TO FIND SADISTO'S GANG.

WOULDN'T THIS BE EASIER IF I HAD MY OWN JET PACK?

NOT UNTIL YOU'RE EIGHTEEN, YOU KNOW THAT.

A JET PACK'S NO SAFER THAN STRAPPING A BOMB TO YOUR BACK.

IS THAT A MONSTER? ON THE GODEL'S BRIDGE?

NO...

97

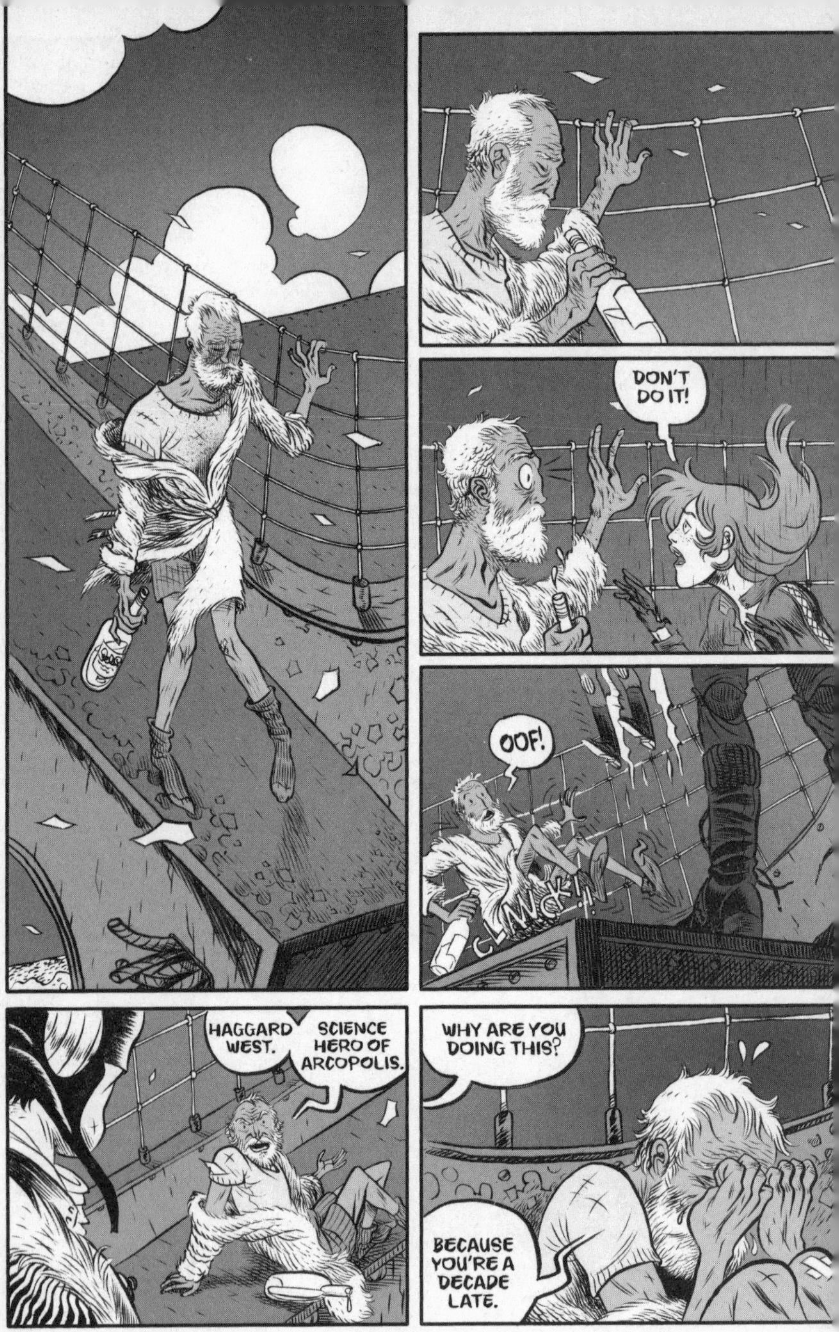
DON'T DO IT!
OOF!
CLWCK!!
HAGGARD WEST.
SCIENCE HERO OF ARCOPOLIS.
WHY ARE YOU DOING THIS?
BECAUSE YOU'RE A DECADE LATE.

99

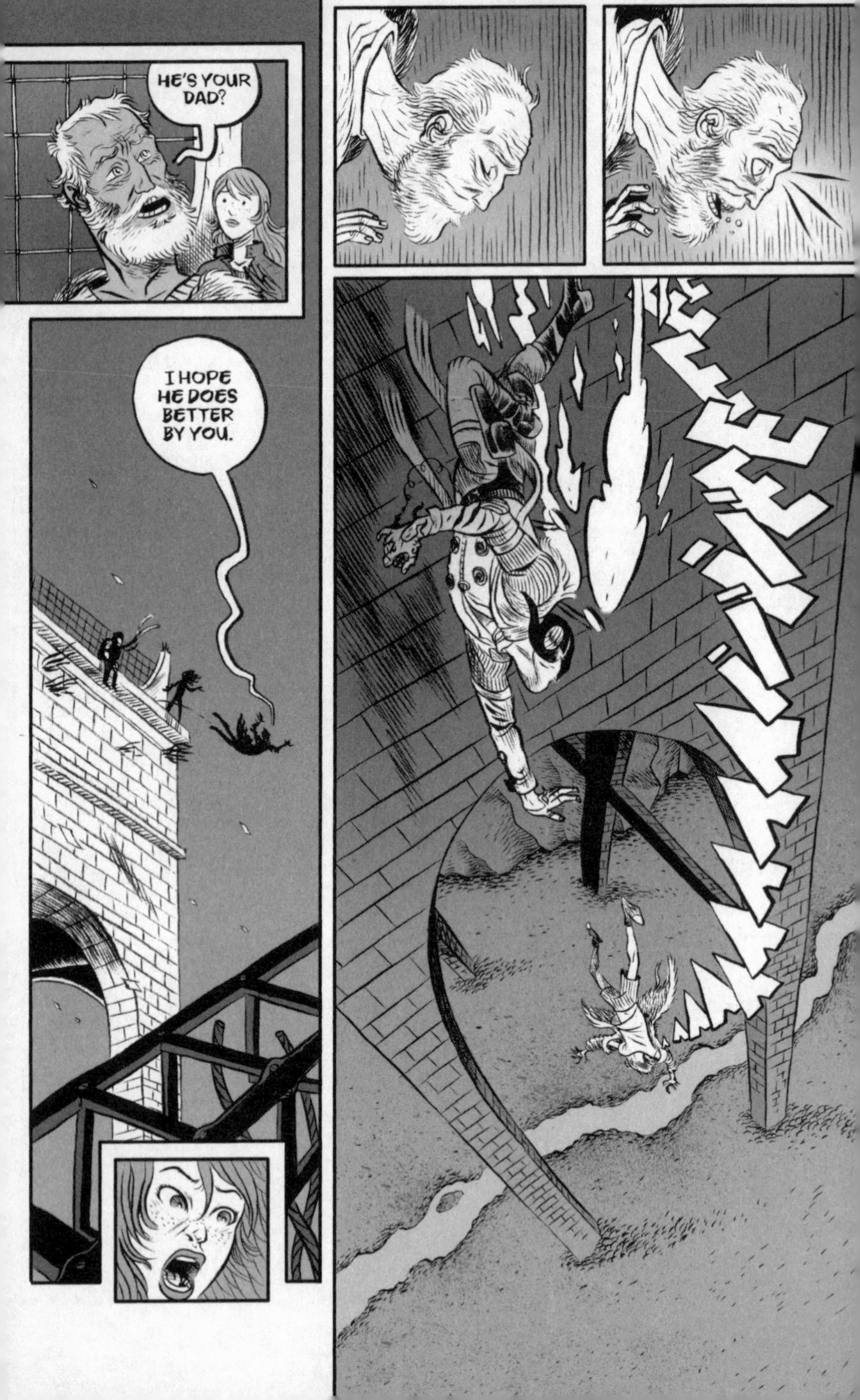
HE'S YOUR DAD?
I HOPE HE DOES BETTER BY YOU.

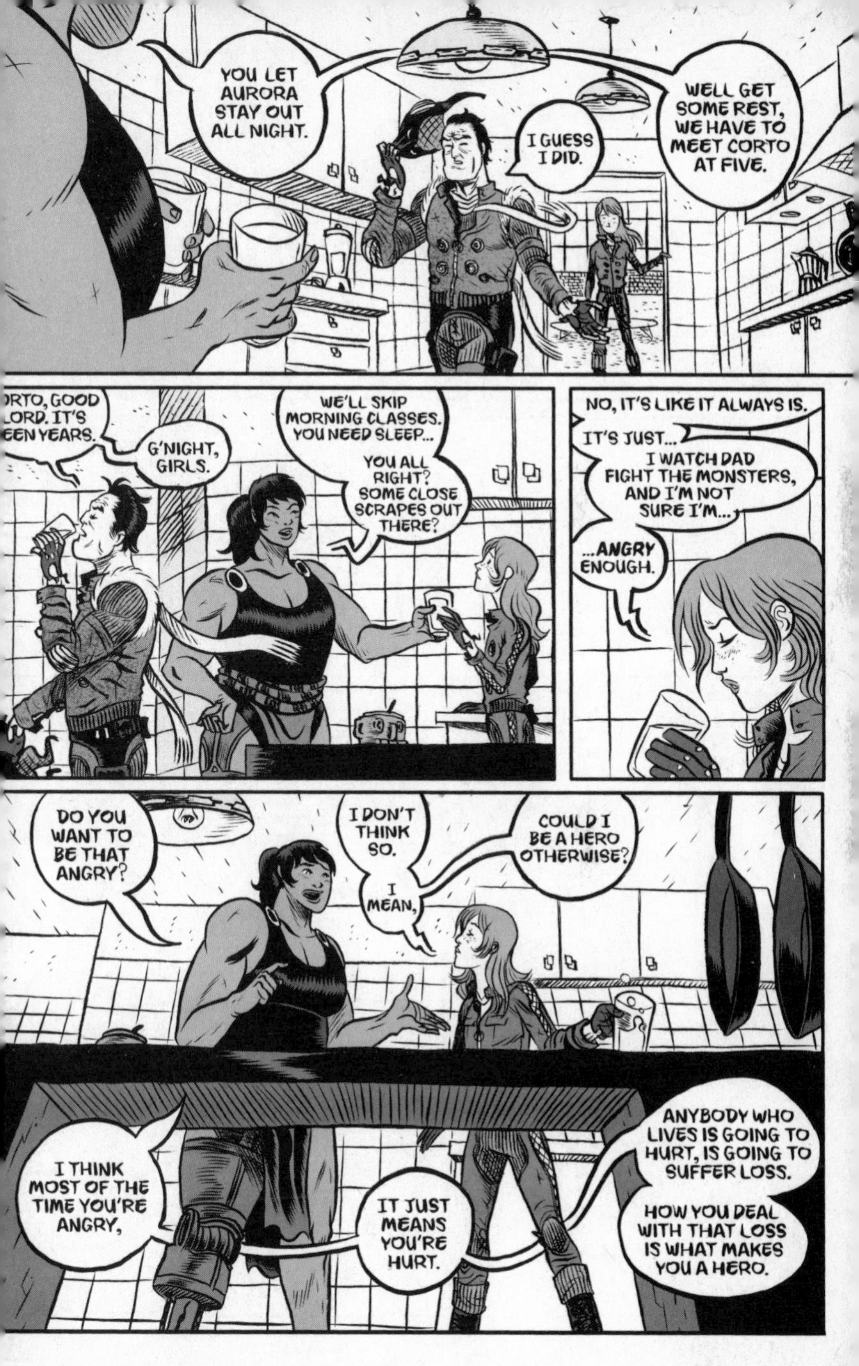
YOU LET AURORA STAY OUT ALL NIGHT.
I GUESS I DID.
WELL GET SOME REST, WE HAVE TO MEET CORTO AT FIVE.
ORTO, GOOD LORD. IT'S EEN YEARS.
G'NIGHT, GIRLS.
WE'LL SKIP MORNING CLASSES. YOU NEED SLEEP...
YOU ALL RIGHT? SOME CLOSE SCRAPES OUT THERE?
NO, IT'S LIKE IT ALWAYS IS.
IT'S JUST...
I WATCH DAD FIGHT THE MONSTERS, AND I'M NOT SURE I'M...
...ANGRY ENOUGH.
DO YOU WANT TO BE THAT ANGRY?
I DON'T THINK SO.
I MEAN,
COULD I BE A HERO OTHERWISE?
I THINK MOST OF THE TIME YOU'RE ANGRY,
IT JUST MEANS YOU'RE HURT.
ANYBODY WHO LIVES IS GOING TO HURT, IS GOING TO SUFFER LOSS.
HOW YOU DEAL WITH THAT LOSS IS WHAT MAKES YOU A HERO.

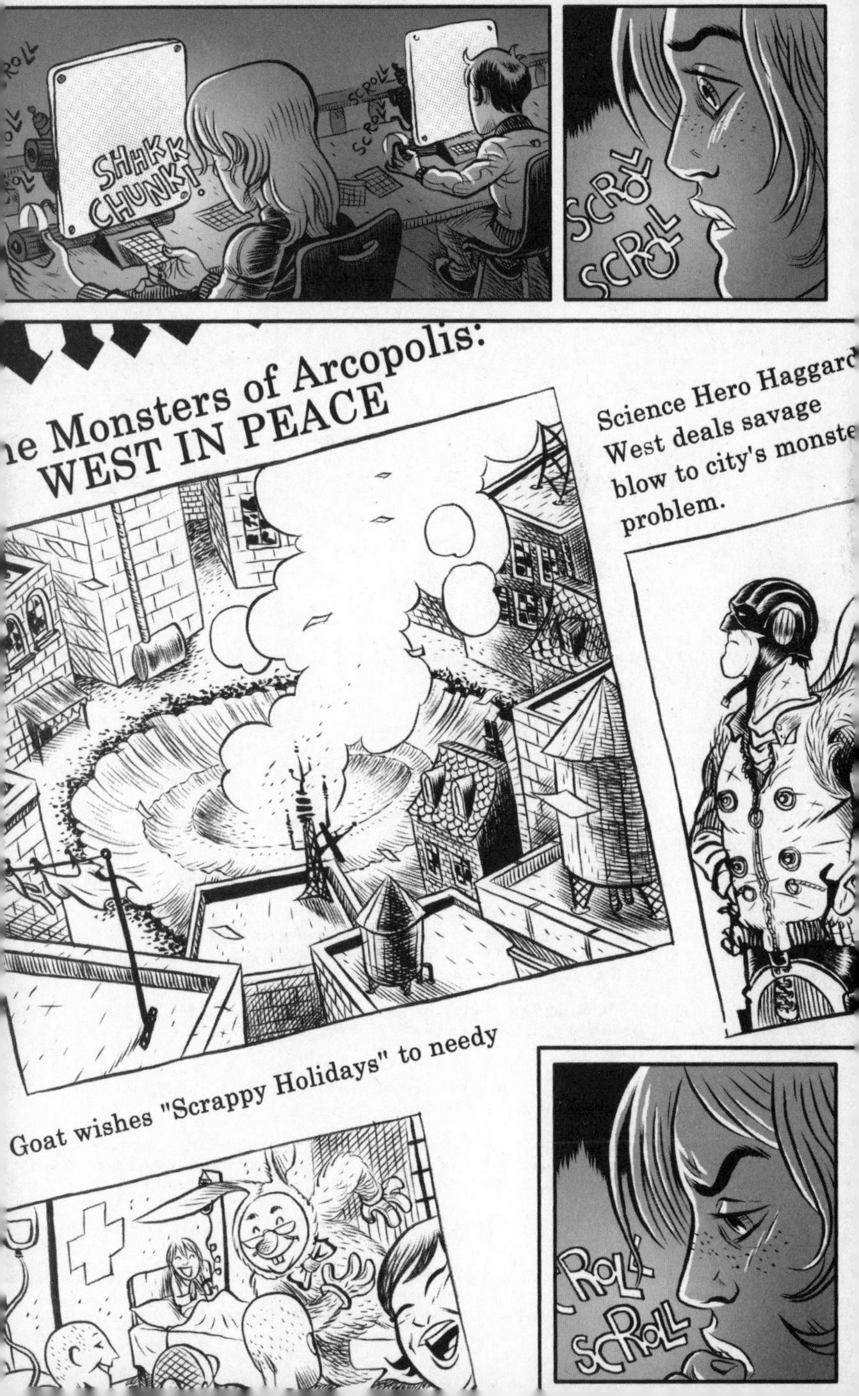

SCROLL
SHHKK CHUNK!
SCROLL
SCROLL
SCROLL
SCROLL
SCROLL
...he Monsters of Arcopolis:
WEST IN PEACE
Science Hero Haggard West deals savage blow to city's monste... problem.
Goat wishes "Scrappy Holidays" to needy
ROLL
SCROLL

MONSTER MASI

HEROIC HAGGARD WEST DEFEATS MONSTERS WITH SCIENCE AND MUSCLE

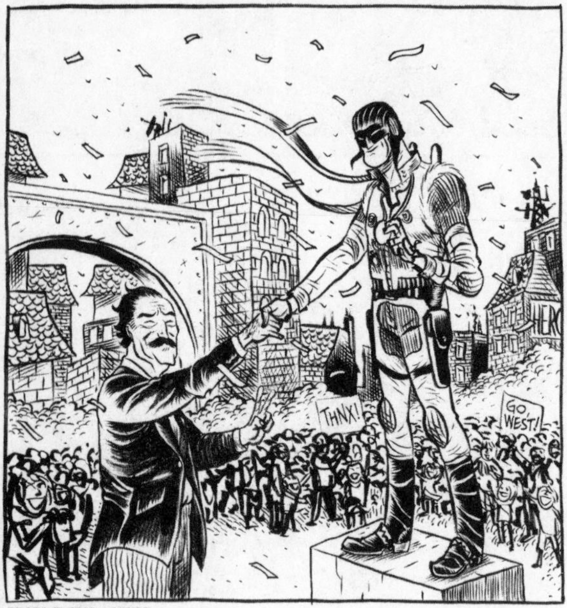
THNX!
GO WEST!

PHOTO CREDIT: AC WIRE

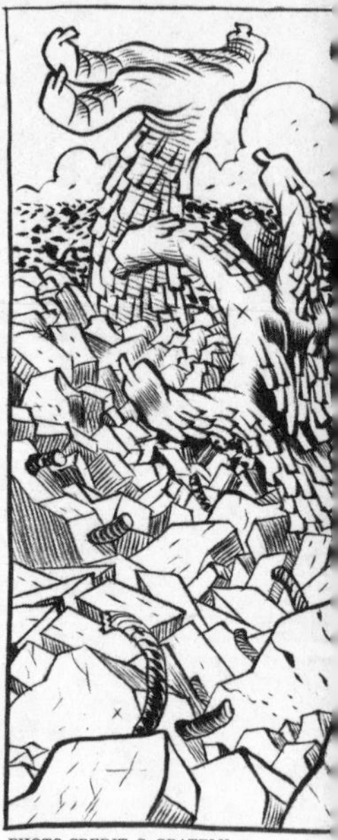

PHOTO CREDIT: S. GRATELY

After years of struggle, Arcopolis' own son Haggard West may have finally put an end to the inhum menace threatening our city's children.

Using what he describes as a "Plasma Cannon," Haggard destroyed the entrance to the monsters' underground lair.

Dozens were surely killed in the initial blast, without the loss of a single human life.
The remaining monsters, a reckless and uneducated mob of swarthy psychopaths, will certainly succumb to starvation, infighting, or fatal despair in the coming months.

The Mayor described Mr. West as, "An inspiration and model for our young people. A self-made mar he exemplifies all the wealth and glory you can achieve through education, calisthenics, and a ceas dedication to the public good."

The people of Arcopolis have lived in the spreading shadow of the monster problem for nearly a dec now. Tonight those good people can rest a little easier.

Mr. West made his fortune through inventions as varied and invaluable as the Westwave Oven™, Carbon Copy™, West-o-Matic Gearbox™, and Catlick Straps™. But with the rise of the monsters, he found a new calling and turned his inestimable brain to the welfare of our children.

"I have a daughter," he said from the podium, "I know the fear we've had to live with for too long. Today, that ends."

He also gave credit for the conception and construction of the Plasma Cannon to his wife and partn Rosetta West, and their assistant and photographer, Svetlana Goodley. The comely ladies of the We Manor were unfortunately delayed at the last moment and unable to attend the ceremony.

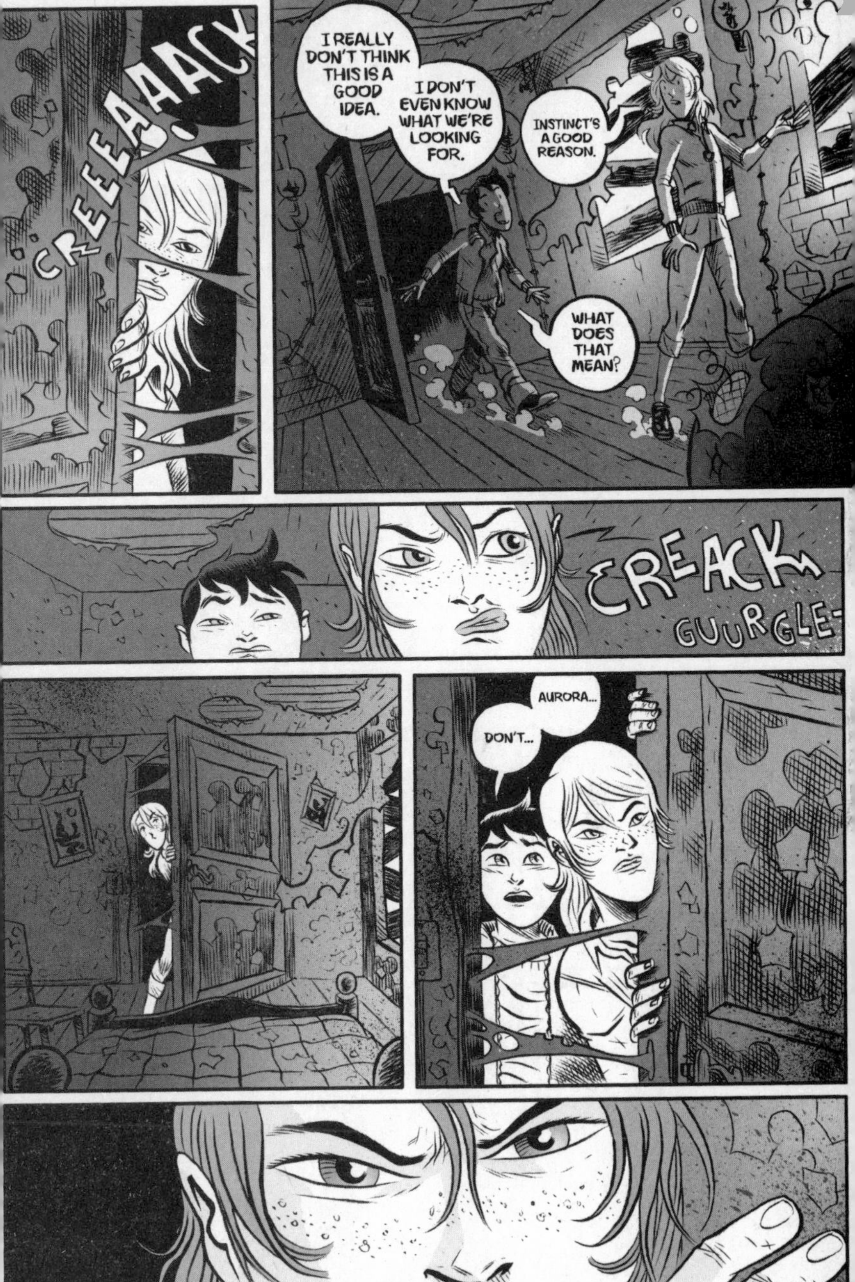
CREEEAAACK
I REALLY DON'T THINK THIS IS A GOOD IDEA.
I DON'T EVEN KNOW WHAT WE'RE LOOKING FOR.
INSTINCT'S A GOOD REASON.
WHAT DOES THAT MEAN?
CREACK
GUURGLE-
AURORA...
DON'T...

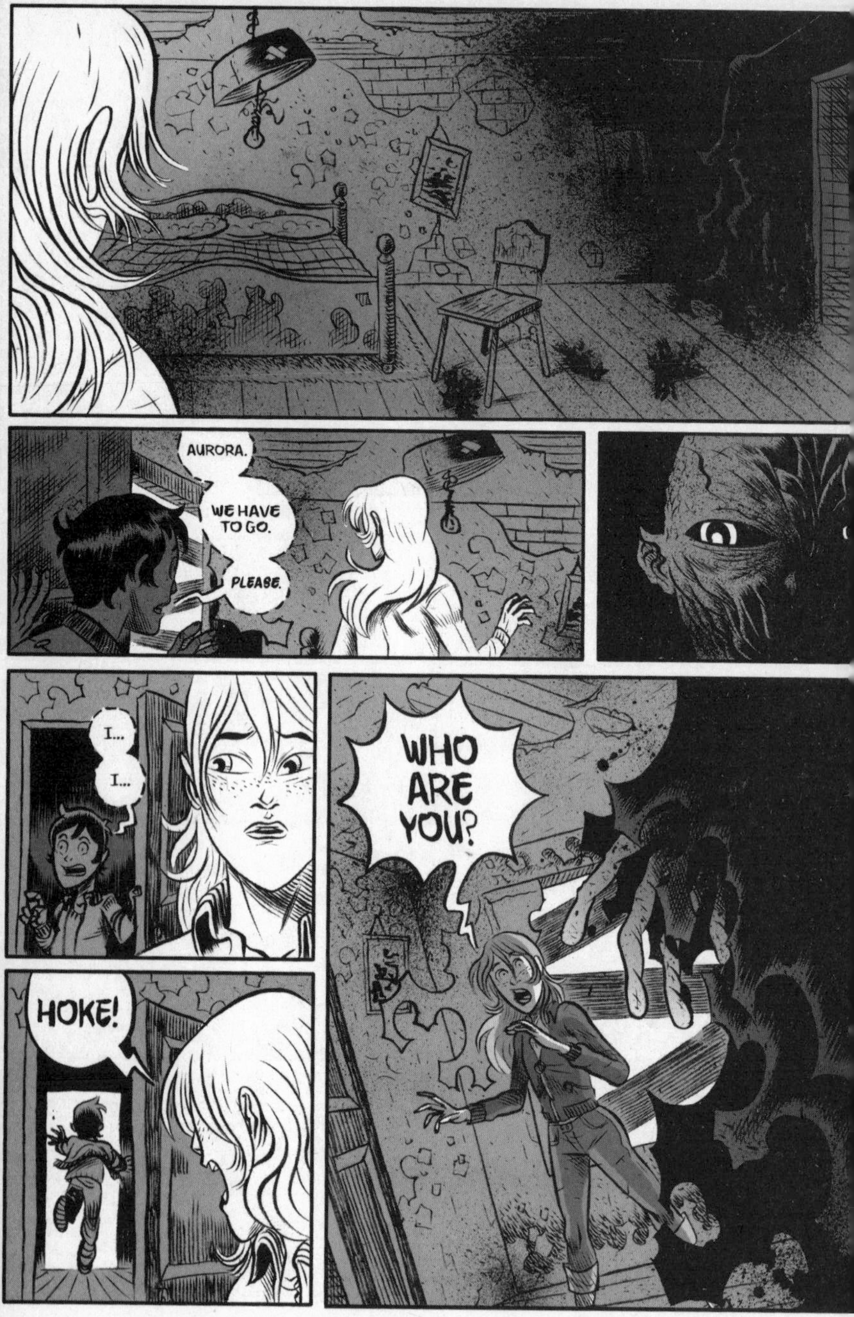
AURORA.
WE HAVE TO GO.
PLEASE.
I...
I...
WHO ARE YOU?
HOKE!

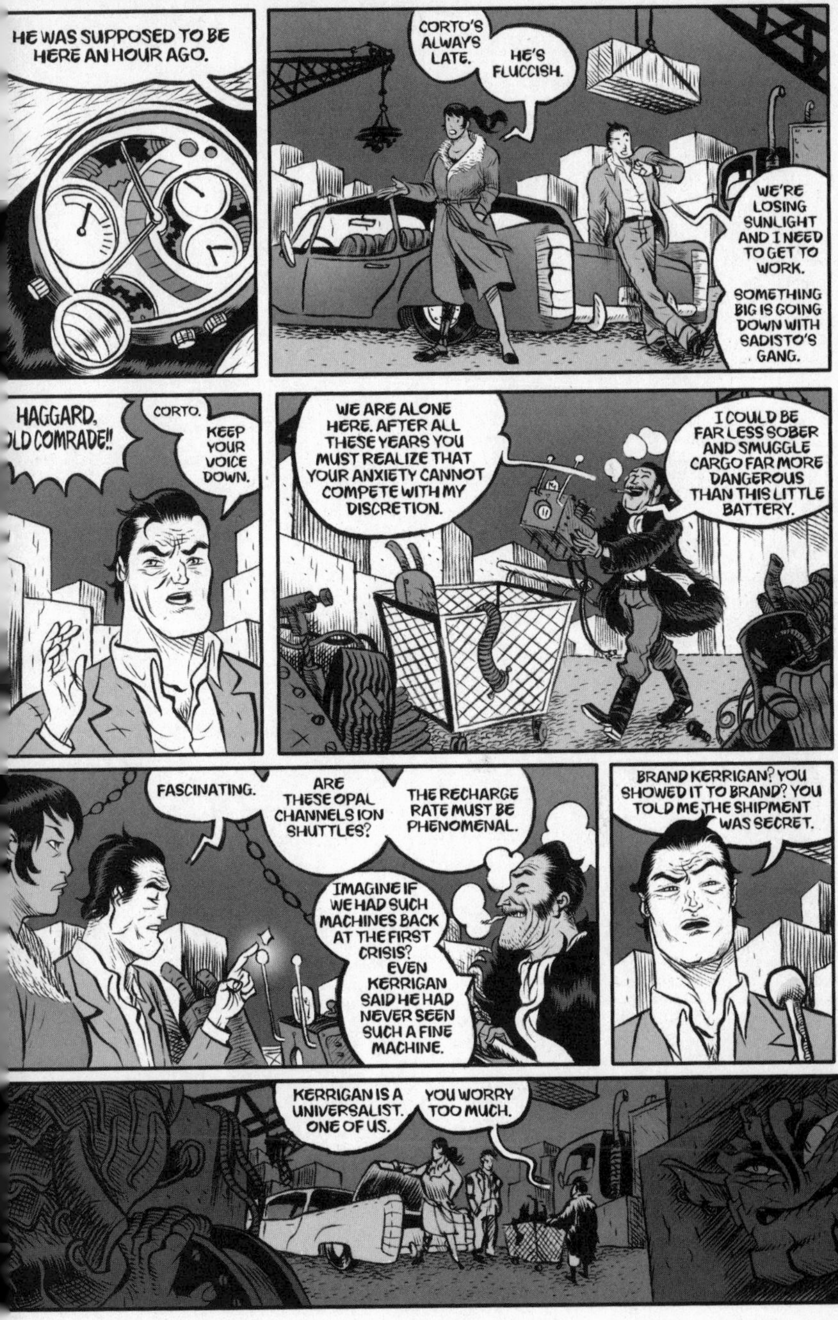
HE WAS SUPPOSED TO BE HERE AN HOUR AGO.
CORTO'S ALWAYS LATE.
HE'S FLUCCISH.
WE'RE LOSING SUNLIGHT AND I NEED TO GET TO WORK.
SOMETHING BIG IS GOING DOWN WITH SADISTO'S GANG.
HAGGARD, OLD COMRADE!!
CORTO.
KEEP YOUR VOICE DOWN.
WE ARE ALONE HERE. AFTER ALL THESE YEARS YOU MUST REALIZE THAT YOUR ANXIETY CANNOT COMPETE WITH MY DISCRETION.
I COULD BE FAR LESS SOBER AND SMUGGLE CARGO FAR MORE DANGEROUS THAN THIS LITTLE BATTERY.
FASCINATING.
ARE THESE OPAL CHANNELS ION SHUTTLES?
THE RECHARGE RATE MUST BE PHENOMENAL.
IMAGINE IF WE HAD SUCH MACHINES BACK AT THE FIRST CRISIS?
EVEN KERRIGAN SAID HE HAD NEVER SEEN SUCH A FINE MACHINE.
BRAND KERRIGAN? YOU SHOWED IT TO BRAND? YOU TOLD ME THE SHIPMENT WAS SECRET.
KERRIGAN IS A UNIVERSALIST. ONE OF US.
YOU WORRY TOO MUCH.

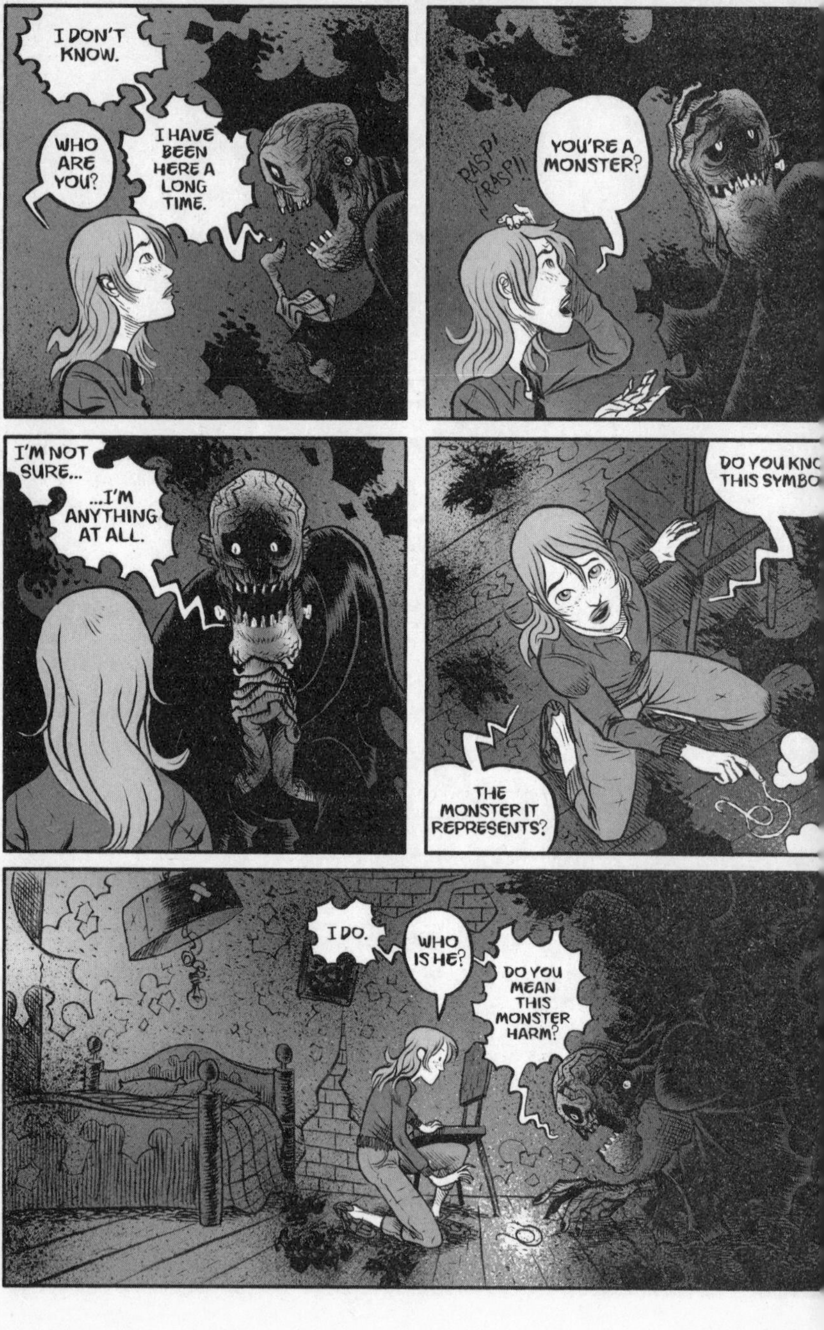
I DON'T KNOW.
WHO ARE YOU?
I HAVE BEEN HERE A LONG TIME.
RASP! RASP!!
YOU'RE A MONSTER?
I'M NOT SURE...
...I'M ANYTHING AT ALL.
DO YOU KNO
THIS SYMBO
THE MONSTER IT REPRESENTS?
I DO.
WHO IS HE?
DO YOU MEAN THIS MONSTER HARM?

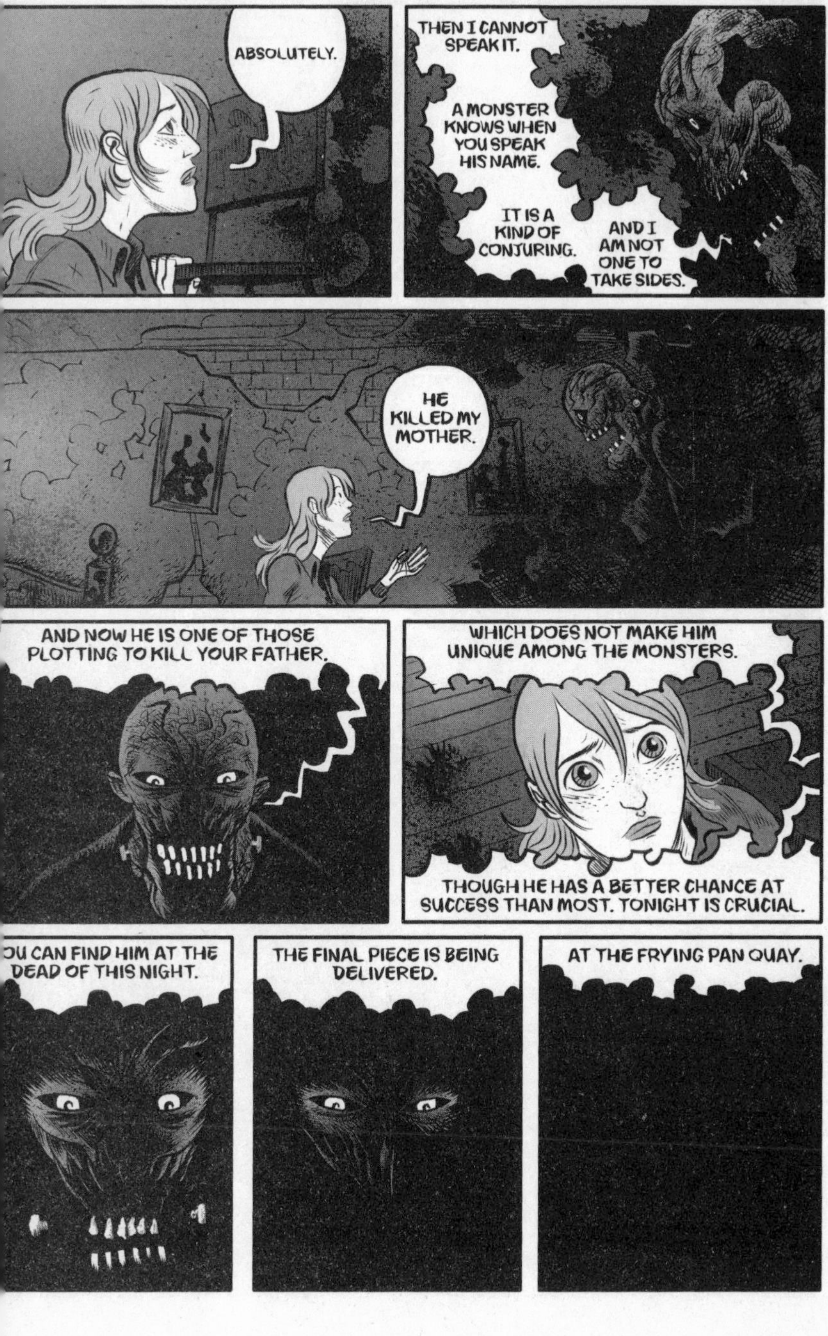
ABSOLUTELY.
THEN I CANNOT SPEAK IT.
A MONSTER KNOWS WHEN YOU SPEAK HIS NAME.
IT IS A KIND OF CONJURING.
AND I AM NOT ONE TO TAKE SIDES.
HE KILLED MY MOTHER.
AND NOW HE IS ONE OF THOSE PLOTTING TO KILL YOUR FATHER.
WHICH DOES NOT MAKE HIM UNIQUE AMONG THE MONSTERS.
THOUGH HE HAS A BETTER CHANCE AT SUCCESS THAN MOST. TONIGHT IS CRUCIAL.
OU CAN FIND HIM AT THE DEAD OF THIS NIGHT.
THE FINAL PIECE IS BEING DELIVERED.
AT THE FRYING PAN QUAY.

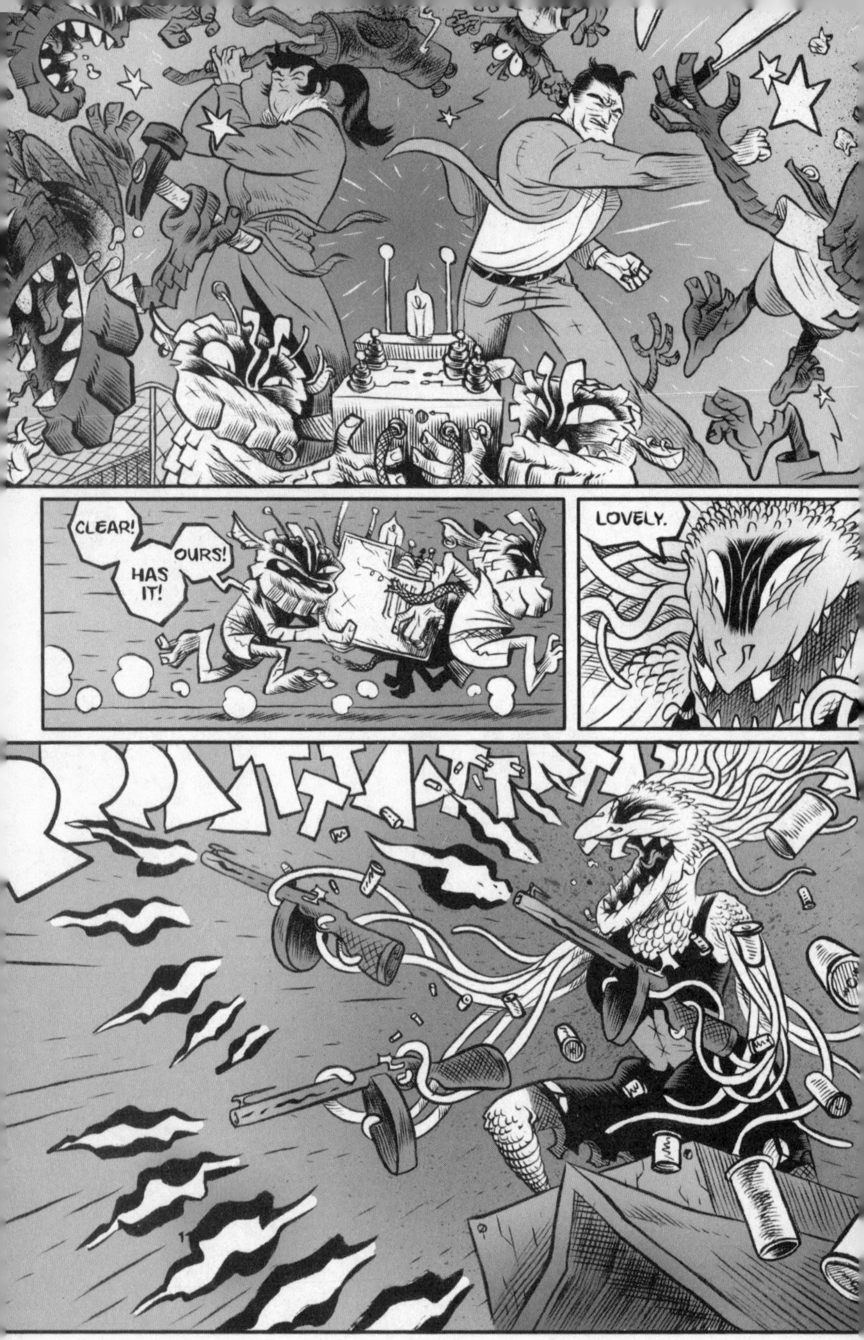
CLEAR!
OURS!
HAS IT!
LOVELY.

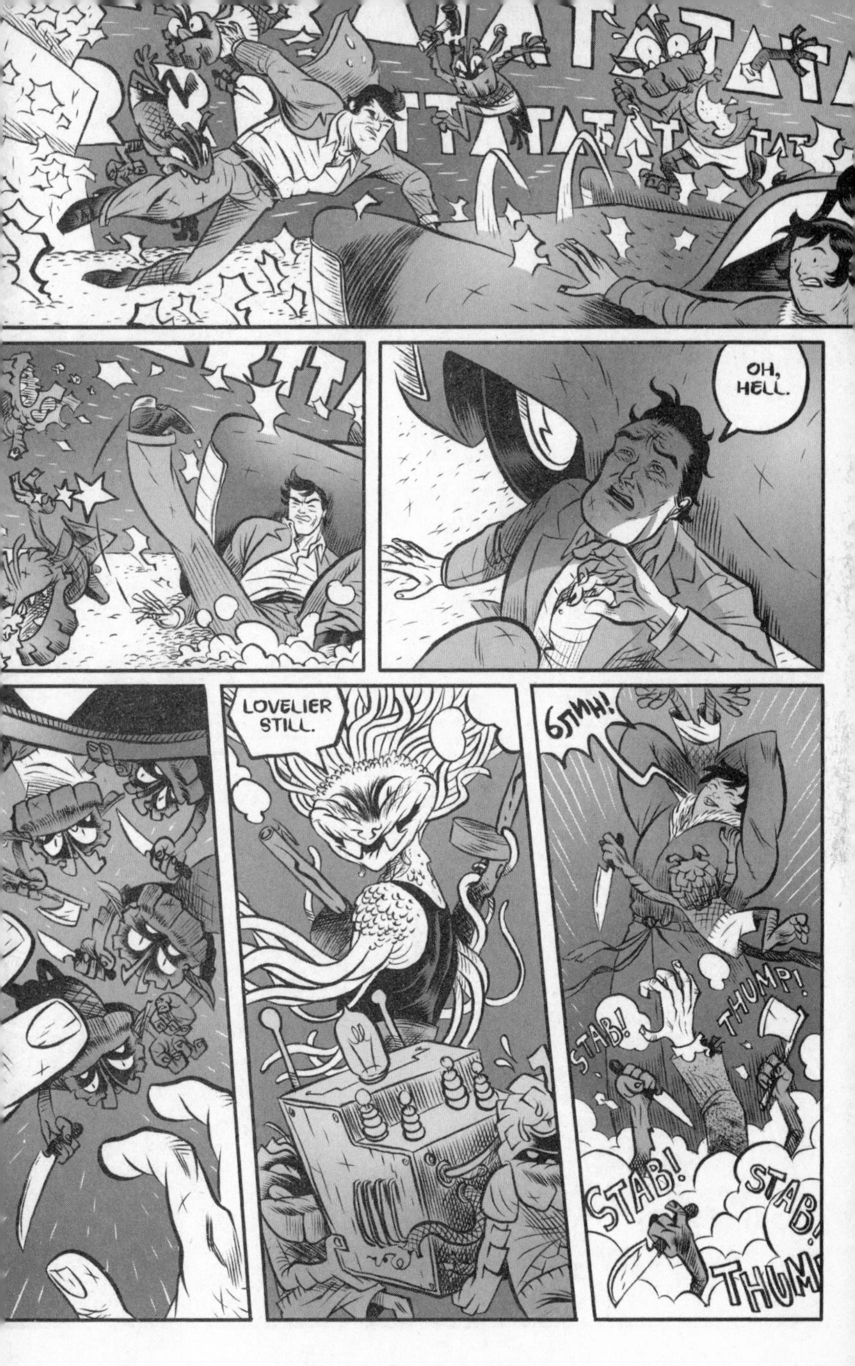
OH, HELL.
LOVELIER STILL.
бЛИН!
STAB!
THUMP!
STAB!
STAB!
THUM

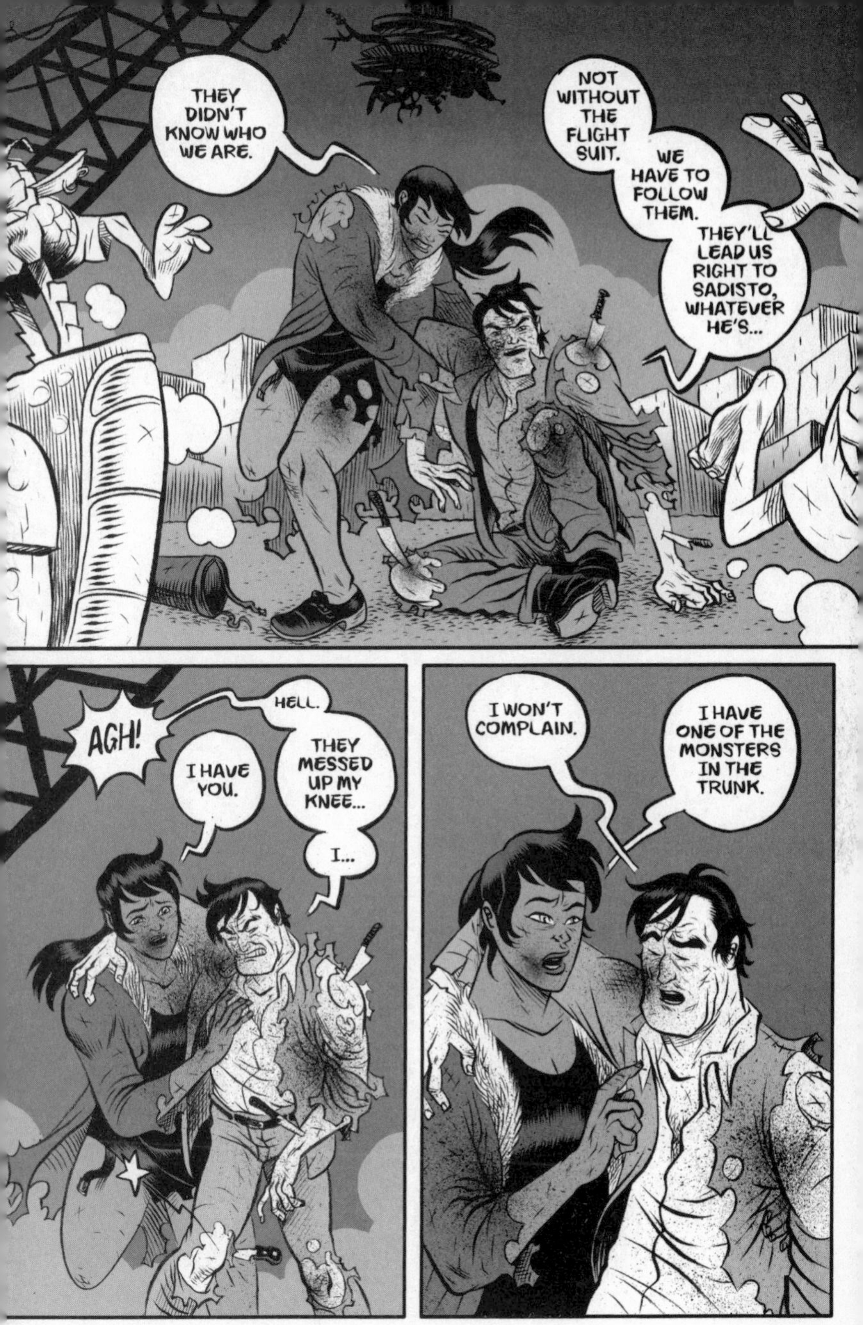
THEY DIDN'T KNOW WHO WE ARE.
NOT WITHOUT THE FLIGHT SUIT.
WE HAVE TO FOLLOW THEM.
THEY'LL LEAD US RIGHT TO SADISTO, WHATEVER HE'S...
AGH!
HELL.
THEY MESSED UP MY KNEE...
I...
I HAVE YOU.
I WON'T COMPLAIN.
I HAVE ONE OF THE MONSTERS IN THE TRUNK.

THE FRYING PAN QUAY.

YOU'VE NEVER ACTUALLY KILLED A MONSTER BEFORE. UNLESS I MISSED SOMETHING?

I NEVER HAVE.

YOU THINK YOU'LL HAVE ANY PROBLEMS WITH IT?

I DON'T THINK SO.

THEY'RE NOT LIKE PEOPLE. NOT LIKE ANIMALS, EVEN.

WHEN I WAS STILL A BOY, TWELVE MAYBE, I SHOT A FOX THAT WAS GOING AFTER OUR CHICKENS.

WATCHED IT STOP BREATHING. THAT FELT WRONG, STILL KIND OF BOTHERS M

BUT MONSTERS DIE BY MY HANDS...

IT'S LIKE SCRAPING DOG'S BUSINESS OFF MY HEEL.

IT'S WHAT HUMANS WERE MADE TO DO.

I'M GIVING YOU A BLASTER FOR TONIGHT.

YOU'RE GOING TO BE MY SUPPORT FROM ABOVE.

BUT SHE HAS TO KNOW.

127

ZAAPP

SCRAEE!!

GET THE BATTERY IN THE TRUCK AND ROLLING!

NAILS!

NET HIS WINDSCREE

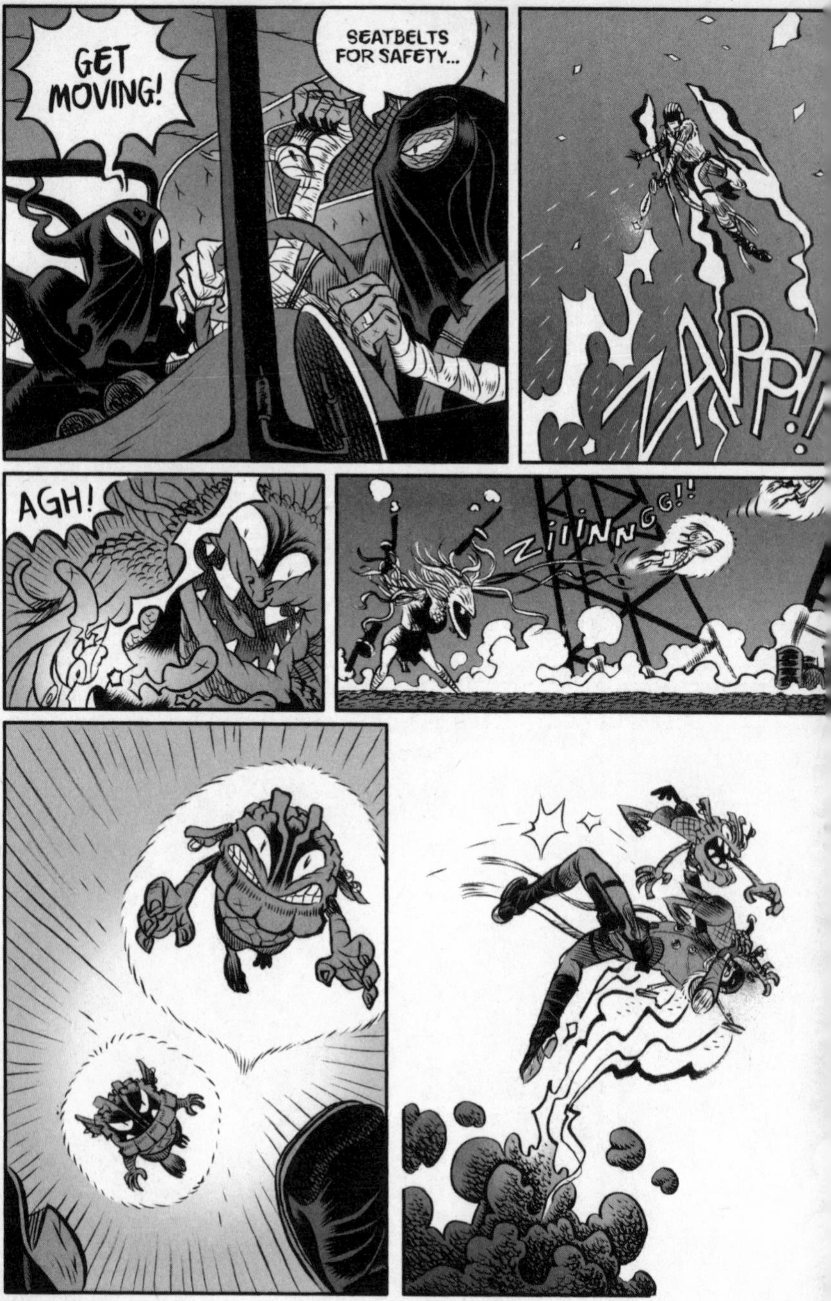
GET MOVING!
SEATBELTS FOR SAFETY...
ZAPP!!
AGH!
ZIIINNGG!!

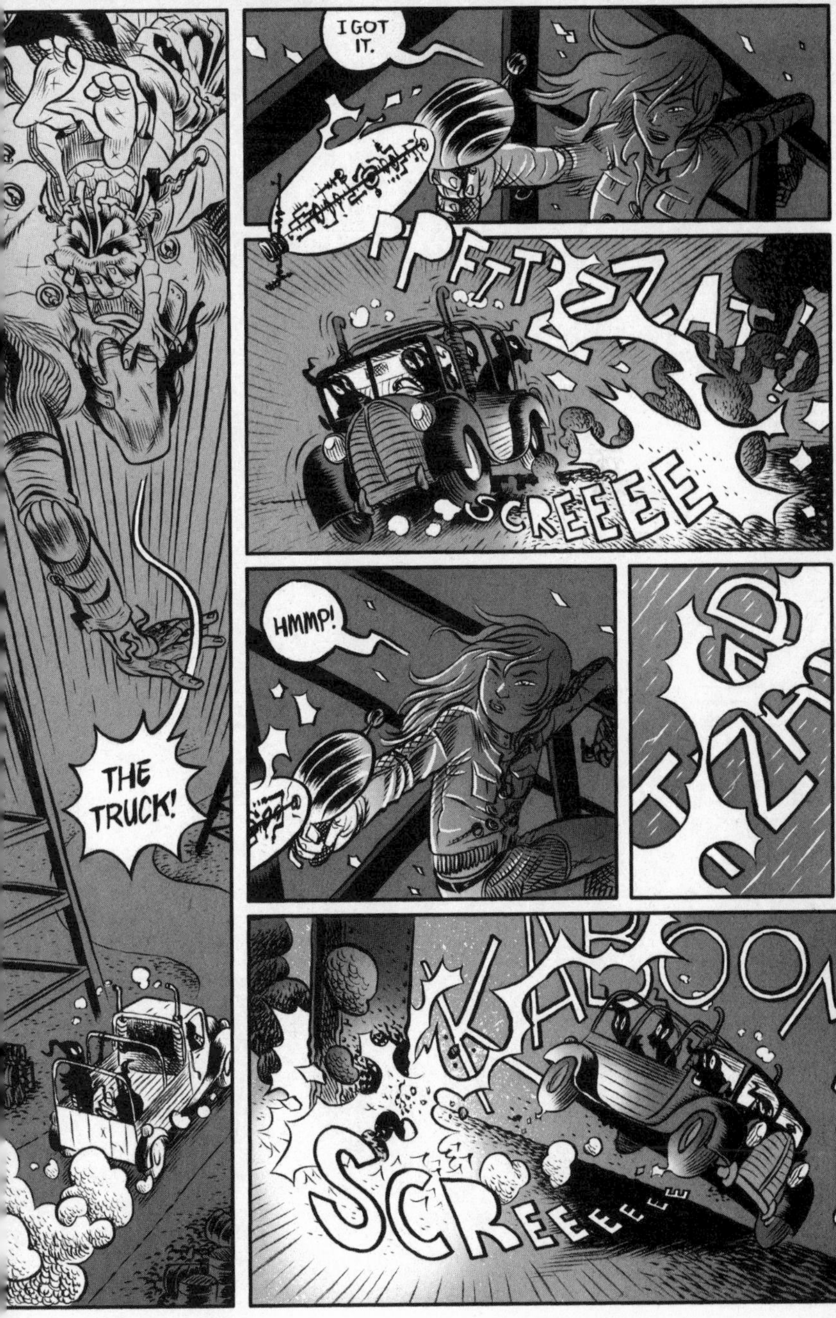
I GOT IT.
PFFT'SPLAT!
SCREEEE
HMMP!
THE TRUCK!
KABOOM
SCREEEEE

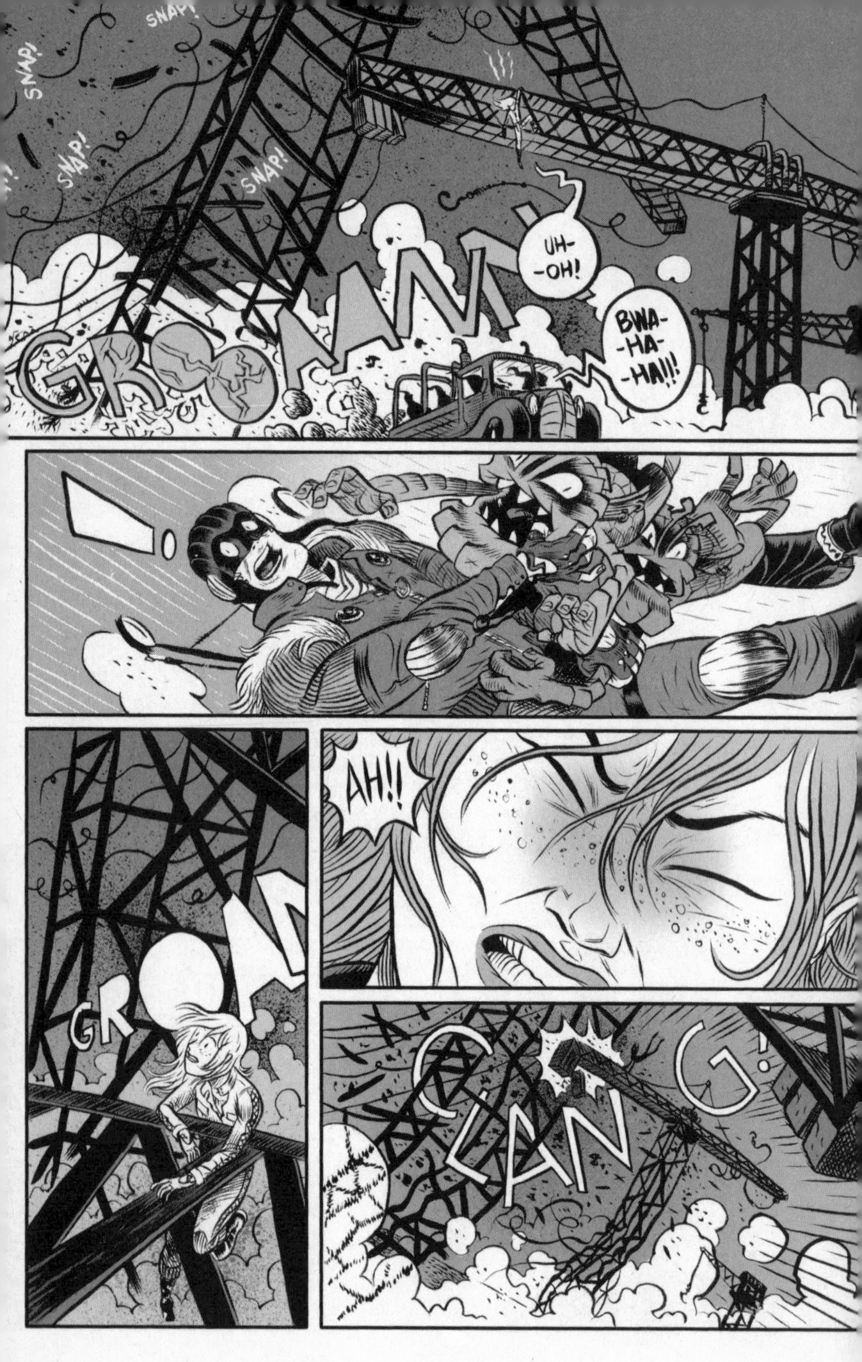
SNAP!
SNAP!
SNAP!
SNAP!
GROAN
UH- -OH!
BWA- -HA- -HA!!
!
AH!!
GR
CLANG!

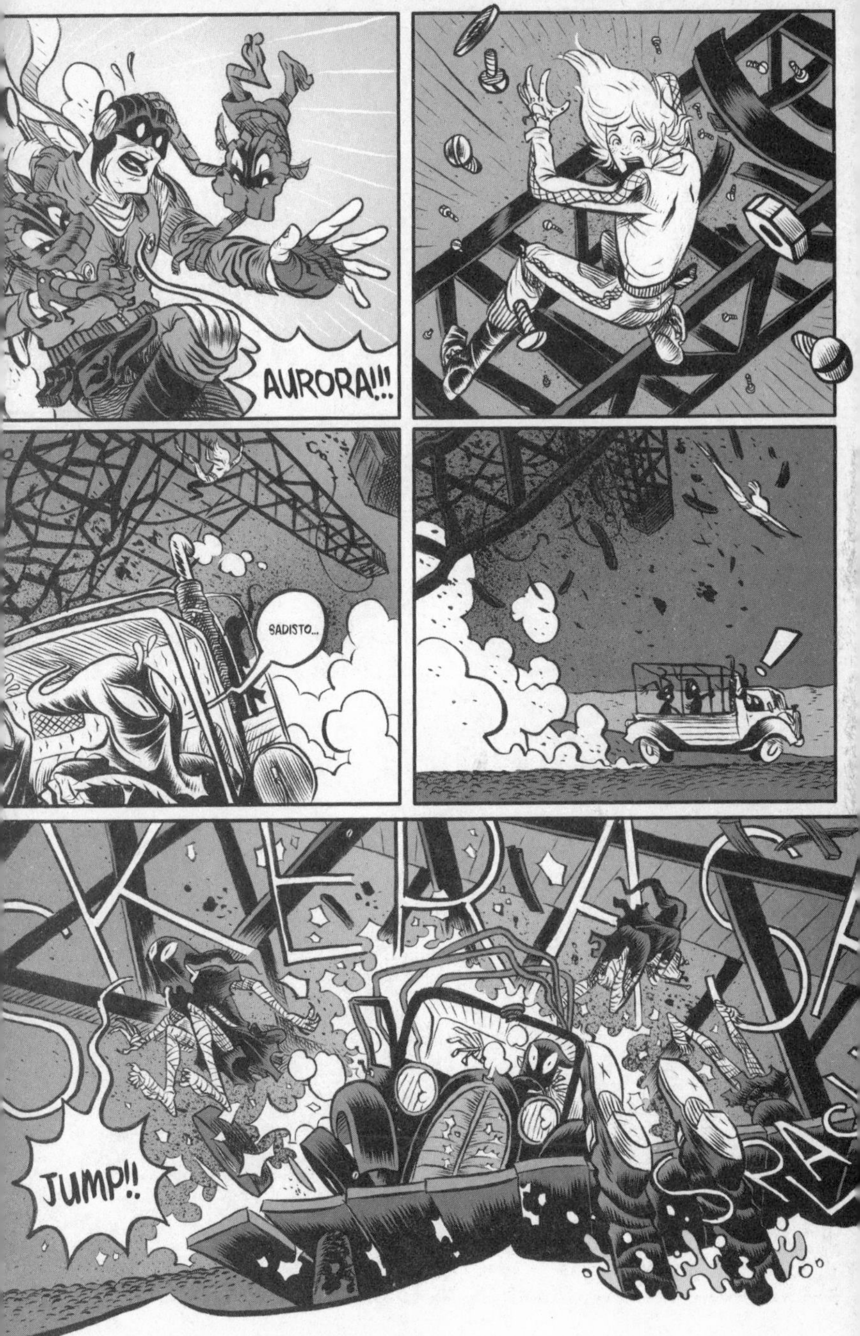
AURORA!!!
SADISTO...
!
JUMP!!

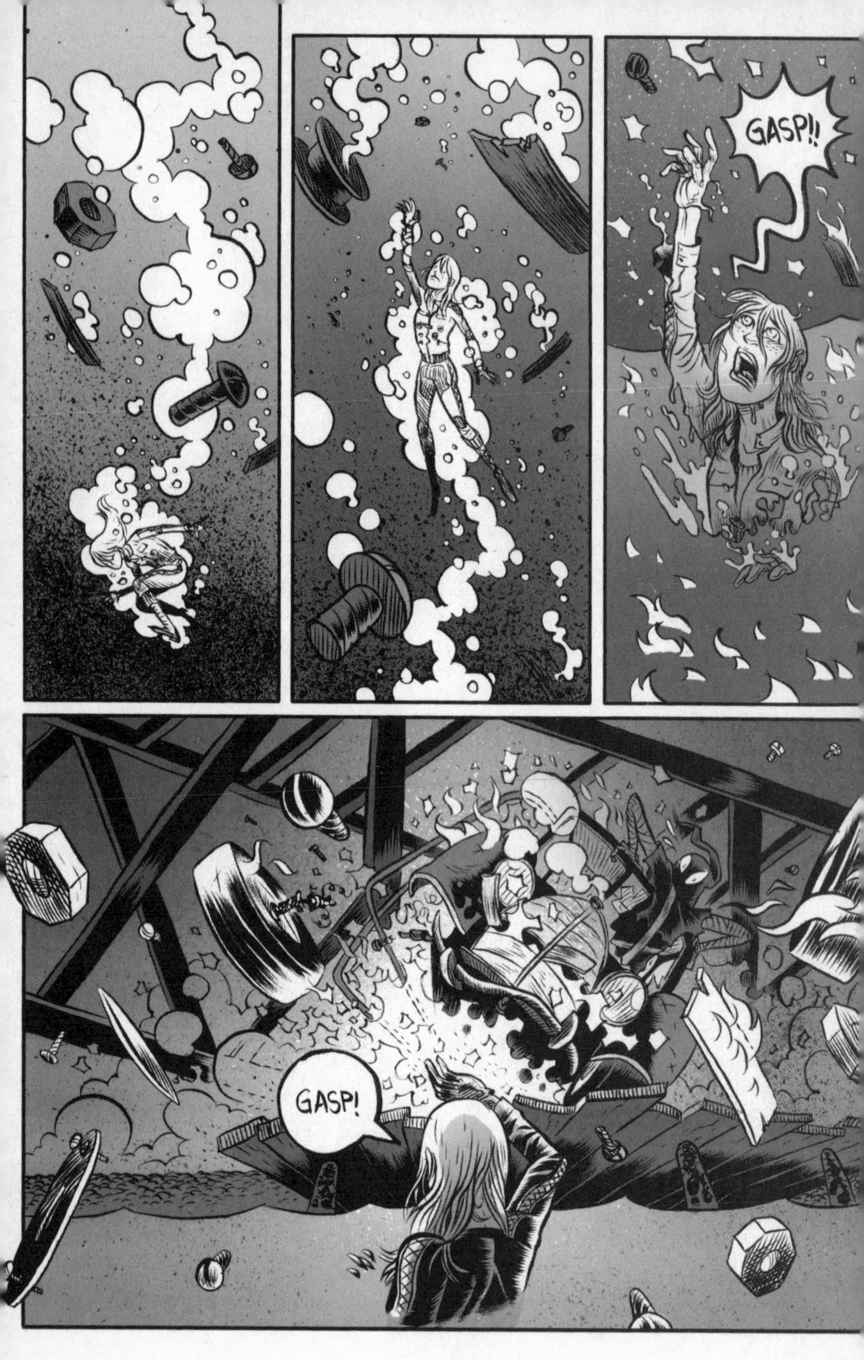
GASP!!
GASP!

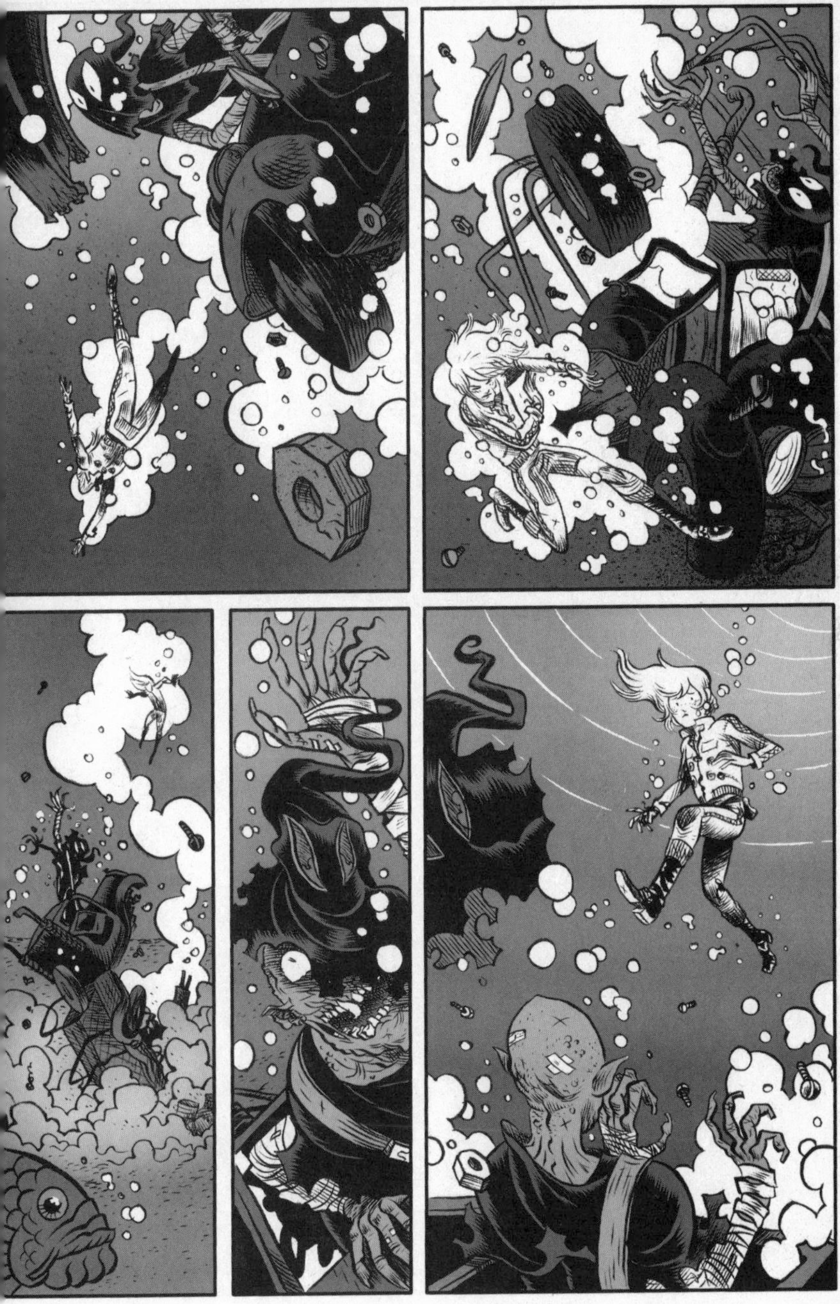

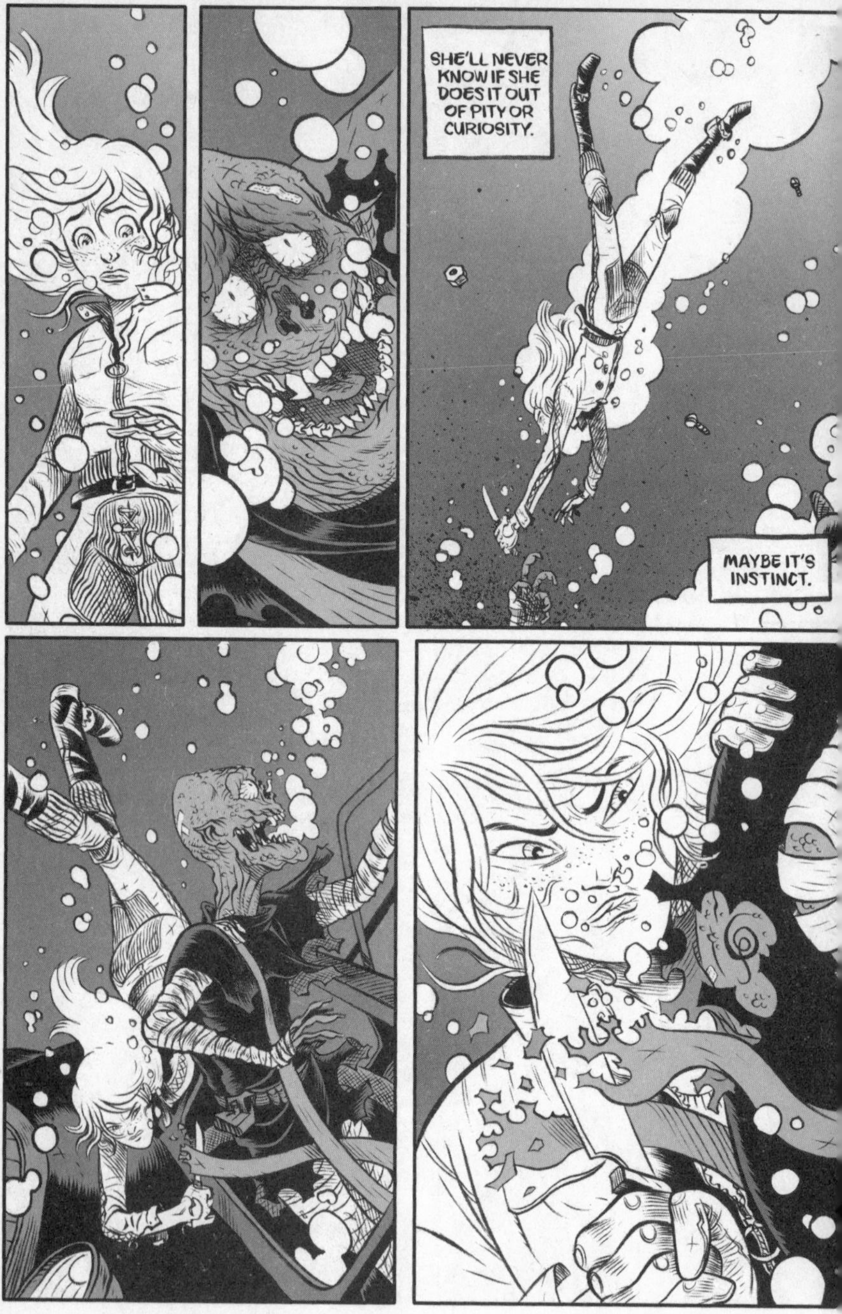
SHE'LL NEVER KNOW IF SHE DOES IT OUT OF PITY OR CURIOSITY.
MAYBE IT'S INSTINCT.

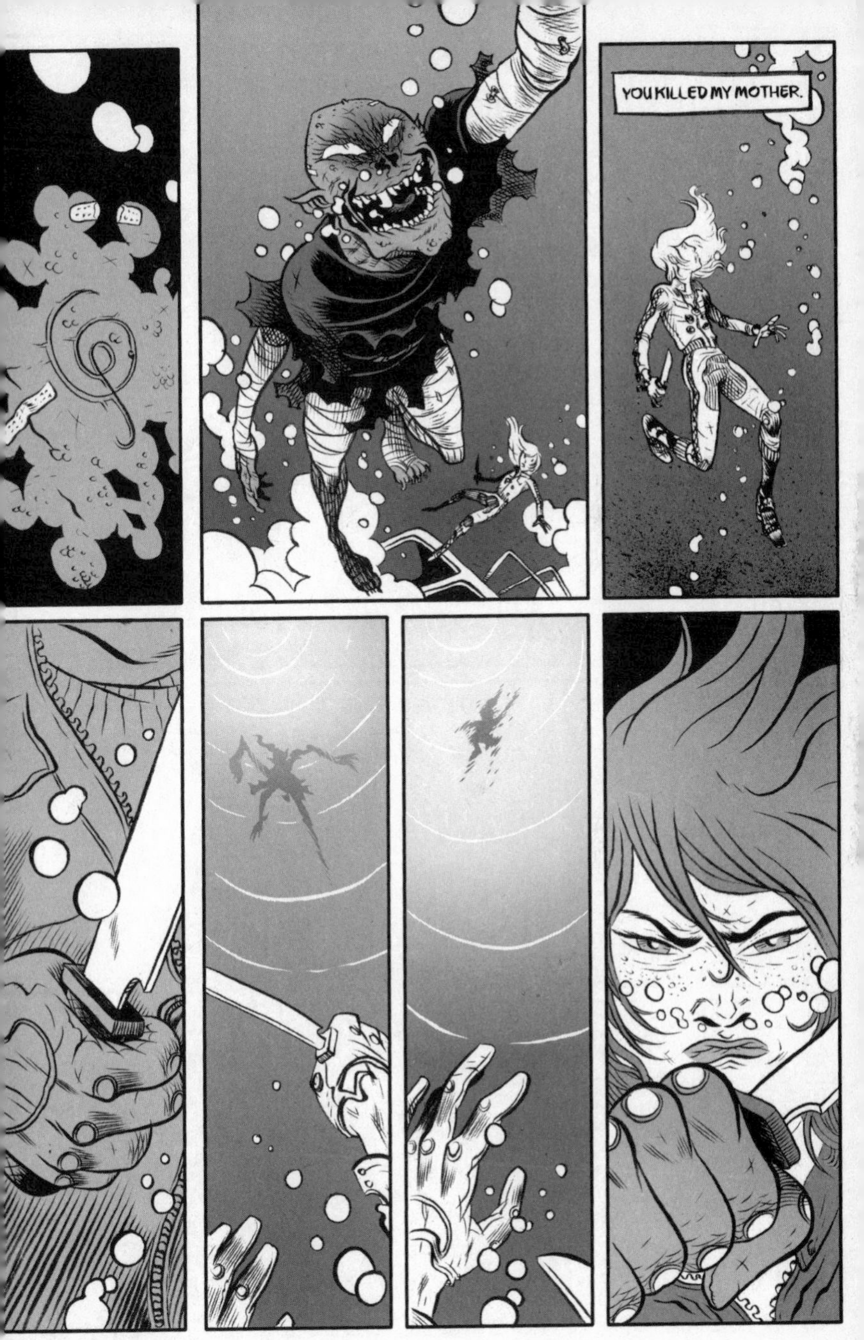
YOU KILLED MY MOTHER.